Murder

in the

Mews

A Redmond and Haze Mystery

Book 10

By Irina Shapiro

Copyright

Cover created by MiblArt.

Table of Contents

Prologue

Thomas Grady left by the servants' entrance and headed toward the stable block, his breath escaping in great vaporous puffs as he hurried across the snow-covered yard. It was still pitch-dark, sunrise two hours off, and colder than a witch's tit, the moon hovering above the dark outline of the trees as if it were the middle of the night. *To some people, it may as well be*, Thomas thought angrily. The family would remain abed for hours yet, warm and snug under their eiderdowns, with fires blazing through the long hours of darkness to keep them comfortable, a far cry from his freezing room in the attics. He might have snatched another half an hour of sleep had the earl not entrusted him with the well-being of the new filly.

The Arabian was as skittish as a teetotaling virgin and about as likely to show him any affection. That damn horse had cost more than Thomas would earn in a lifetime, but such was life. Some were born to inherit great wealth, others to shovel shit until they either retired from a life of service with a little something put by or wound up in a workhouse, where the only thing they had left to look forward to was the tender embrace of the pauper's grave.

Thomas's boots left deep footprints in the fresh snow, and the cold seeped through the worn soles, reminding him that he'd have no choice but to spend his wages on a new pair. He peered at the low brick building, suddenly noticing that the door was not only unlatched but partially open. His heart sank. The earl would have his guts for garters if the Arabian had escaped.

Thomas rushed toward the stable and burst through the door, his gaze leaping to the Arabian's stall. The horse was there, as were the grays, but their restless snuffling, along with the awful smell emanating from the other side of the building, immediately put Thomas on his guard as he looked around for the source of the stench. He cried out in horror when he spotted the earl, the man's ashen face illuminated by the feeble moonlight streaming through the narrow window set high in the wall.

Thomas edged closer until he could see around the partition. It was clear the earl was dead. His head had lolled to the side, and his torso was caked with dried blood, a pitchfork sticking out of his belly as if he were a Sunday roast. The straw-covered floor was smeared with congealed blood. The earl's gaze appeared to shift, and Thomas rushed forward, thinking the man might still be alive. But as he drew closer, he realized that the man's eyeballs were shiny with frost, the ice simply reflecting the silvery moonlight.

Heaving with fear and disgust, his mouth filling with bile and his empty stomach threatening to turn itself inside out, Thomas erupted out of the stables and ran back the way he'd come, puffing like a locomotive as he exploded into the warm servants' hall and sprinted toward the butler's pantry.

"What's the matter with you, boy?" Mr. Simonds exclaimed, ready to subject Thomas to a tongue-lashing, but Thomas was in no mood for the well-deserved reprimand.

"It's his lordship," he cried, tears running down his chilled cheeks. "He's been murdered."

Chapter 1

Wednesday, December 23, 1868

The morning was bitterly cold, the ground covered with a thin layer of snow that crunched beneath the wheels of the carriage. Jason Redmond stared out the window, enjoying the drive despite the macabre reason for this foray into Surrey. The frosty fields sparkled in the weak winter sunshine, and the bare branches formed an intricate latticework against the pale blue sky, the crows that dotted the landscape like charcoal smudges on a nearly finished canvas. They'd passed several neat cottages, ribbons of smoke curling from stone chimneys and the lowing of cows in the barn carrying on the wind.

As Jason surveyed the peaceful scene, he wondered why it was that people never got tired of killing each other. Surely most grievances that led to murder were not that serious, the sort of conflicts that could be peacefully resolved should the injured party consider diplomacy rather than violence. The more pressing question, however, was why he'd been summoned to a sleepy village that lay more than twenty-five miles from London. According to Constable Napier, who'd been dozing for the past half hour, his helmet in his lap and his head resting against the side of the carriage, Surrey had its own police service that was headed by a well-respected and experienced superintendent and was based in Guilford, but surely there was a parish constable who could have taken charge until reinforcements arrived.

The answer to Jason's question materialized a short while later as the peaked roof of Langley Hall came into view. The palatial house sat proudly amid acres of lawn and parkland and could be accessed only via the mile-long lane, which culminated in a circular driveway that wound its way around a marble fountain worthy of a Roman piazza. Built in the Palladian style, the house boasted a triangular portico supported by six massive columns that was reminiscent of an ancient temple. Romanesque statues gazed down their prominent noses from the roof, and massive urns flanked the steps that led to the front door. The victim was too wealthy and influential for the handling of his killing to be left to the local police.

The splendor of the house and grounds made the method of the murder seem incongruous. What sort of individual skewered the lord of the manor with a pitchfork, and what had tipped him or her over the edge? Jason could conceive of a few reasons someone would resort to such savagery, but now wasn't the time to analyze the mindset of the killer. A boxy police wagon, a blight on an otherwise picture-perfect scene, was parked at the top of the drive, awaiting the victim's earthly remains, which Jason was here to examine.

Jason grabbed the medical bag he'd brought just in case, thanked Joe for getting him to his destination without getting lost, and alighted from the carriage, followed by the bleary-eyed constable. Joe would seek shelter from the cold in the servants' hall until it was time to leave, and Jason hoped they'd be gracious to an outsider.

"Good morning, my lord," Constable Collins called out as he came around the side of the house. "This way, if you please."

"Good morning, Constable," Jason said. "Is Inspector Haze here?"

"Indeed, he is, sir. Just getting acquainted with the dead cove," the constable answered flippantly.

Jason didn't approve of making jokes at the expense of the deceased, but everyone dealt with violent death differently, and some people, especially someone as young as the constable, needed a way to come to terms with the carnage they so often faced.

Jason's boots crunched on the snow as he followed the constable to the stable block located a good way behind the stately mansion. He wished he'd have listened to Katie and worn woolen socks. His feet were growing numb with cold. Jason hunched his shoulders against a sudden gust of wind and grabbed his top hat, which was about to fly off his head.

"It's a cold one," Constable Collins observed as they trudged toward the stables, Constable Napier lagging a few steps behind in order to right the helmet that slid into his eyes with every blast of wind. Jason couldn't conceive of less practical headgear for policemen, who often had to run to apprehend a suspect, but kept that opinion to himself.

"Have you seen the victim?" he asked instead.

"Oh, aye," the young constable replied. "It's not a pretty sight."

"It rarely is."

Jason couldn't help but smile as Inspector Daniel Haze emerged from the stables, his cheeks ruddy with cold and his glasses reflecting the ray of sunshine that broke through the clouds and illuminated Daniel in a heavenly halo. He wore his usual bowler hat, but today, he sported a red and green tartan muffler, which Jason could just bet was a birthday present from a certain someone they never discussed openly.

"Jason," Daniel said, his pleasure at seeing Jason obvious. "Thank you for coming. I do hope the superintendent's message didn't interfere with your hospital commitments."

Jason had been volunteering at St. George's Hospital since moving to London in the spring, but although he had been repeatedly asked to join the staff full-time and had been offered a wage due an experienced surgeon, he preferred to both operate and teach on a volunteer basis, a decision that allowed him to determine which patients he chose to help and which surgeries he was willing to open to the medical students. He liked the flexibility of the arrangement and the satisfaction of being able to help those in need without the suffocating restrictions of the bureaucracy that dominated every medical institution. He often took on cases other surgeons elected to pass on, deeming the effort either futile, since the chances of survival were minimal, or unnecessary.

“I had an operation scheduled for this afternoon, but Mr. Harris was kind enough to offer to perform the procedure in my stead,” Jason replied.

Daniel’s brows furrowed and his nose wrinkled with obvious disgust. “Is he not the one who walks around in a soiled apron and adds a notch to the handle of his blood-spattered saw for every limb he amputates?”

“He is,” Jason replied curtly.

Jason was forever advocating the benefits of cleaning the surgical instruments between surgeries and washing hands before and after an operation but most of his British counterparts either laughed at him outright or attributed his eccentricity to being American and simply ignored him. They believed the key to survival was the timing of the surgery rather than the method. It was said that certain surgeons could amputate a limb in as little as thirty seconds, hacking through the bone as if it were a hunk of firewood.

Jason supposed speed was imperative in situations where the unfortunate patient was conscious, but with the use of ether, the operating surgeon could afford to take his time and try to minimize the damage to the remainder of the limb as well as the possibility of infection.

“I expect the operating theater will be full,” Jason mused. “The students admire Mr. Harris’s decisiveness and strive to copy his technique. They don’t much care if postoperative infection kills half his patients.”

“Surely, who lives and who dies is not entirely up to the surgeon,” Daniel said. “Unless the individual dies by suicide, the outcome is determined by divine will.”

“I’m not so sure about that,” Jason replied bitterly. In his opinion, the most basic of hygienic practices would go a long way toward saving more patients, but no one at St. George’s paid much attention to his opinion on the subject.

Daniel seemed poised to disagree but changed his mind, since this was neither the time nor the place to engage in a discussion on the role of science versus the will of God, when a fresh corpse awaited their attention.

"Let's see our man," Jason said.

Daniel led Jason into the stables and toward the back. Several horses, one of them a snowy white beauty, occupied the stalls on the right side, their restlessness and loud snorting evidence of their distress. The sooner the victim was removed, the better for the poor animals that were clearly agitated by the comings and goings and the reek of the blood that accosted Jason's senses the moment he entered the building.

Despite the brightness of the day, the interior was dim, which explained the oil lamps strategically positioned to illuminate the crime scene.

Jason let out a low whistle when he saw the body slouched against the wooden partition separating two stalls. The tines of the pitchfork had been driven in so deep as to securely affix the victim to the wood. The man had to be nearing forty and had shaggy dark-blond hair and a long, thin face that was frozen in the serene expression of a Biblical saint. Saint Sebastian, who'd been tied to a post and shot with arrows, sprang to mind, but this was no Bible lesson, this man no Christian martyr.

Setting down his Gladstone bag on a bale of straw, Jason approached the victim and studied him closely, noting the thin layer of frost on his skin and the blood on his clothing and hands. He must have touched his perforated abdomen either in shock or in an effort to free himself, perhaps believing there was still a chance of survival.

"Has the victim been positively identified?" Jason asked.

"Yes. This is Damian Langley, the Earl of Granville, close friend and advisor to Her Majesty the Queen." Daniel looked so tense as he made this pronouncement, if his spine grew any stiffer,

Jason thought it just might crack. “There’s much at stake, Jason,” Daniel added.

“I understand. Has Mr. Gillespie taken photographs of the crime scene?”

Daniel shook his head. “He hasn’t been sent for. Superintendent Ransome wants this one kept quiet until we know more of what happened here.”

“To have a photographic record of the crime scene would have been helpful,” Jason replied.

“I agree, but I can’t go against Ransome on this.”

Jason nodded, then turned to the two constables hovering in the doorway. “You may take him down.”

Worried the constables might inflict postmortem injuries that would cloud the results of the autopsy, Jason grabbed onto the pitchfork and pulled, extracting the murder weapon from the body. The mortal remains of the earl, now freed from the partition, slid sideways, falling onto the bloodstained straw at their feet.

“Take this too,” Jason told Constable Napier as he handed him the pitchfork.

“Can you perform the postmortem right away?” Daniel asked. He stepped aside to allow the constables to lift the body onto a canvas stretcher, then placed the bloodied pitchfork atop the corpse, lest the constables forget to take it.

Jason shook his head. “He needs to thaw.”

“Are you suggesting—” Daniel sputtered.

“The corpse is partially frozen,” Jason replied.

“How long will he take to defrost? The countess is beside herself, and Ransome will be breathing down my neck like an enraged bull as soon as I return to the Yard, demanding answers I don’t have.”

"I understand that, but I can hardly perform an autopsy on frost-hardened remains, and the body is not likely to thaw on the way. It's too cold. I suggest we interview the countess and the staff, then find an establishment where we can get something to eat. By the time we return to London, the earl should be ready, if the body is kept upstairs in one of the warmer parts of the building," Jason said as he reached for his bag. "Oh, and please instruct the constables not to leave the earl too near the hearth," he added, worried the constables might think that slowly roasting the corpse might speed up the process.

"Yes, of course," Daniel said, nodding in agreement. "I've already taken a statement from the groom who found the body."

"What did he say?"

"Nothing that can be of any use in finding the killer. Tom Grady arrived at the stables well before dawn, as usual, to check on the horses. His lordship was very fond of his grays, apparently, and the white horse is a new acquisition, a Christmas gift for his daughter. The groom came upon his employer, correctly assumed that he was beyond earthly help, and ran back to the house to inform the butler, Mr. Simonds. The butler had the presence of mind to dispatch a rider to Scotland Yard once he ascertained there was no need to summon the family physician and to keep the matter quiet in order to prevent gawkers from contaminating the crime scene."

"Clever man," Jason said as they saw off the earl's remains and headed toward the grandiose entrance Jason had passed earlier.

"He is that," Daniel agreed. "Ex-military. Seems he and the earl go back a long way."

"Have you interviewed him?"

"Very briefly. I thought it was more important to keep the murder scene intact until you arrived."

"And the family?"

"Safely indoors."

"Were there any footprints when you arrived?" Jason asked.

"Yes, but they belong to the two people who were first on the scene, Grady and Simonds. Grady is certain he did not see any footprints in the freshly fallen snow."

"Which means the earl was murdered before it began to snow," Jason mused. "That's good to know, since it will be difficult to determine the exact time of death. What time did the groom leave the stables last night?"

"Six. He went up to the house to clean up for supper and then headed to bed around ten."

"Is there just the one groom?" Jason asked. In a house this size, he'd expect an army of employees.

"No, but the second man wasn't needed and left an hour before, since he'd been feeling unwell. The earl and his family only came to the house for the Christmas holiday and were due to leave after Boxing Day. They did not bring the entire staff, only the individuals they needed for the duration. The Langleys reside in Park Lane for most of the year."

"Will you permit them to leave if they wish?" Jason asked.

"I don't see any reason to keep them here, and it will make it easier for us to investigate from a geographical perspective."

"Yes, I agree."

"Jason, would you say he died quickly?" Daniel inquired as he used the ornate knocker to announce their presence.

"I hope so," Jason said. "For his sake."

In truth, given the amount of blood on the victim's hands and the floor, Jason thought the earl had remained conscious long enough to experience not only great pain but terrible fear as the realization that he was about to die dawned on him. He may have suffered for as long as an hour before passing out due to blood loss, but Jason didn't want to commit to any answers before he had a chance to open up the body and base his suppositions on scientific evidence rather than guesswork. He unwittingly squared his shoulders as the bolt was drawn back and the door opened. A new investigation was about to begin in earnest.

Chapter 2

Simonds had to be in his late forties or early fifties. His hair, which was snow-white and contrasted sharply with his deeply tanned skin, made his exact age difficult to gauge. He had a wary dark gaze and a posture so erect, he might have had a length of rail track for a spine. His suit was neatly pressed, and his shoes shone with polish. Whether the death of his master had rattled him was impossible to tell, since on the outside, he was a pillar of decorum.

"Mr. Simonds, this is my associate, Lord Redmond. We would like to speak to the countess," Daniel announced as they surrendered their things to a maidservant hovering nearby.

"I'm afraid that's impossible," Simonds replied. "Her ladyship had suffered a nervous collapse on hearing that her husband is dead. The housekeeper, Mrs. Frey, administered smelling salts and then we helped her ladyship to her bed."

"I see," Daniel said. "Then we shall start with you, Mr. Simonds."

"Very well, Inspector. We can speak in the butler's pantry, if you have no objection."

"Are any other members of the family at home?" Jason asked.

"Only the children."

"And how old are the children?" Daniel asked.

"Lord Robert is eleven, and Lady Viola is sixteen."

"Have they been informed of their father's death?" Jason asked, hoping the children were not in shock.

"Not yet. We thought it best to wait until we had more information."

"Will they not ask after their father?" Daniel inquired as they followed the butler through the green baize door into the servants' domain.

"They don't expect him back until tomorrow, so no."

"Where do they think he is?" Daniel asked once they were seated in the cane chairs that faced the butler's desk. Simonds took his place, his expression that of a schoolmaster facing his pupils.

"His lordship left early Monday morning to visit his aunt in Hastings. She's quite elderly, and he pays her a visit once a month. He was expected back tomorrow," Simonds added. "In time for Christmas Eve dinner."

"Did anyone know the earl had returned early?" Jason asked.

"No. He did not come to the house, nor is his brougham here."

"But the horses are," Daniel pointed out. "We saw them in the stables."

"The family had arrived in two separate conveyances, Inspector. His lordship took the bays to Hastings, as was his habit."

"And the family was meant to return to London after Boxing Day?" Daniel asked.

"They were. The countess detests the country and wished to return as soon as possible."

Daniel nodded and flipped his notebook open to a clean page. He imagined that after the brutal death of her husband she wouldn't be too fond of Christmas either. Christmas had certainly lost its magic after the death of Sarah, but now wasn't the time to dwell on his personal feelings. "Mr. Simonds, did the earl have any enemies that you know of?" Daniel asked instead.

"I wouldn't know, sir," Mr. Simonds replied. "He never discussed his private business with me."

"It was my impression that you served together," Jason said, recalling Daniel's earlier comment.

"We did. Saw action during the Indian Rebellion of fifty-seven. I was his lordship's batman until he sold his commission in fifty-nine."

Jason wasn't sure what a batman's role was, but it didn't sound an enviable position based on the title alone.

"You must have grown close," Daniel said, shifting his bulk in the flimsy chair and making it squeak in protest.

"Hardly," Simonds replied. "But the earl saw fit to reward me for my service."

"There must be a reason for such loyalty," Jason interjected.

Simonds's expression turned bashful. "It was my honor to assist his lordship in his greatest hour of need."

"Meaning?" Daniel demanded.

"I saved his life," Simonds said, his gaze sliding away in obvious embarrassment. "I carried him to safety when a shed used for storing munitions was blown up while he was inside. The injury I suffered eventually led to my discharge from the army."

"Was the earl injured?" Jason asked.

"His lordship had suffered a head wound and minor burns when he was thrown by the blast."

"And you?"

"I suffered burns to my back and arms," Simonds replied quietly. "Spent months in hospital."

Daniel jotted that down and looked back up, evidently ready to move on to an alternative line of questioning. "Were the earl and his wife happily married?"

"Are you suggesting that the countess did that to him?" the butler asked, his shapely brows lifting in astonishment.

"Not personally, but perhaps there was an interested party," Daniel suggested.

"You mean a jealous lover?"

"I do."

"I can assure you there isn't one."

"How can you be so certain?" Jason asked.

"Her ladyship is—was a devoted wife. You won't find anyone who'll tell you different."

Daniel nodded. "I'd like to speak to her ladyship's lady's maid. May we interview her in here?"

"Of course. I will send Adams in."

Simonds hoisted himself to his feet, his distaste for Daniel's line of questioning blatant in the pursing of his lips and the angry sidelong glance the butler directed at him as he left the room.

"You think the earl was killed by a jealous lover?" Jason asked once they were alone.

"I think it was a crime of passion," Daniel replied. "Whoever killed the earl did so on the spur of the moment, with whatever he had to hand. The brutality of the attack speaks of murderous fury."

"I agree with you there," Jason remarked. "This was not planned, unless the murderer wanted it to look like a spontaneous attack."

"Could this have been done by a woman, do you think?"

"It would have taken a great deal of strength to drive the pitchfork so far in as to nail the victim to the wall. I suppose a strong, angry woman might have managed it, but just now, I'm leaning toward a male killer."

"As am I," Daniel agreed.

They paused in their speculation when a young woman of about twenty-five entered the room. She had shiny chestnut hair, parted in the middle and tightly pulled back beneath a lace cap, and a hazel gaze that passed over the two men before she lowered her eyes.

"I'm her ladyship's lady's maid," she announced.

"Have a seat, Miss Adams."

The maid looked utterly scandalized at taking the butler's seat, so Daniel moved behind the desk, offering her the guest chair.

"What is your full name?" he asked.

"Leanne Adams, sir."

"And how long have you been with her ladyship?"

"These three years, sir."

"Where were you employed before?"

"With Lady Benton, sir. She had me trained up as a lady's maid. She passed," Miss Adams added.

"When was the last time you saw the earl?"

"Just before he left for Hastings, sir. He came in to say goodbye to her ladyship. I was in the room."

"Did your mistress ever complain about her husband to you?" Upon seeing the maid's closed expression, Daniel hastened to warn, "If you lie to me, you can be charged with obstructing an investigation. Anything you tell me will be kept in confidence," he promised, understanding only too well that the young woman would be in fear of losing her position if she revealed anything unflattering about her mistress.

"No, sir. Their lordships were devoted to each other. A well-suited couple if ever I saw one."

"Did your mistress keep secrets from her husband?"

"What sort of secrets, Inspector?"

"Did she perhaps have an admirer?" Daniel clarified.

"She was admired by many, but not in the way you're suggesting."

Daniel turned to Jason, silently encouraging him to ask his own questions, since he seemed to have exhausted his own line of inquiry.

"Miss Adams, did the earl and his wife engage in marital relations regularly?" Jason asked.

Adams colored and averted her gaze. "Yes, sir. His lordship came to my lady's bedroom twice a week."

"And did the countess welcome his visits?"

"Why, yes, sir. She was hoping for another child."

"Did she tell you that?"

"She did. She would have liked to have another son."

"A spare?" Jason asked.

The maid nodded. "Lord Robert is hale, but things happen, don't they?"

"Indeed, they do," Daniel agreed. "Lord Robert is now an eleven-year-old earl."

Miss Adams looked momentarily shocked, as though she hadn't realized the boy had inherited the earldom the moment his father breathed his last, although as the son of an earl he probably held a courtesy title as well. "The poor mite," Miss Adams muttered. "What a responsibility to care for his mother and sister at such a young age."

"Did the earl have any siblings?" Jason asked. "Perhaps someone who can guide Lord Robert until he's of age."

"No, sir. His lordship was an only child." Miss Adams leveled a questioning look at Daniel, clearly hoping to be excused. "I need to check on my mistress, sir," she said when Daniel failed to dismiss her. "May I go?"

"Yes. Please send down the earl's valet."

"He's not here, sir. He'd gone off with his lordship."

Daniel nodded. "You may go, Miss Adams. Please send for me if you think of anything pertinent."

"I will, sir."

"It seems that neither the coachman nor the valet have returned. Might they have had a hand in the murder?" Daniel asked, his expression thoughtful.

"I think we need to discover where they are in order to answer that," Jason replied.

"I think that's me off to Hastings tomorrow," Daniel said as he heaved himself to his feet. "Perhaps they're still at the aunt's house. I'll get the address from Simonds."

Mr. Simonds seemed to have forgotten his earlier pique when they found him in the servants' hall, enjoying a cup of tea. Jason's coachman, Joe Marin, silently sipped his own brew, an empty plate before him.

"Mr. Simonds, I will need the name and address for the earl's aunt. And is there a place near here where we can get coffee or a spot of lunch before we head back to London?" Daniel inquired. He'd obviously noted the time on the clock mounted on the wall.

"I will write down the address for you," the butler said as he pushed to his feet. "Cook will be happy to make you coffee and sandwiches," he offered.

"That would be most kind," Jason replied.

"I will have the refreshments sent to the drawing room," Simonds announced, glancing toward Jason surreptitiously. He was probably still trying to figure out Jason's role in the investigation and how his American accent tied in with a British title, but being a well-trained butler, he knew that to offer him refreshments in the servants' hall would not reflect well on the family.

"There's really no need. We'll take our coffee right here, if that's all right, and then we'll be on our way," Jason said, not wishing to waste time repairing to the other side of the house and waiting for the refreshments to be brought when the servants' hall was a stone's throw from the kitchen. Daniel seemed taken aback by Jason's response but didn't bother to argue.

Jason didn't usually eat before performing a postmortem, but if he didn't have lunch, he would suffer a dip in his blood sugar levels and experience a bout of dizziness and weakness. Despite all the recent medical advancements, there was no cure or treatment for hypoglycemia, so Jason had been compelled to figure out for himself how to manage the condition. He found that eating at regular intervals, partaking of a protein with every meal, and monitoring his sugar intake helped to manage the episodes.

"May we return to London tomorrow, if that is her ladyship's wish?" Mr. Simonds asked once he'd instructed one of the kitchen maids to ask Cook for coffee and sandwiches.

"You may," Daniel replied. "Please notify me as soon as you arrive. I will no doubt have more questions, and I intend to speak to the countess as soon as she feels up to it."

Simonds left to write down the address, and Joe sprang to his feet. “I’ll fetch the carriage round, shall I?” he muttered, and headed for the door without waiting for an answer.

Jason and Daniel settled at the long oak table, mindful that they’d have to finish before the staff came down for their midday meal. Jason inhaled deeply as the smell of freshly brewed coffee wafted from the kitchen, followed by a maid with a silver pot and a plate of sandwiches. She made sure they had everything they needed before leaving them on their own, but as if by silent agreement, neither man mentioned the case, instead speaking of trivialities and gauging what time they would arrive back in London if the weather held.

Since the constables had taken the body and the police wagon, Daniel would travel back to London with Jason, which would give them an opportunity to speak privately. There was nothing more to learn at Langley Hall just then, and a partially thawed corpse awaited them in London.

Chapter 3

By the time they returned to London, Jason concluded that the earl, who'd been left to thaw in the middle of a back corridor, was as ready as he'd ever be, and asked for the body to be moved to the mortuary so that he could begin the postmortem. He hoped to finish by six o'clock, which would give him enough time to get home, clean up, and dress for dinner. Katherine had invited a new acquaintance and her husband to dine and would be upset if Jason failed to join them. Jason wasn't really in the mood to socialize, given the day's events, but Katherine so rarely asked anything of him, he wouldn't want to disappoint her or put her in an awkward position.

Jason removed his coat and hat, tossed his scarf and gloves onto a small table next to his medical bag, then donned a leather apron and the linen cap he used to keep the hair out of his face while working. Once ready, he fixed his attention on the victim, whose skin was still icy to the touch and unpleasantly damp. Jason began by checking the man's pockets, which yielded a few coins, a train schedule, an inexpensive watch, which was scratched and dented, and a hardboiled sweet. An odd assortment of items, but he supposed there was no accounting for what people stuffed in their pockets. Once all the items had been examined and placed in a cardboard box, Jason began to undress the corpse.

Much like the contents of the pockets, the garments didn't fit with what he knew of the man, which was that he was not only wealthy but highly influential and widely respected. Jason had seen a photograph of the earl in *The Times* several months ago, the man meticulous in his appearance—his clothes immaculate, his face cleanly shaven, and his hair neatly trimmed and gleaming with oil. The clothing he wore at present was inexpensive, the workmanship second-rate. The shoes were scuffed, the soles nearly worn through, and the earl's cravat was yellowed from repeated washing and threadbare with age. The shirt was neither very clean nor starched. Constable Napier had brought the earl's coat and hat, which were also rather shabby, but there was no walking stick or gloves, items that the earl would be sure to carry.

Jason carefully folded the clothes and set them aside, then took some time to examine the body's exterior before commencing with the postmortem. The man's skin was pallid. Not surprising in the winter months, but the earl looked borderline malnourished, his ribs clearly visible and his hip bones jutting out from a narrow waist. The nails were bitten to the quick, and his hair was greasy and lank, his lean cheeks coated with thick stubble a shade darker than the follicles on his head.

Whatever the earl had been up to the last few days, he hadn't been living in luxury, and given his unkept state and clothes, he might have been mistaken for a tramp. Jason's gaze slid toward the man's belly. There were three distinct holes where the pitchfork had entered the body and bruising where the base of the implement had met the skin. The earl's lower stomach and pelvic area were covered in blood as well as a yellowish-brown substance that smelled strongly of excrement. Since there hadn't been a great deal of blood at the scene, Jason concluded that most of the bleeding was internal. The gastrointestinal tract had been perforated, the contents leaking into the abdominal cavity and oozing from the wounds. Turning the earl over, Jason fixed his attention on the exit wounds. As with the stomach, there was some bleeding, but it hadn't been significant.

Jason rolled the body onto its back and reached for a scalpel, making a Y-shaped incision in the earl's chest. Three hours later, he tied off the thread he'd used to close up the corpse and pulled a sheet over the dead man, ready to make his report to Daniel and Superintendent Ransome, who'd wish to be present.

Chapter 4

Jason stopped by Daniel's desk, and the two men made their way to Superintendent Ransome's office. Ransome didn't even pretend to be busy, leaning forward eagerly in his seat when they entered. His hair was neatly combed, and his moustache carefully waxed, but his demeanor belied his well-groomed appearance. He was distinctly on edge, and understandably so. Ransome barely looked at Daniel, all his attention focused on Jason, who settled in a guest chair and waited for Daniel to take a seat before sharing the results of the postmortem.

"My lord," Ransome said by way of greeting. "I don't need to tell you that what we are dealing with is a very delicate situation. The Earl of Granville was a personal friend of Her Majesty and had been quite close with the late prince. If we fail to apprehend his killer, we will not only embarrass ourselves but possibly lose a significant portion of our funding. Did the postmortem provide any leads?" Ransome asked, his voice almost pleading.

"Not of the variety you're seeking, Superintendent," Jason replied. "The victim died sometime between six last night and three this morning. Given the low temperatures, I was not able to conclusively determine that from the postmortem, but we know that Thomas Grady, the earl's groom, left the stables at six to go to the servants' hall for his evening meal and did not return until the morning. Since it started snowing around three, and there were no visible footprints in the snow other than those of the groom and the butler, it stands to reason that our window falls between those hours."

Ransome nodded in acknowledgement but remained silent, so Jason continued. "The man was shabbily dressed, unkempt, and underweight." He looked to Ransome, wondering if he had known the earl in person.

"The Earl of Granville was a slender man, but he was always well dressed, his clothes fashionable and of the finest quality. He also wore several pieces of jewelry. Did you find anything on his body?"

"Just a battered pocket watch and a few coins."

"The motive must have been robbery," Ransome speculated. "Please, continue."

"The murder weapon was the pitchfork the killer had helped himself to in the stables. He drove the fork in with such force that he nailed the victim to a wooden partition. The fork entered at midriff, just below the ribcage. That's the softest part of the body and the area least likely to offer resistance, even if the victim tensed at the time of the attack. The tines punctured the bowel, and the middle tine penetrated the spine. That alone might have paralyzed the victim from the waist down had he survived."

"Was that what killed him?" Ransome asked, clearly shocked by the brutality of the attack.

"The victim died of cardiac arrest, but if his heart hadn't given out, he would have died from massive internal hemorrhage, as well as exposure. Even if the earl had received medical attention at once, he would not have survived the day."

Jason paused for a moment, then continued. "There were no other bruises on the body, nor were there any defensive wounds. The victim's hands were covered in blood, but his nails were not torn, nor were there any abrasions to the hands. The blood came from the wound to his abdomen. He did not try to fight off his killer."

"Can you tell anything from the manner of the attack?" Ransome asked dejectedly.

"I would speculate that the person who murdered him was of about the same height as the earl, given the position of the wound. The pitchfork would have been angled upward by a shorter assailant and downward by one who was significantly taller. The person wielding the fork was strong, and possibly very angry or scared. If pressed, I would say that the killer was a man, but as I have told Inspector Haze, it might have been a strong woman. Given that the earl was of middling height, she wouldn't have been unusually tall for a woman."

"Is there anything else you can tell us, my lord?" Ransome begged. "Once I inform Commissioner Hawkins, he'll have to apprise the Home Secretary. It would be immensely helpful if I could propose several lines of inquiry rather than admit that we have nothing to go on."

"I'm sorry, Superintendent, but that's all I can commit to at this time." Jason was about to rise when he remembered a small detail. "The victim had a train timetable in his pocket."

"You think he took the train from Hastings?" Ransome asked, his gaze instantly brightening.

"He may have, since there's no sign of his carriage. Perhaps he returned in secret, leaving his coachman and valet in Hastings, where he was meant to be visiting his aunt."

"Might the attack have been premeditated?" Ransome asked.

"I suppose so," Jason replied. "If the killer had been waiting for him in the stables, the earl might have had no time to react, but then the person wielding the fork would have to have known that the earl would make an appearance."

"They might have had a prearranged assignation," Ransome mused. "If the earl had known the killer, he'd have no reason to expect an attack."

"Why would the Earl of Granville go creeping about on his own property, dressed as a pauper, when everyone believed him to be in Hastings?" Daniel asked, chiming in for the first time.

"That's what we need to find out." Ransome pinned Daniel with a less-than-admiring stare. "How do you intend to proceed, Haze?"

"I wasn't able to question the countess, but I will attempt to speak with her this evening. I just received word that the family have returned to their Park Lane residence. Then first thing tomorrow, I will travel to Hastings and question Lady Seton, the earl's aunt. I hope to find both the coachman and the valet in residence, which would go a long way toward clarifying the earl's state of mind in his final days, as well as his plans."

"I would advise you to be very gentle with the countess, Haze. Kid gloves."

"Yes, sir. Understood."

"Report back to me as soon as you return from Hastings, Inspector."

"Yes, sir."

"This case must not make it into the papers, not until we've apprehended the killer," Superintendent Ransome said, glaring at the two men. "You are not to discuss it in public, nor are you to give any interviews to the newspapers. Is that clear?"

"Yes, sir," both men answered in unison, and pushed to their feet.

"Are you in a rush to get home, or can you accompany me to Park Lane?" Daniel asked once they had stepped outside. It was just past six, but it was dark, the sky overcast, a soupy fog swirling around the gas lamps and making them glow like disembodied orbs floating through the night sky.

"Katherine invited a friend to dinner. She'll be upset if I don't join them."

"Then, of course, you must go home. I'll speak to the countess on my own."

"Would you like me to accompany you to Hastings?" Jason asked.

"Your assistance would be most welcome, as always," Daniel added. "Shall we meet at Charing Cross, at say, seven a.m.?"

"How long does it take to get to Hastings?"

"Let's allow three hours for the journey," Daniel said. "I've never been to Hastings, but it's at least seventy miles from London, and there are several stops along the way."

"Can I offer you a lift to Park Lane?" Jason asked when his carriage materialized out of the foggy gloom, Joe huddled on the bench. Jason had asked to be collected at six, so the coachman must have been waiting just down the road.

Daniel shook his head. "You go on. I'd rather walk."

"See you tomorrow, then," Jason said, and climbed in.

Chapter 5

Turning up his collar against the bitter wind, Daniel set off at a measured pace. It wouldn't take long to reach Park Lane, and he needed time to think. What Jason had said about the deceased's physical condition struck Daniel as paradoxical. Why would an earl, a longtime favorite of the queen and a well-known and respected man about town, be dressed in shabby clothes and appear malnourished? That didn't make sense, especially since the earl had been last seen by his family and staff a mere two days ago, when he'd left the tender ministrations of his devoted minions.

Daniel had never met the man in person but had seen a photograph on the drawing room mantel when he'd arrived at Langley Hall that morning. The specimen in the picture had looked well-groomed and robust, his smile a smirk of confidence. What had happened to him between the time he'd left for Hastings and the moment of his death? Had he known his killer? Had the meeting been prearranged? If it had been, then the earl must have wanted to keep it secret, since he'd returned to Langley Hall using public transport and appeared to have walked from the nearest station, given the state of his shoes. Had he not been murdered, how would he have explained his unexpected presence to his wife, or had he intended to return to Hastings and then come home on Christmas Eve as expected?

And the poor countess. What must it have been like to discover that her husband had been murdered in such a savage way and had died an agonizing and possibly slow death? Unexpectedly widowed, she would now have to defer to her eleven-year-old son, unless he allowed her to hold the purse strings until he reached his majority and was ready to take on the running of the estate.

Somewhere, a clock struck the half hour. It was only half past six, but it seemed to Daniel that he had left his house yesterday instead of that morning. He was tired, hungry, and disheartened, but the promise of seeing his darling Charlotte and Miss Grainger—Rebecca, he thought with an inward smile—after the interview with the countess spurred him on. Once home, he'd enjoy a strong drink, a hearty meal, and the welcoming smiles of his all-female household. Daniel's hand subconsciously went to the tartan muffler Miss Grainger had given him for his birthday. It was not only striking but warm, made of the finest Shetland wool. She'd spent her hard-earned wages to buy him a gift, and Daniel had felt a mixture of deep pleasure and embarrassment when she'd given it to him over breakfast a fortnight ago. It was the first time a woman who was not his wife or mother had given him a birthday present. He found the thought strangely exhilarating.

As he paused to admire the waxing moon that was briefly revealed by the parting of the thick clouds, Daniel realized that it had been days since he'd thought of Sarah, who had died by suicide in early summer. Nor did he feel as broken inside. Perhaps it was because he had finally made peace with her death, or perhaps because he'd found comfort in Rebecca Grainger's uncomplicated presence. As Charlotte's nurse, Miss Grainger spent quite a lot of time with Daniel, and since they were the only two adults in the house besides Grace, the maid-of-all-work, it seemed silly for Miss Grainger to take a tray in her room instead of joining Daniel in the dining room. The meals had been a bit awkward at first, but after the first few days, Daniel and Rebecca had found their footing and talked easily to one another, discussing the day's happenings, Charlotte's activities, and just life in general.

Daniel never dared to ask any personal questions or utter anything that might sound even remotely flirtatious, but when he went up to his lonely bedroom at night, he often found himself smiling at something Rebecca had said or recalling how she had looked in the firelight when she read in the parlor after supper. Or how her eyes sparkled in her rosy face when she came in from the cold and declared that she could murder a cup of tea—an odd expression she'd learned from her father—and then giggled adorably when she recalled what Daniel did for a living and asked if she would be the prime suspect if the tea tin went missing.

Rebecca was so different from Sarah, Daniel reflected. She was lively, and so easily pleased. Of course, he could hardly compare, given what Sarah had suffered after their son's death, but for some reason, he thought that had something of a similar nature happened to Rebecca Grainger, she would have handled it quite differently. At the very least, she wouldn't have downed a bottle of laudanum to end her pain without any regard for the small child and loving husband she was leaving behind.

Having reached the earl's exclusive address, Daniel put all thoughts of the winsome Miss Grainger from his mind and walked through the gate set into the high stone wall that fronted the street. The house, which overlooked Hyde Park and was built in the Palladian style, could have passed for a smaller version of Buckingham Palace, and the size of the household staff had to be significant. It always struck Daniel as deeply unfair that some Londoners could barely afford enough food and coal to survive the winter while others lived in such hedonistic splendor, blessed with more than they could ever hope to need or consume in a lifetime. It was obvious from the numerous chimneys billowing smoke into the overcast winter sky that more rooms than could be in use at any given time were being heated on this frigid day, the cost of coal irrelevant, the waste inconsequential.

Daniel approached the stately double doors and knocked, relieved when he was instantly admitted by the butler. The house was already decked out for mourning with a black bow on the front door and black crape adorning the windows and covering the mirrors, paintings, and clocks. Despite the countess's malaise, the family had wasted no time, leaving Surrey within hours of the murder and setting the wheels of mourning in motion. The earl would no doubt have an elaborate funeral, possibly after the New Year, so that the maximum number of mourners could attend without having to forgo their Christmas and New Year celebrations.

Perhaps an emissary from the palace would be sent to represent the queen or maybe the home secretary would make it his business to pay his respects to a man he must surely have known well. Regardless, if a culprit was not apprehended and charged with murder by then, it would reflect very badly on the police service, Commissioner Hawkins, Superintendent Ransome, and, in turn, Daniel himself. He might even lose his place, since someone would have to pay for such catastrophic failure and Ransome would simply shift the blame in order to shield himself from the criticism and calls to defund the police that were sure to follow.

There were still those who would be happy to see the police service dismantled since they saw the brave men who often risked their lives to keep the peace and prevent crime as nothing more than blundering clodhoppers who were paid more than they were worth and only got in the way of activities that made thousands of pounds for those who flooded the city with opium and illegal pornographic material imported from France, and recruited boys and girls as young as eight to service middle-aged clients who had a penchant for children and didn't care for anyone to get in the way of their pleasure.

Daniel was distracted from his morbid thoughts by a maidservant who waited patiently to take his things. Once she'd taken his coat, hat, muffler, and gloves, Simonds led him directly to the drawing room, where the Countess of Granville reclined on a damask-upholstered chaise. The room was decorated entirely in chinoiserie, with blue and white wallpaper printed with whimsical pagodas, porcelain vases on spindly tables and the marble mantel, and both the carpet and the upholstery picking up the Oriental theme with a dark blue and gold motif.

The countess, who appeared to be in her mid-to-late thirties, looked pale and drawn, her dark hair severely pulled back into a low chignon and covered with flimsy black netting. There were shadows beneath her eyes, and her lips were almost devoid of color. She wore a string of jet beads with matching earrings that dangled from her ears and swayed gently as she moved her head to size up the new arrival. Daniel couldn't help noticing that the satin gown of unrelieved black appeared to be new and was cut in the latest style. As he advanced into the room, Daniel wondered if rich people ordered mourning clothes regularly just to have them on hand for when tragedy struck.

"My lady," Daniel said as he bowed from the neck.

"Inspector Haze," the countess said weakly. "Please, make yourself comfortable. I do apologize for not speaking with you earlier. I'm afraid I simply wasn't up to the task."

"No apology necessary, my lady," Daniel assured her. "I am deeply sorry for your loss."

"Thank you. Would you care for some refreshment?"

"No, thank you," Daniel said as he settled in an Oriental chair, which proved supremely uncomfortable, and took out his pencil and notebook.

The countess shifted on the chaise, assuming a half-sitting position. "Inspector, I would like to get this over with as quickly as possible, if you don't mind, so please ask your questions. I will not be offended, nor will I refuse to answer, no matter how intimate the inquiry."

"Very well," Daniel said, relieved that the woman intended to be forthcoming and he wouldn't have to beat around the bush for a quarter of an hour before getting to the crux of the matter. "My lady, when was the last time you saw your husband?"

"Two days ago, just before he left for Hastings. Damian would have liked to bring Aunt Hermione to us for Christmas, but he said she was too frail and wouldn't wish to make the journey," she added. "She hasn't visited us in quite some time, either in Surrey or in London."

"When was his lordship due back?" Daniel asked, even though Simonds had already told him the earl was due back on Christmas Eve. Perhaps the countess was aware that her husband meant to come back sooner.

"He was due back tomorrow. Damian loved Christmas, and it was our longstanding tradition to spend it in the country, where there were fewer social obligations, and we could enjoy the festivities in peace."

The cool succinctness of her answers surprised Daniel, given the circumstances. The countess looked bereft, but there was not a trace of the histrionics some women might have indulged in had they found themselves in her very fashionable shoes.

"Can you think of any reason your husband would have returned early, and on his own?"

The countess shook her head. "I've been puzzling over that. Neither the coachman nor Hannity—that's my husband's valet—have come back. It's most perplexing, Inspector."

"My lady, was the earl in reasonably good health?" Daniel asked carefully.

"He was. Why do you ask?"

"It's only that he was rather thin," Daniel dissembled, deciding it was best not to alarm the woman with the brutal truth of her husband's physical condition at the time of his death.

The countess made a dismissive gesture, her hand a pale wing against the crow-black of her gown. "Damian was never one to overindulge when it came to food. He liked to remain fit and took regular exercise."

"He looked rather down at the heel, if you'll pardon me saying so," Daniel remarked, still diluting the reality of what he had seen.

The countess looked surprised. "I don't know how to account for that. Perhaps Hannity wasn't on hand, and he dressed himself. Damian was hopeless when it came to such things." Her face suddenly crumpled, and silent tears slid down her pale cheeks.

"I don't know what I will do without him," the countess wailed. "I've known Damian my whole life. I always knew we would marry. There was never anyone else for me."

"I'm very sorry, my lady. I know how difficult it is to suddenly lose one's life partner." Daniel wasn't sure why he'd said that. What did an earl's wife care about his loss?

"Are you widowed as well?" the countess asked, fixing him with a watery stare.

"Yes. My wife and I had known each other since we were children as well," Daniel offered. Why was he telling her this? He wasn't here to talk about Sarah.

"Oh, I am sorry, Inspector Haze," the countess said through delicate sniffles. "Tell me, does it get easier?"

"It does," Daniel replied truthfully. "With time."

"I haven't even told the children their papa is dead. I keep hoping it was all a dreadful mistake and Damian will walk through that door," she said, giving the door a pointed stare.

"Your butler and groom have both identified the deceased as the Earl of Granville," Daniel said apologetically.

"I want to see him," the countess said. "When will you release the body for burial?"

"The undertaker can collect it tomorrow," Daniel replied.

The countess looked thoughtful. "I rather doubt my dear Damian will be ready for viewing until after Christmas. Even undertakers celebrate our Savior's birth. Perhaps I should come to Scotland Yard."

"My lady, I strongly advise you against such a course of action," Daniel said.

"You mean the sight is too gruesome for a lady?" she asked, smiling wanly.

"It will haunt you," Daniel said. "And I'm sure that's not how you would wish to remember your husband."

"No, you're right," the countess said. "I would rather pretend he's sleeping than see him in such sterile surroundings, and I know that he would have hated for me to see him that way. I will do whatever Damian would have wished," she said with obvious resolve. "I will allow him that final dignity."

"Very wise of you, my lady," Daniel agreed.

"Please, find his killer, Inspector Haze. I know it won't bring Damian back, but it will give me some semblance of peace to know that the scoundrel met his end at the end of a rope."

"I will do everything in my power to apprehend the killer," Daniel promised.

"Thank you. I believe you will," the countess replied. "I have a good feeling about you."

Daniel thanked the countess for her assistance and took his leave. He had no wish to walk and wasted no time in finding a hansom, eager to get home.

He arrived at home half an hour later and stepped into the warm foyer that smelled wonderfully of baking, pine boughs, and roasting meat. Daniel hung up his coat and scarf, carelessly tossed his hat onto the hat stand, and hurried into the parlor, where he found Miss Grainger sitting in her favorite chair, an open book in her hand. She smiled widely, her pleasure at seeing Daniel reflected in her eyes.

"Good evening, Inspector."

"Good evening, Miss Grainger. Something smells wonderful," Daniel said, inhaling deeply as he poured himself a large brandy.

"Grace made your favorite, mutton chops with mint jelly and roasted potatoes." Rebecca glanced at the clock. "Shall I tell her you're ready to dine?"

"Yes, please. But first, join me in a drink."

Rebecca inclined her head in agreement, and Daniel poured her a small sherry. He handed her the glass, and she accepted with thanks. Daniel sank into the other chair, a twin to the one Rebecca occupied, glad to be near a warm fire after the chilly ride home.

Rebecca took a dainty sip and fixed all her attention on Daniel. "How was your day, Inspector?"

"Frustrating," Daniel replied with feeling.

"Oh, dear," Rebecca replied with a gentle smile. "Then you must tell me all about it."

And he did.

Chapter 6

Katherine's new friend, Adelaide Powell, was a charming woman who had a sweet smile and a sharp wit. Her husband, Andrew, wasn't nearly as diverting but seemed a solid sort of fellow who was well informed and not nearly as stodgy as some of the men Jason came across in his professional life, who often saw themselves as godlike due to their perceived power over life and death. Andrew Powell was deeply interested in the United States and asked many questions about how the political and social conditions had changed since the end of the American Civil War. Jason was grateful that he didn't ask about his imprisonment or wartime experiences. He had no desire to recount either.

Although he valiantly tried to keep his mind on the conversation, Jason's thoughts kept drifting toward the case, especially once the topic of social reform had come up. Mrs. Powell devoted much of her time to charitable works, but her ideas for improving conditions for the city's poor were somewhat naïve, and her husband was clearly nervous that she was going too far in her criticism of the status quo in the presence of someone of Jason's stature. Jason smiled politely, nodded, and responded when addressed, but lost the thread a few times and earned himself a stern look from his wife, who tried to make up for his graceless ways by being extra charming and supportive of Mrs. Powell's ideas.

"I'm sorry, Katie," Jason said contritely as soon as their guests left, and they had retired to their bedroom.

"Really, Jason," Katherine huffed. "You were borderline rude."

"I didn't mean to be, but I couldn't stop thinking about the victim."

"It's dreadful what happened to the earl, but our life can't revolve around murder," Katherine admonished him. "We do need to have friends who are not policemen or surgeons."

"You are absolutely right," Jason agreed, his gaze sliding toward the carriage clock on the mantel. He was tired and would have liked nothing more than to go to sleep.

"Oh, just go to bed," Katherine said, but there was no heat in her voice, only resignation. "You must be exhausted."

"I'm sorry," Jason tried again.

"I know you are." Katherine wrapped her arms around his waist and pressed her cheek to his chest. Jason pulled her close and rested his cheek against her head, marveling at how perfectly they fit together.

"I love that you want to help people and don't expect any reward. It's what makes you you," Katherine said into his shoulder, and he could hear the smile in her voice.

"I haven't even seen Lily today," Jason complained as Katherine stepped out of his embrace and sat down at the dressing table, ready to unpin her hair. "I miss her. And I must leave early tomorrow."

At eight months old, Lily was a delight, and Jason longed to feel her chubby arms around his neck as she hugged him. She had just started saying "Mama" and he was eagerly waiting for her to ask for him. But she always smiled and stretched her arms out when he came into the room, and for now, that was good enough. It was better than good. It was heaven.

"Go look in on her before you go to bed," Kathrine suggested.

It would take her at least a quarter of an hour to get ready for bed, so Jason took her advice and went up to the nursery, where he settled in a rocking chair next to Lily's crib and watched his daughter sleep. He longed to hold her but didn't want to disturb her. She was a light sleeper and would take a long while to get back to sleep if woken.

Unwittingly, Jason's mind turned to the Langley children, whose world had turned upside down today. Even if they didn't yet know the details of their father's death, they'd find out soon enough. The story was sure to make the papers in the coming days, and some publications, like *The Illustrated Police News*, would report the crime in all its gory detail. Neither the children nor the countess were likely to read the papers, but if they so much as left the house, they were sure to come across newsboys shouting the headline in the streets.

Going back to the postmortem, Jason couldn't help feeling that something wasn't quite right, and he had missed something vital, but he couldn't think what that might be. Perhaps he would figure it out in the coming days. For now, he had to put the murder from his mind if he hoped to sleep through the night, but as he left the room and headed toward the master bedroom, he knew the gory scene would revisit him in his dreams.

Chapter 7

Thursday, December 24

Hastings was probably lovely in the summer, but on this frigid day in late December, it was desolate, the inhabitants keeping inside and enjoying the warmth of their fires as an army of chimneystacks belched black smoke into a lowering gray sky. Daniel and Jason huddled deeper into their coats as gusty wind tore at their mufflers and hats, even inside the hansom they'd taken from the station.

Lady Hermione Seton's house was situated on the seafront in St. Leonards, a location that had to be highly desirable during the heat of the summer months but was downright arctic at this time of year. The hansom rolled passed a number of nearly identical fronts before finally stopping at the correct address. Daniel paid the cabbie, whose caped greatcoat, voluminous woolen muffler, and bowler hat that was pulled down low to keep it from blowing off, made his face nearly impossible to find among the layers of clothing.

A middle-aged servant in black bombazine answered the door and invited them inside, shutting the door hastily behind them to keep out the cold. The house seemed unusually quiet, all the doors leading off the foyer closed, presumably to keep in the heat.

"We'd like to speak to Lady Seton," Daniel said as he held up his warrant card. "Inspector Haze of Scotland Yard, and this is my associate, Lord Redmond."

The woman looked stunned but nodded and hurried off, leaving them in the foyer to await her return. A few moments later, she took their things and directed them to a lovely drawing room decorated in lemon yellow and silver. Despite the overcast, windy day outside, the room looked sunny and bright, and was marvelously warm and welcoming.

An elderly woman sat before the fire, her gray hair covered with a black lace cap and her outdated gown unrelieved black satin. A cameo depicting the silhouette of a woman hung around her scrawny neck, secured by a black velvet ribbon. She offered them a small smile, but despite the reserved reaction her gaze was bright with curiosity.

"Good morning, gentlemen. Do sit down," she invited. "Would you care for a hot drink? I hear it's rather blustery out there this morning."

"That's very kind," Daniel said. "A warm drink wouldn't come amiss."

"Gladys, bring us some coffee. I think you had better explain the reason for your visit," Lady Seton said once Gladys had departed.

"My lady, I'm very sorry to inform you that your nephew, the Earl of Granville, was found dead yesterday morning."

The woman looked perplexed, her bony fingers clasping the cameo at her throat in her confusion. "Inspector, my name is Lydia Hammond, and I am no lady," she added with a wry twist to her mouth. "Lady Seton died more than three years ago and had bequeathed her home to me. We were lifelong friends, and when we both found ourselves widowed, decided to set up house together. It was more companionable than living alone. I am sorry about his lordship, of course, but I'm not sure what his death has to do with me or his deceased aunt."

Daniel and Jason exchanged looks. "Lady Seton is dead?" Daniel asked, just to make certain he had understood correctly.

"Yes. The earl attended her funeral."

"So why would he tell his wife that he regularly visited his elderly aunt?" Daniel asked, hoping Mrs. Hammond might offer an explanation that made sense.

"I wouldn't wish to speculate, Inspector, but if I had to guess, I'd say it made for a convenient excuse," Lydia Hammond said with a knowing smile.

"Are you suggesting that the earl was visiting his mistress?" Daniel asked, annoyed when Gladys entered the room bearing a laden tray. She set a silver coffeepot, cups and saucers, a cream jug, and a sugar bowl on the low table and added a plate of sliced cake that filled the room with an aroma of vanilla and citrus.

"Shall I pour?" Glady asked her mistress.

"Please," Mrs. Hammond replied. "I'm afraid my hands are a bit shaky these days," she explained unnecessarily.

Gladys poured each of them a cup of coffee, fixed Mrs. Hammond's the way she liked it, and handed it to her on a saucer, waiting patiently to make sure the old woman had a firm hold on the plate.

"Would you like a slice of cake, madam?" she asked.

"No. But do serve the gentlemen before you leave."

Once Daniel and Jason were furnished with cups of coffee and slices of cake, Gladys finally departed, leaving them to speak in private.

"Mrs. Hammond, was the earl unfaithful to his wife?" Jason asked, clearly intrigued by this new possibility.

"I don't know for certain, but Hermione didn't hold her nephew in the highest regard. She thought him something of a libertine."

"When was the last time he'd visited his aunt before her death?" Jason asked.

"That would have to be more than five years ago now. He had his minion, Simonds, check on us from time to time, just to make sure we were still breathing, but Damian rarely came in person."

"But he was aware that his aunt had died and attended the funeral," Daniel reiterated.

"Of course he was aware, Inspector," Mrs. Hammond scoffed. "He came to the funeral, all right, but he did not bring his family. He came alone and then tried to evict me immediately after the burial."

"Did he own this house?" Jason asked.

"No, but he thought it unseemly that I remain here. I asked him to respect his aunt's wishes and leave me in peace. I haven't heard from him since."

"Would the earl keep the news of Lady Seton's death from his wife?" Daniel asked, trying to get a clearer understanding of the earl's character.

"If it suited his purpose, I don't see why he wouldn't," Mrs. Hammond replied. "Damian was the sort of man who siphoned every event through the funnel of his own needs, and if Hermione's death offered him a way to deceive his wife, then he would be sure to make use of it."

"Do you happen to know the identity of the earl's mistress?" Daniel asked, wondering if the woman lived in Hastings or the earl had simply used the town to keep his wife off the scent and went somewhere else entirely, rendering this journey to Hastings futile since neither the coachman nor the valet were here.

"I do not," Mrs. Hammond replied. "And he might have had several mistresses since Hermione's passing. That man did not let the grass grow under his feet."

"Thank you for your help, Mrs. Hammond," Daniel said. "We're sorry to have troubled you."

"Not at all," Mrs. Hammond replied, her fingers still stroking the cameo. "I get so few visitors these days, especially in the winter months. It was my pleasure to speak with you."

Having bid Mrs. Hammond goodbye, the men returned to the foyer and waited in silence for Gladys to bring their things. They were just about to leave when Gladys, who had been sneaking urgent looks at Daniel, finally spoke up.

"Inspector, may I have a word?"

"Of course," Daniel replied.

Gladys clasped her hands before her, as if she were about to sing. "I couldn't help but overhear what you asked Mrs. Hammond just as I brought in the coffee, and I think I might be able to help."

"How?" Daniel asked, surprised by her offer.

"I have seen the earl several times this past year when I went to purchase some items for Mrs. Hammond. Both times in the company of a young woman."

"Do you know who the woman might be?"

"I do. Her name is Rosamunde Lillie, and she keeps a house in George Street."

"How do you know that?" Jason asked, regarding Gladys with renewed interest.

Gladys looked embarrassed. "It gets rather lonely here with just the two of us," she explained. "Sometimes, when the mistress asks me to run an errand, I stop in at a tearoom in Pelham Crescent. I've lived in Hastings all my life, so I often run into an acquaintance or two, and we enjoy a quiet chat."

"You mean you're privy to local tittle-tattle," Daniel summarized, pleased that the servant had decided to speak up.

"Yes," Gladys replied, coloring slightly.

"Thank you," Daniel said heartily. "You've been most helpful, Miss… eh, Gladys."

"I'm glad," Gladys replied, visibly pleased to have her contribution acknowledged. "And I'm glad that scoundrel is dead," she hissed. "He was beastly to his aunt. Just beastly."

Having said her piece, she marched to the door and held it open, inviting them to take their leave before her mistress began to wonder why the men were still there when they'd bid her goodbye more than ten minutes ago.

There was no cabstand nearby or a convenient hansom rolling down the street, so Daniel and Jason set off on foot, the pleasant warmth of Mrs. Hammond's drawing room quickly forgotten as a chill wind whipped their trouser legs and snatched at their hats.

"Well, I certainly didn't expect that," Daniel observed as he clutched at his hat to keep it from flying off.

"Neither did I," Jason replied. "But if the earl used his dearly departed aunt as an excuse to visit his mistress and the countess discovered the real reason behind his forays into Hastings, that would certainly give her a motive for murder."

"Yes, it would, but would the countess be strong enough to nail her husband to a wall?" Daniel mused.

"The earl was borderline malnourished," Jason replied. "Perhaps he suffered from an illness that I wasn't able to detect during the postmortem. If he was considerably weakened, a strong, angry woman would be able to skewer him."

"Yes, I suppose you're right, but I can't see the Countess of Granville murdering her husband in such a brutal manner because of his infidelity. Plenty of men keep a piece on the side. It's not uncommon, nor is it frowned upon by members of your class," Daniel said apologetically. "The attention such an act would cast upon her family would do more lasting harm than a fleeting romance that might be over in a few months."

"Perhaps not so fleeting," Jason remarked. "Lady Seton died three years ago, yet he was still coming to Hastings. Had he found a new mistress closer to home, the ruse would no longer be necessary."

"Miss Lillie might have been one of many. Hastings is a popular seaside resort during the summer months. A man of the earl's standing would have no trouble finding a host of willing females here, and who is to say that every time he said he went to Hastings, he actually did? He might have gone anywhere and kept a string of mistresses."

"Let's see what Miss Lillie has to say. At this stage, we're simply jumping to baseless conclusions."

Daniel sighed, knowing Jason to be right. But he did hope Glady had got it right and Miss Lillie had been the earl's current mistress. Identifying the reason for his visits to Hastings would go a long way to figuring out what he'd been up to in the months leading up to his death.

Chapter 8

Rosamunde Lillie's house was an oasis of comfort and style. A huge vase filled with fresh flowers—rather an extravagant indulgence in the dead of winter—served as the focal point for the black-and-white tiled foyer. The parlor, to which Daniel and Jason had been led by a crisply uniformed maid, was decorated in shades of peach and cream, the elegant furniture and lovely paintings a testament to the owner's good taste and obvious wealth. A small Christmas tree stood on a spindly table, the fanciful baubles reflecting the light from the windows.

Miss Lillie, when she finally joined them, was a vision in dove-gray silk, her fair hair arranged into a fashionable hairstyle and her silvery eyes fringed with lashes too dark to be natural in one so fair. She appeared to be in her early twenties, but the look in her eyes gave the impression of an older, more worldly woman. Daniel wondered if Miss Lillie had been rescued from a brothel by the besotted earl.

"How can I help you, gentlemen?" the young woman asked as she sat down and arranged her skirts in a way that made her look like a delightful confection.

"Miss Lillie, I'm Inspector Haze of Scotland Yard, and this is my associate, Lord Redmond," Daniel said. He'd learned to gauge when it was beneficial to use Jason's title and when a simple *Mr. Redmond* would do. In this case, he thought the title might be of use.

"Yes, Mary told me who you are, but I don't quite understand the purpose of your visit," Miss Lillie said, looking from Daniel to Jason as if their appearance could alleviate her confusion.

"We are investigating the death of the Earl of Granville," Daniel said, watching her closely.

Miss Lillie's hand flew to her bosom as her eyes grew huge with shock. She cried out, the sound reminiscent of an injured animal that knew the wound to be fatal. Unless she was a very fine actress, her distress appeared genuine. Chest heaving as she struggled to draw breath, she sprang to her feet and began to pace, drawing in deep, calming lungfuls of air.

Jason was immediately at her side, while Daniel called for the maid to bring a glass of sherry. Miss Lillie took a few small sips, then handed the glass back to Mary and sank onto the settee, seemingly exhausted. But the crisis had passed. She was breathing normally, and her gaze was clear, if troubled.

"Forgive me," she said weakly. "The news came as a dreadful shock. Please, tell me what happened to Damian."

Miss Lillie's reaction all but confirmed what Gladys had deduced about the relationship. Daniel relayed an abbreviated version of events, sparing Miss Lillie the worst of the gruesome imagery. She nodded miserably when he finished but didn't ask any probing questions.

"Miss Lillie, how long have you been the earl's mistress?" Daniel asked without preamble.

"Nearly three years," she replied.

Daniel was glad she'd decided not to play coy and deny the obvious. "And he leased this house for you?"

"Damian purchased it for me outright."

"That's very generous," Daniel remarked. The earl must have been besotted, indeed.

"Damian was a generous man."

"How did you two meet?" Jason asked, smiling at the woman kindly.

Miss Lillie looked very sad, a faraway expression on her lovely face. She clasped her hands in her lap and stared at them for a long moment before raising her head to meet Daniel's inquisitive gaze and Jason's sympathetic one.

"When I was a child, my father, who was a third-rate musician at best, realized I had a good singing voice and an aptitude for music. He spent every farthing he had to engage the best voice coaches to develop my talent, and once he judged me ready, he found a way to get me into the drawing rooms of the nobility. Something about my voice must have pleased them because the number of bookings increased steadily over the years, as did my fee. I became my father's meal ticket. There were weeks when I performed at a different house every night, sometimes taking an afternoon and an evening booking for the same day."

Miss Lillie sighed heavily. "I suppose I'd still be singing for my supper if I hadn't met Damian. He approached me after a performance at Lady Downing's musical evening. We got to talking, and he asked if he might see me again. I knew my father would order me into Damian's bed in order to further his own ambitions, so I politely declined," Miss Lillie said.

"Over the next few months, Damian appeared at nearly every event my father booked for me and tried to charm me every time. I continued to refuse him, so he arranged for a private event and had me sing just for him." She smiled at the memory. "After the first few songs, he dismissed my father and asked me to join him for supper. It was a lovely evening, and he treated me with the utmost respect. We continued to meet for the next few months, and eventually I agreed to become his mistress. I didn't do it to benefit my father. I did it because I fell in love and thought I deserved some happiness," she said defiantly.

"And your father?" Jason asked.

"Doesn't know where I am. That was one of my conditions."

"Did the earl make any promises to you regarding the future?" Daniel asked.

"Damian said he'd always look after me."

"Did his wife know of your relationship?" Jason inquired.

"Damian said she didn't. He told her he was visiting his aunt, and she seemed to accept that."

"Would she have murdered him if she found out?" Daniel asked.

"I highly doubt it," Miss Lillie replied. "The countess is a practical woman. An unfaithful husband is better than no husband, and Damian made sure no one knew of our liaison. He had no wish to cause the countess any embarrassment or emotional distress."

"But people did know. That's how we came to find you, Miss Lillie," Daniel pointed out.

Miss Lillie shifted in her seat, her gaze sliding toward the window, where watery sunshine was trying to break through the clouds.

"Damian had grown careless of late. He was tired of sneaking around."

"And might this carelessness have cost him his life?" Daniel asked.

"Do you seriously think that the Countess of Granville would run her husband through with a pitchfork, knowing the sort of scrutiny that would invite?" Miss Lillie challenged him. "If not to preserve her own reputation, she would at least think of her children, who would no doubt suffer should their family name be dragged through the muck."

"She might have found someone willing to do the deed. And the scandal will soon die down if the story is kept out of the papers, which it will be."

Miss Lillie shook her head stubbornly. "I hope you will forgive my impertinence, Inspector, but I think you're barking up the wrong tree."

"Perhaps," Daniel agreed, "but I must explore every possibility, and your affair certainly gave the countess a motive."

"Did the earl use his own carriage when he came to see you?" Jason asked.

"Sometimes. And at other times, he took the train from London."

"So where did his coachman and valet go when he opted to take the train?"

"For a jolly jaunt," Rosamunde Lillie replied, a smile tugging at the corner of her mouth. "They were given a few days off to make themselves scarce, and then they would collect Damian at the railway station at the appointed time and bring him home."

"Where are they now?" Daniel asked.

"I don't know. I haven't seen Damian since October."

"Did he simply show up on your doorstep, or did he inform you of when he was coming?" Jason asked.

"He usually notified me. We wrote to each other regularly."

"And did you send the letters to his home?" Daniel asked.

"Yes, but I used his aunt's name on the envelopes, in case his wife saw the letters."

"Did you know that Lady Seton passed three years ago?" Jason inquired.

"Yes, I did, but Damian never told the countess of his aunt's passing."

"Miss Lillie, did the earl ever speak to you of any enemies or conflicts that might have led to a physical altercation?' Daniel asked.

Miss Lillie appeared to be considering the question, then, having seemingly made up her mind, faced Daniel head on. “Damian once told me that his happiness was bought with the suffering of another. He seemed almost frightened when he said that, as if he were anticipating a reckoning of some sort.”

“Did you ask him about it?” Daniel asked.

“I did, and he said that his father told him that when Damian had dared to complain about some minor injustice inflicted on him as an adolescent.. I had no wish to upset him, so I didn’t probe any deeper. Damian was not someone who liked to dwell on unpleasantness. He enjoyed the finer things in life and believed that it was up to the individual to make their time on earth as happy and fulfilling as their circumstances would allow.”

“What will you do now that the earl is gone?” Jason asked.

“I don’t know,” Miss Lillie replied, her uncertainty palpable. “I suppose I will remain in Hastings for the time being. I am safe here, as long as no one knows my real name.”

“What was your identity before you met the earl?” Daniel asked.

“Do I have your word that my privacy will be protected, Inspector?”

“I can’t make such a promise, Miss Lillie. That all depends on where the investigation takes us.”

“Then I’m afraid I can’t tell you my real name. I will not go back to slaving for my father. Damian made sure I was well provided for, and I will be happy enough on my own,” she stated with steely resolve. “When will the funeral be held?”

“I really couldn’t say,” Daniel replied truthfully. “That depends on the countess.”

"Can I ask you to let me know once you do?" the young woman asked, her tone pleading. "I know I should probably stay away, but I would like to pay my respects."

"Certainly," Daniel replied, and pushed to his feet. "Thank you, Miss Lillie. You can write to me care of Scotland Yard if you think of anything relevant to the investigation."

"I will be sure to do that," Miss Lillie replied as she followed the men to the door.

"If we hurry, we'll just make the London train," Jason said as soon as he and Daniel stepped out into the gale-force wind blowing off the sea. "It seems our business here is done."

"Let's go," Daniel said, and they set off at a trot.

Chapter 9

Finding an empty compartment with no great difficulty, Daniel and Jason settled in for the long ride. Jason set his topper and gloves on the seat beside him but kept the scarf on. The compartment was only marginally warmer than the outdoors. Daniel did the same and watched with some relief as the station rushed past them, then faded from view, the outskirts of Hastings giving way to frost-covered fields and sleepy hamlets.

It was Christmas Eve, but Daniel felt as if it were an ordinary day and wished he could skip over Christmas altogether. If not for Charlotte, he would have, but he owed it to his precious girl to acknowledge the holiday no matter how wretched he felt. This would be their first Christmas without Sarah, the first of many, and they had to forge their own traditions and create their own joy.

"What are your thoughts?" Daniel asked, turning his attention back to Jason. It was much safer to focus on the case rather than his own feelings.

"I think Miss Lillie knows more than she's saying," Jason replied without hesitation.

"I agree, but she's either protecting someone else or herself."

Jason nodded in agreement. "She said the earl always notified her when he was going to come and see her, but she hadn't seen him since October and didn't appear to be expecting him. That's a long time not to see one's mistress," Jason theorized.

"I wouldn't know. I've never kept a mistress," Daniel replied, grinning despite himself.

Jason laughed. "Neither have I, but I would imagine that a man who's enamored of his paramour would wish to see her more than once per quarter."

"Do you think the earl might have been visiting someone else?"

"It's entirely possible that he had tired of Miss Lillie, which would give her a motive for murder."

"I don't see the beautiful and delicate Miss Lillie attacking him with a pitchfork," Daniel pointed out.

"Neither do I, but there are always those who will happily do any deed if sufficiently paid. And then there's her father. She seems very frightened of him. If he had finally discovered where his daughter resides and at whose expense, he might have decided to dispose of her lover in the hope that she would be forced to resume her singing career."

"We must find out the name of Miss Lillie's father and verify his whereabouts at the time of the murder," Daniel said.

"I'll check with Katherine. She likes to read the society columns. Perhaps she can point us in the right direction. But there might be another possibility," Jason mused.

"Which is?"

"If we are to take Miss Lillie's statement that the earl's happiness had come at the expense of someone else at face value, then we need to consider whose happiness or well-being had been sacrificed."

"Perhaps he had been referring to his wife, but then downplayed the remark when he realized that he'd let down his guard and brought his marital problems into his lover's bed," Daniel replied.

"If there's a time when a man will let down his guard, it's in the moments of postcoital bliss," Jason said, an amused smile tugging at his lips. "But it is possible that he meant someone else and that his father's rebuke had stayed with him all this time."

"Yes, it is," Daniel agreed. "We must track down the valet and coachman. No one knows more about a man's private affairs than his faithful servants."

"Well, they're either enjoying a jolly jaunt, unaware their master is dead, or they're dead as well," Jason said.

"Let's hope it's the former and they will turn up within the next few days when their master fails to appear at the appointed time."

"It would certainly help if the story made it into the papers. The news might bring them back sooner."

"Or drive them away. They might be implicated in the earl's death," Daniel mused.

"How do you intend to proceed?"

"I would like to speak to Lord Elton," Daniel said. "I believe the two were close friends, and I would very much appreciate it if you would accompany me."

"Did the countess point you in Lord Elton's direction?" Jason asked.

Daniel shook his head. He'd rather not admit to it, but he enjoyed reading the society columns as well and had seen the two men mentioned in the same sentence more than once. They were devoted cronies, if the gossip could be believed, and were often spotted out on the town together.

"I heard they were well acquainted," Daniel said. "I should think he'd want to help us find his friend's murderer."

As a rule, the nobility weren't eager to help the police, even when it was in their best interests to be forthcoming. Everyone had their secrets, and they guarded them jealously against becoming public domain. Lord Elton was a notorious womanizer and man-about-town. He might not wish to reveal anything about his good friend for fear of unwittingly implicating himself—not that the ton wouldn't forgive him any transgression. Lord Elton was still one of the most eligible bachelors in London, and any ambitious mama would be happy for her daughter to marry him, even if he kept a harem of concubines on the side.

Jason pulled out his watch and flipped it open to check the time. "We can either try our luck with Lord Elton this afternoon or wait until after Christmas. Speaking of which, what are you and Charlotte doing tomorrow?"

Daniel swallowed the sizeable lump that seemed to have formed in his throat, threatening to choke him.

"We'll have Christmas dinner after church. Grace has been cooking and baking mince pies for the past two days. Miss Grainger will, of course, be joining us. You?"

"Same," Jason replied with a joyful smile. "It's Lily's first Christmas, and what makes it even better is that the very pious Reverend Talbot can't join us because he has to take the Christmas service at St. Catherine's. Even Katherine is relieved that her father won't be there. He does tend to suck the air out of the room with his mere presence, and he would be outraged by the presence of the staff and make his feelings known. Very loudly, I might add.."

"Are you celebrating with the staff?" Daniel asked, scandalized.

Grace would be joining in the celebration, but Daniel's household wasn't nearly as hoity-toity as Jason's, and he had just the one maidservant, so it would be rather cruel to banish her to the kitchen.

"The staff will have their own Christmas dinner tomorrow, but we will have a small party tonight, and I will pass out my gifts."

"You do know that's what Boxing Day is for, don't you?" Daniel teased.

Jason knew all about the tradition of giving the staff gifts the day after Christmas, since Sarah had explained it to him when he'd first arrived on English shores.

"I do, but I like doing it on Christmas Eve. Our servants are like our family, and I prefer to treat them as such. Besides, my parents always included the servants in our Christmas Eve celebration, and I would like to continue the tradition."

"Do you give them a bonus, or have you actually bought gifts?" Daniel asked, curiosity getting the better of him.

He intended to give Grace a small bonus, but he had purchased a gift for Rebecca, and the mere thought of it made his cheeks burn. Not because it was in any way inappropriate, but because it felt rather intimate to be buying a gift for any woman other than Sarah. He hoped Rebecca would like the silk shawl embroidered with bluebells that had reminded Daniel of her eyes.

"Katherine and I bought individual gifts. And I will give the staff a bonus as well. They richly deserve it," Jason said.

"Putting up with you, you mean?" Daniel joked.

"It's not an easy feat," Jason replied, smiling widely. "They might never find respectable employment again, having demeaned themselves by working for the upstart American and his lowborn wife."

"They won't need future employment, as they'll never leave you."

Jason's expression wasn't lost on Daniel. The staff might never leave him, but it wasn't impossible that he'd leave them.

Chapter 10

Lord Elton received them with alacrity but decided to conduct the interview in the billiards room, where the irritating clicking of colliding balls set Jason's teeth on edge, as did the man's cocky attitude and good looks. Jeremy Elton was in his mid-thirties and boasted the physique of a man who spent hours at the gymnasium, and the grooming of someone who spent the rest of his time with his tailor and barber. His auburn hair was fashionably cut and artfully arranged, and his cornflower blue eyes were fringed with lashes any woman would envy. His hands were elegant, his long fingers tipped by perfectly manicured nails, and Jason wouldn't have been surprised to learn that Lord Elton's shapely copper eyebrows were regularly plucked.

"I gather neither one of you has better things to do on Christmas Eve?" Lord Elton asked playfully as he chalked the tip of his cue stick and continued with his solitary game, a glowing cheroot dangling from the side of his mouth and filling the room with smoke.

Daniel couldn't afford to anger the man, but Jason felt no such compunction, being his equal. "Some people work for a living," he said tartly.

"Surely not you, my lord." Lord Elton grinned, as if recalling an amusing joke. "Oh, but you do work. In a hospital. Is that an American thing, or did your grandfather burn through the family fortune, leaving nothing but the title?"

"I enjoy my work," Jason replied truthfully.

"I could never resist a do-gooder," Lord Elton said, clapping Jason on the shoulder in a condescending manner. "You have my undying admiration, Lord Redmond. I would never soil my hands if I found myself in your position, but then again, I'm both lazy and selfish. I'm keenly aware of my faults," he said with a disarming wink. "Would either of you be willing to give me a game?" He gazed eagerly from Daniel to Jason as he stubbed out his cigar.

"I'll play," Jason replied, and picked up a cue stick.

He'd played countless games of billiards in Newport, Rhode Island, where he and his former fiancée had spent time during brutally hot New York summers. He hoped he could still manage to sink a ball. Daniel settled in a chair and pulled out his notebook, ready to take notes.

"So, what's this about, then?" Lord Elton asked once he'd taken the opening break shot.

"The Earl of Granville was found dead yesterday morning at his Surrey estate. Murdered with a pitchfork," Jason said, watching his opponent for any sign of awareness, but Lord Elton's face went slack, the cue stick nearly slipping from his hand.

"Damian is dead?"

"He is," Daniel replied.

"But who would wish to kill him? Damian was as amiable a chap as one could ever hope to meet."

"That's what we're trying to discover," Jason replied. He thought Lord Elton would no longer wish to play, but he turned to Jason, eyebrow raised.

"Your turn, old son," he said.

Jason surveyed the table, looking for an easy shot. He was in no mood to play but wanted to keep Lord Elton talking, and this seemed to be the best way. "Do you know of anyone he might have disagreed with recently?" Jason asked before taking his turn.

"No, I don't. Damian got on with everyone."

"Have you ever met Miss Lillie, my lord?" Daniel asked, taking the man by surprise. His cue stick glanced off the ball, and he pitched forward, then instantly righted himself. "Yes, of course

I've met Miss Lillie. Damian and I had no secrets from each other."

"Was the earl perhaps tiring of her?" Jason asked after he'd taken an angle shot and pocketed the ball.

"No." Jeremy Elton smiled wistfully. "Damian was an honorable man. Had been since he was a boy. Fair play was important to him."

"And you see remaining faithful to one's mistress as fair play?" Jason asked, knowing that Daniel, not being Lord Elton's equal, could hardly ask such an insolent question.

Lord Elton shook his head, then set down his cue stick. "I don't really feel like playing," he said. It was obvious the news of Damian Langley's death had shaken him to the core. "How about we have a drink instead, to old Damian's memory."

He walked over to a drinks cabinet and opened it to reveal several cut crystal decanters. "What's your tipple of choice?" he asked.

"Whatever you're having," Jason replied.

"I prefer Scotch whisky. Inspector?" Lord Elton turned to Daniel.

"Yes, thank you."

Lord Elton poured two fingers' worth of Scotch into crystal tumblers and passed out the drinks as if he were a footman, then invited the men to sit on a studded green leather sofa, taking a seat in a matching club chair that stood opposite. He raised his glass. "To Damian. The best friend a chap could have."

Daniel and Jason raised their glasses and took a sip. Jeremy Elton drained his glass in one go and set it down on a table at his elbow.

"Now, to address your question, Lord Redmond," Lord Elton said. "Damian always knew he'd marry Euphemia. His father deemed her a suitable bride, and they're second cousins, so keeping the bloodline pure and all that," he said, making an expansive gesture with his hand. "Damian loves—loved Effie, but it wasn't until he met Rosamunde that he truly fell in love for the first time. I would be lying if I said he didn't suffer a crisis of conscience, but a man is entitled to one great love affair in his life, is he not?" Elton asked. "So, he set up Rosamunde in Hastings, an arrangement that suited them both. Effie need never know, and Rosamunde could enjoy the respectability she wasn't going to get in London, where she was known to quite a few people. Everyone was happy."

"Clearly not everyone," Jason interjected.

"Are you suggesting that Effie murdered her husband?" Lord Elton asked, his eyebrows lifting comically.

"I'm suggesting nothing of the sort, but someone clearly had a motive, and given the method they employed, they were driven by strong feeling rather than a cool head."

"Effie knew nothing of the affair, and Rosamunde was only too happy to remain in the shadows."

"Do you happen to know her father?" Jason asked.

Lord Elton looked genuinely surprised. "She told you about him, did she?"

"She did. She seems rather frightened of him," Daniel said.

"I do know her erstwhile sire, but I promised Damian I would not reveal Miss Lillie's true identity. Her father is a brute and would repay her bid for independence with his fists."

"Miss Lillie's father has a motive for murder, sir," Daniel stated.

Lord Elton inclined his head. "Yes, I suppose he does. But why would he wait until now to come after Damian?"

"Perhaps his financial situation has deteriorated further and he's desperate to get his daughter back," Daniel speculated. "Especially since the earl had been generous to her."

Lord Elton looked from Daniel to Jason. "You must give me your word as gentlemen that Rosamunde's whereabouts will remain secret from her father. Damian would want me to protect the woman he loved."

"You have my word that Miss Lillie will not be betrayed to her father by either of us," Jason said, knowing it was his word as a nobleman that Lord Elton wanted.

"Rosamunde's father's name is Harry Quimby. Damian detested the man. Used to refer to him as Hairy Quim," Lord Elton said with a rueful smile that turned into a grimace of grief. His eyes misted with tears. "Dear God, I can't believe I'll never see Damian again. He was always such fun."

"And where might we find Mr. Quimby?" Daniel asked, trying valiantly not to betray his amusement.

"He used to keep rooms in Clerkenwell, but that was years ago, before Rosie ran out on him."

"Do you think Mr. Quimby is capable of murder?" Daniel asked.

"Without a doubt. As I said, he was the sort of man who resolved all of life's problems with violence. He never hit Rosie in the face, or the stomach because that might prevent her from singing, but he took a belt to her most nights, after he'd been drinking. Damian was shocked to see her back and thighs striped with red welts the first time… Well, you know what I'm referring to. He wanted to protect her, to keep her safe from the abuse. That's when Rosie Quimby died, and Rosamunde Lillie was born. Damian renamed her and gave her a new life. I really should go see her," Lord Elton said under his breath. Jason didn't think his motive was entirely altruistic.

"Was his lordship upset or worried about anything in the weeks leading up to his death?" Daniel asked.

"Not that I know of, but he had been down at the mouth since his father passed last February. Cancer of the pancreas," Lord Elton said, lowering his voice as if he feared to utter the words. "Brutal illness. Martin Langley went from being a hale and hearty man to hardly more than skin and bones in a matter of months. He would have died in agony had Damian not ordered the nurse he'd hired to ply him with morphine."

"Was the earl close with his father?" Jason asked.

"Yes, he was. He had great respect for his father and had always done his bidding without question."

"And his mother?"

"Lady Cecily died when Damian was four. She suffered from melancholia and had all but retired from society." Lord Elton averted his gaze and stared into his empty glass.

"My lord?" Jason said gently, interrupting the man's reverie. He was sure there was more.

Elton sighed. "She hanged herself. She was twenty-five at the time."

Jason stole a peek at Daniel, whose head was bowed, his expression inscrutable. Given his own wife's suicide, this couldn't have been easy for Daniel to hear, but he was a professional, and his task was to uncover who had killed the Earl of Granville.

"Was there anyone at all the earl had been at odds with recently?" Jason asked, more to give Daniel a moment to compose himself than because he thought Lord Elton had the answer.

"Not that I know of," Elton replied, shaking his head. "Damian was a lovely chap. He got along with everyone, even back at school, when bullying was rampant among the boys. There is always a hierarchy in such places. It's bully or be bullied."

"And which group did Damian Langley belong to?" Jason asked.

"Neither. That's my point. Damian was no bully, but he wouldn't allow himself to be bullied either. He knew just how to navigate a complex situation and come out the moral winner."

Jeremy Elton leaned back in his chair and fixed Daniel with a speculative stare. "I don't presume to tell you how to do your job, Inspector, but given that Damian was killed on his own property, I would think that you should be looking at the people who were at the house rather than at some perceived slights that go back years. Perhaps one of his servants had a grievance against him, or perhaps someone from the village had trespassed on the property and mistook Damian for one of the servants."

Daniel nodded. It was certainly a valid point. "We are pursuing all lines of enquiry," he said, adopting one of Ransome's favorite phrases when being interviewed for the papers. It smacked of confidence and unlimited resources, when in fact it was simply another way of saying that the police were blundering in the dark, in Jason's opinion.

"When found, the earl appeared to be underweight, and wore tatty clothing," Daniel said. "And his valet and coachman are still unaccounted for. Any thoughts on that, my lord?"

Elton shook his head. "Damian always dressed well, and although slender, he was in fine health. I saw him at Mr. Gideon's gymnasium only last week, and he was in top form. Something awful must have happened to him. Something awful, indeed."

Lord Elton grew silent, his expression morose, and Jason took that as their cue to leave. There was nothing more Elton could tell them at this time. Jason pushed to his feet, and Daniel followed suit.

"Thank you for your assistance, Lord Elton," Daniel said as he returned his notebook and pencil to his breast pocket.

"Happy to help, Inspector. You will find whoever did this, won't you?" Lord Elton asked, looking like a child that needed to be reassured that everything would be all right. His earlier cockiness had evaporated, leaving behind a bereaved and vulnerable man.

"I will do everything in my power to bring this case to a satisfactory conclusion," Daniel replied, once again resorting to one of Ransome's useless placating phrases.

"See that you do," Elton said, clearly needing to reestablish dominance over the interview. "I will call on Superintendent Ransome after Christmas for an update on the investigation."

"That is your prerogative," Jason said, and strode toward the door. He was more than ready to leave, and it was time he found his way home. Katie would be expecting him back by now.

A winter twilight had replaced the sullen daylight of earlier, and gentle gaslight illuminated the square, casting pools of light onto the ground below. Stars twinkled in the purpling heavens, and the moon seemed to hang unnaturally low, nearly scraping the chimneypots that appeared black against the darkening sky. Daniel turned to Jason, his brows knitted with obvious disappointment.

"Not much to go on," he said.

"No, but at least we now have the name of Miss Lillie's father. How does one find someone in a city of thousands?"

"I will stop by Division E first thing on Boxing Day. That's the nearest station to Mr. Quimby's last known residence. If he's as violent as Lord Elton says he is, then they might have had dealings with him in the past."

"That sounds like a reasonable plan," Jason replied. "I'm afraid I'm due at the hospital on the twenty-sixth, but perhaps we can meet up later."

"May I call on you in the afternoon?" Daniel asked.

"Of course. Merry Christmas, Daniel."

"And to you. My regards to Katherine."

Jason tipped his hat and headed toward his house only a few streets away. Daniel would find his own way home.

Chapter 11

Friday, December 25

Christmas Day

Jason gently smoothed a dark curl off Lily's face. She looked so peaceful now that she was finally asleep. The child had been fractious all evening, and he had worried that she might be coming down with something, but her forehead was cool and her airways clear. Perhaps she had been overexcited by the lavish gifts and Micah's return from school for the Christmas holiday. Lily adored Micah but was too little to understand why he appeared and disappeared from her life. Or maybe she'd had too many sugary treats, sneaked to her by both Katherine and Mrs. Dodson, who wanted to make sure the child enjoyed her first Christmas and sampled something of the seasonal puddings, as they liked to refer to dessert.

Jason always downplayed any concern about Lily's health in front of Katherine, but he worried incessantly and checked on her more often than his wife realized. How could he not be when he was faced with death every day? In some cases, it was unavoidable, but in others—most of them, in fact—early detection and timely medical assistance might have saved the patient. So many children died needlessly, and even those that survived were often underfed, nearly frozen to death, and very frequently neglected by parents who were busy scratching out a living and couldn't devote the time or resources to their numerous offspring.

Looking down at his precious daughter, it was difficult for Jason to comprehend how a father could intentionally hurt his child. Lord Elton's words echoed in his mind. *He took a belt to her most nights*. He couldn't imagine raising a hand to Lily, even if she had done something he deemed unforgivable. But so many people saw their children not only as a punching bag but as a lifelong burden, especially girls, who required more vigilance from their parents than boys of the same age. Miss Lillie was so delicate, so lovely. How could any man wish to hurt her?

But some parents' behavior was beyond comprehension, something Jason had learned when he'd first met the Donovans at a Union Army camp in Virginia. What sort of man took an eight-year-old boy to war, or left his only daughter at home alone and unprotected? Jason had judged Liam Donovan harshly when he'd first made his acquaintance, but later came to realize that Liam loved his children fiercely and had been unable to part from his youngest after his wife died, choosing to keep Micah with him despite the danger.

Jason was the closest thing the Donovan children had to a parent these days, and although Mary was in Boston, reunited with her son and making plans to marry a beau Jason had yet to meet, and Micah was away at school, Jason still felt a sense of responsibility and worried about them as if they were his own children. He had much to learn about being a parent and often prayed that he wouldn't get it wrong, as he had with Mary, whose pride was wounded by Jason's offer of financial support. Were there any parents that didn't make mistakes? His own parents had been loving and kind, but they'd had their share of disagreements, especially when it came to Jason's grandfather, whom he'd never met due to his father's mulish refusal to entertain any possibility of a reconciliation. Geoffrey Redmond couldn't forgive his father's rejection of his American wife, and he'd cut his father off completely, refusing to so much as pen an occasional letter to the parent who'd failed him. And now both men were gone, Jason the only bridge between the past and the present.

Jason sighed and carefully pushed to his feet, mindful of waking the child. He laid Lily in her cot and covered her with a goose-down blanket, tucking in the edges to prevent Lily from pulling the thick blanket over her head in her sleep and to keep her warm. He spared no expense on coal, but the house was still chilly.

Taking one last look at his daughter, Jason let himself out of the room and moved down the corridor toward the master bedroom. Katie refused to hire a nanny, determined to look after

Lily herself, so they kept the baby near them instead of on the upper floor, where a nursery was usually located. If Katie had to leave Lily for a couple of hours, she asked Fanny or Kitty to mind the child. The staff doted on the little girl and were only too happy to help out. Even Dodson, a curmudgeonly old bugger, as his wife affectionately called him behind his back, hovered nearby when Lily was downstairs and had been known to smile at her in a way that almost made him look grandfatherly.

Katherine was in bed, her spectacles perched on her nose as she read a new book, a gift from Mrs. Powell. A small smile played about her lips, a sure sign that she was enjoying the story.

"What are you reading?" Jason asked as he undressed for bed.

"*Little Women*. It's charming," Katherine replied as she marked her place with an embroidered bookmark and removed her glasses, carefully setting them atop the book. "It takes place in Massachusetts. You might like it," she added.

"I'll read it after you," Jason promised as he slid into bed, glad that his wife had warmed it for him. Usually the sheets were ice cold unless Fanny warmed the bed with a hot-water bottle.

"I can't stop thinking about the case," Katherine said as she snuggled closer to Jason. "The poor woman."

"Which woman are you referring to?"

"Well, both of them, I suppose," Katherine replied. "It's awful to lose one's husband, but the countess is wealthy and influential; she will persevere. But Miss Lillie…" She sighed. "Can you imagine having to change your name to get away from your own father? I tell you, Jason, it's abominable how some people treat their children."

"I was just thinking the same thing. I really believe there should be an inexpensive and effective way to prevent pregnancy. People should only have children if they want them."

"Please don't say that in front of my father," she replied as her lips quirked into an amused smile. "He would have an apoplexy."

"I hardly think the good reverend and I will ever discuss contraception, but you have my word that I will not intentionally irritate your father more than I already do."

"He plans to come to London for Lily's first birthday," Katherine said apologetically. "I hope you don't mind. I was thinking of having a little celebration."

"Of course. Perhaps I can bring Micah from school just for the day. I know he'd like to be there."

Katherine turned onto her side and propped her head up on her hand. "Did you have a chance to speak to him?"

"Not in private, no. Why?"

"He's been writing to us less. Do you think he's unhappy at school?"

Jason considered this for a moment. "He's either unhappy, in which case I think he would tell me, or he's enjoying school and asserting his independence."

"Yes, I suppose that could be a factor," Katherine replied. "I still think of him as a little boy, but he's practically a man. Does he still want to join the police service, do you think?"

"I'd much rather he go into medicine," Jason grumbled.

"You want him to follow in your footsteps?" Katherine quizzed him with a smile.

"It's foolish. I know," Jason conceded. "Micah might not even wish to remain in England once he's done with his studies. I think the arctic freeze between Micah and Mary has begun to thaw. He's been writing to her."

"Has he forgiven her for leaving at last?"

"I think so. He misses her, and now that Mary is settled, Micah might decide to attend college in the States, to be closer to Mary and her new family," Jason speculated. "There'll be another baby before the coming year is out. Mark my words."

"You are probably right. Where there's love, there are babies," Katherine said wistfully. She looked uncertain for a moment, her gaze sliding away from Jason's face. "Jason, what about us?" she asked softly.

"What about us?"

"Do you not want another baby?"

Jason had been taking precautions, unwilling to subject Katherine to another pregnancy until she was ready, both physically and mentally. She was still nursing Lily and was often worn out at the end of the day, falling asleep within moments of getting into bed.

"Of course I do."

"Well, then?" Katherine said, sliding her hand beneath the eiderdown and making her intentions crystal clear.

"I thought we should wait until Lily is at least one," Jason replied, somewhat breathlessly. "But if you're game…"

"Oh, I'm game. I'm okay with it," she added, copying Jason's American expression. Her laugh was throaty as she withdrew her hand and pulled off her prim, ruffled nightdress.

Jason's last coherent thought was that he hoped Lily would stay blissfully asleep for at least an hour.

Chapter 12

Saturday, December 26

Daniel rose bright and early on Saturday morning, glad Christmas was finally over and life could return to normal, or to whatever counted as normal these days. Yesterday's celebration had been awkward, the lack of a festive spirit too difficult to ignore, and Sarah's absence felt more keenly than her unobtrusive presence ever had been. Miss Grainger had done her best to put on a happy face for Charlotte, and Daniel had tried to pretend that this was just like any other Christmas, but he'd felt vastly relieved when Rebecca finally took Charlotte up to bed and then retired to her room, leaving him alone with his brandy and his thoughts.

Rebecca had liked his gift, he was sure of it, but her embarrassment had been palpable, especially since she'd opened it in front of Grace, whose eyes had narrowed in speculation as her gaze flew toward her employer. Perhaps he should have bought a shawl for Grace as well, to minimize the awkwardness, but it was too late to worry about that now. Still, he had no wish to face Rebecca over the breakfast table this morning, and he had a murder to solve.

It was still dark when Daniel left the house, the wind slashing him with icy daggers. He hurried to the cabstand. There was only one hansom, which Daniel climbed into eagerly. It was too cold and too far to walk. Daniel huddled deeper into his coat and muffler and fidgeted impatiently as the hansom made slow progress along increasingly busy streets. The upper echelons of society were still warm in their beds, but the poor were out in full force, heading to their places of employment, making deliveries of milk, meat, produce, and coal to households and local taverns, and farmers and fishermen were streaming into the city to set up their market stalls. Ragged, bleary-eyed boys emerged with their twig brooms to sweep the crossings of horse droppings, and thin, pale girls wrapped in nothing but threadbare shawls against the bitter wind appeared with trays of oranges and steaming pies slung over their scrawny necks, their long day about to begin.

The station at Holborn was just coming to life, with several constables exchanging morning greetings and brewing tea on a potbellied stove in the corner. The desk sergeant turned warily toward Daniel as he walked in, mistaking him for a member of the public.

"Good morning," Daniel said, and flashed his warrant card. "I'm Inspector Haze of Scotland Yard."

Th sergeant's demeanor instantly went from barely contained impatience to grudging respect. "Name's Sergeant Old'am, sir. 'Ow can I 'elp ye, Inspector?"

"I'm looking for a man named Harry Quimby. He's said to have resided in the Clerkenwell area as recently as three years ago."

"Oh, aye. We know 'Arry." The sergeant's lip curled in derision. "Quite a frequent visitor to the cells, 'Arry is."

"On what offense?"

"Brawlin', mostly. And public drunkenness."

"Is he dangerous?" Daniel asked.

"Ye mean does 'e 'ave an 'istory of causing bodily 'arm to unsuspecting patrons of the local establishments? Oh, aye. Pulled a blade on some poor sod only this week. Left 'im with a souvenir the daft cove's wife is not likely to appreciate."

"What was the cause of the disagreement?"

"The clumsy oaf bumped into 'Arry at the Black Dog and caused 'im to spill some of 'is drink. 'Arry tossed the ale in the man's face and pulled a knife on 'im while 'e were sputterin'. Cut the man from ear to mouth." Sergeant Oldham drew his finger across his own fleshy cheek to illustrate the severity of the injury. "Nearly took the man's ear off. Then 'eld the knife to 'is bollocks and instructed ’im to buy a fresh drink, on account of ’Arry’s other drink ’avin’ gone to waste.”

“Good Lord!” Daniel exclaimed. He hadn’t expected this level of volatility from a man who’d sired a creature as delicate and lovely as Miss Lillie, even if he was less than a loving father. “I heard he was a musician,” Daniel said for lack of a more fitting comment.

“’E is at that,” the sergeant replied. “Was a talented pianist in ’is day, but a love of strong drink, a fiery temper, and a runaway daughter ’ave pushed ’im over the edge of reason.”

“Was he arrested for attacking the man at the Black Dog?” Daniel asked.

“That ’e was. In fact, ’e’s down in the cells, if ye’d like a word. I reckon that’s the safest place for ’im, and for ye if ye mean to question ’im. What’s ’e meant to have done any’ow?” Sergeant Oldham asked.

“A man of some distinction was murdered on Tuesday night. Harry Quimby had as good a motive as any for wanting him dead. That’s all I’m at liberty to say,” Daniel explained.

“Well, couldn’t ’a been our ’Arry. ’E were right ’ere, safe and sound.”

“When was he taken up?”

“Monday evenin’. Been ’ere since. ’E’ll be on ’is way to Fleet Prison this afternoon. Deluxe accommodation.” The sergeant chuckled at his own wit. “I doubt ’e’ll be seeing the inside of a tavern anytime soon. The poor sod ’e slashed, ’is wound’s festered, according to ’is missus. If ’e dies, it’s the noose for ’Arry.”

“I’d like to speak to him,” Daniel said, exceedingly grateful that the man was behind bars and that he had found him so quickly

“Sure thing, guv. Eccles, take Inspector ’Aze down to the cells. Our ’Arry is a person of interest.”

He laughed again, but Daniel's attention was no longer on the sergeant. He was relieved to have found Harry Quimby, but if Sergeant Oldham was correct, there was no way Quimby could have been anywhere near Langley Hall on Tuesday night. Still, Daniel needed to be sure. Perhaps Harry had an associate.

Chapter 13

Harry Quimby sat on a narrow cot, his gaze fixed on the tiny window high up in the wall. Weak winter sunshine streamed into the cell, illuminating a face that seemed as placid as a frozen lake. Harry turned when Daniel called his name, looking at him without a glimmer of interest.

Daniel studied the man before him. Even when seated, it wasn't difficult to tell that Harry Quimby was tall and slender. His lank hair was a shade darker than his daughter's, but the eyes were just the same, silvery gray and elongated like a cat's, and his lips were full and shapely, like hers. His clothes were filthy and threadbare, but they must have been of fine quality once, before Harry had fallen on hard times.

"Mr. Quimby?"

"Who's asking?" His voice was velvety and cultured, and it was hard to reconcile this man with the violent thug who'd open a man's face for accidentally bumping into him in a tavern.

"I'm Inspector Haze of Scotland Yard. I'm investigating a murder."

Quimby tilted his head, the pose making him look like a curious bird. "Oh, yes? Who's been murdered?"

"The Earl of Granville," Daniel revealed against his better judgment.

Quimby's face lit up. "Thank you, oh Lord!" he exclaimed. "My prayers have been answered."

"You don't deny you wanted him dead?"

"Not for a second."

"Why do you feel such animosity toward the earl?" Daniel asked. It felt strange to talk to someone through bars, but Daniel didn't care to join Quimby inside the cell.

"If you are here, questioning me about his murder, then you already know, Inspector," Harry Quimby replied, smiling coyly.

"Why don't you tell me anyway?"

"And why don't you bugger off!" Quimby snarled, baring his tobacco-stained teeth.

"Where were you on Tuesday night?" Daniel asked, even though he already knew.

"Right here. Enjoying Her Majesty's boundless hospitality." The coyness was back again, accompanied by an engaging smile.

"Did you pay someone to kill the earl?"

Harry Quimby laughed at that. "Inspector, I barely have enough tin to buy a half-pint, much less pay someone to murder an earl. I attacked the man in the Black Dog on purpose," he said, his gaze boring into Daniel with surprising intensity.

"Why would you do that?"

"Because I'm skint and have nowhere to go. I'd have frozen to death sleeping on the streets, so I got myself arrested. Warm cell, regular meals, and guaranteed accommodation for the foreseeable future. I was even treated to Christmas dinner," he added smugly.

"But you might hang for murder."

Harry Quimby shrugged. "So what if I do? Who'll care? I have nothing, and it's all my fault. I had a wife once, and a daughter. And I had talent, which I squandered because I couldn't be bothered to put in the effort needed to become truly remarkable. But now I'm a bitter, lonely man who can't even find employment in a music hall because my reputation precedes me. My life isn't worth a damn, and I'm ready for it to end." He looked at Daniel with a mournful stare, his gray eyes limpid and pleading. "Can I beg a favor of you?"

"What favor is that?"

"If you're investigating Granville's murder, then you might come across my daughter. Rosie Quimby is her name. No doubt she changed it the first chance she got. Hated that name," he said under his breath. "Anyway, if you happen to speak to my girl, please tell her that I'm sorry and I wish things could have been different between us. I don't expect her to forgive me, but it would make me feel better to know that I'd tried to make amends. Have you seen her?" he asked eagerly. "Have you met my Rosie?"

Daniel almost admitted that he had, then realized that the man could be manipulating him. There was a good chance the man he'd attacked would recover, and then Harry Quimby would eventually go free and come after his daughter.

"I have not met anyone of that name."

Harry Quimby wagged his finger at Daniel playfully. "I didn't expect you to tell me. You're too clever for that. Well, I'm sorry her golden calf has died. She'll have to make her own way now. I only hope he'd given her something worth selling." That coy smile again. "Had he?"

"I wouldn't know," Daniel replied, now certain the man was on a fishing expedition.

"She is smart, my Rosie," Quimby went on. "One thing I taught her, always see to your own interests, my girl. And she has. Turned tail as soon as she found herself a wealthy benefactor. I hope she was smart enough not to get with child. A brat would prevent her from finding a new situation, and she's still young enough to snag one of his lordship's posh mates. That Lord Elton is always on the lookout. He'd never marry the likes of her, but he might set her up nice if she plays her cards right. He might even look after her sprat, if she's got one, on account of being Granville's loyal crony."

Harry Quimby's eyes suddenly grew moist. "Do I have a grandchild, Inspector?" His voice sounded almost feminine, as if he were pretending to be a loving mother.

"I don't know, Mr. Quimby," Daniel said. "I have never met your daughter."

Quimby shrugged, his expression hardening. "Maybe the earl threw her over once he tired of her. Men are like that, you know. At least I offered her the means to make a respectable living, not earn her keep by pleasuring any man that's willing to pay the rent. She was still a maid when the earl had her, I made sure of that, but now she can't bargain with her innocence. Once used, a woman has to rely on her experience and make sure her man never wants to leave her bed. I do hope she has learned a trick or two while servicing the earl." Harry smiled lewdly, as if mentally cataloguing the tricks that would please him.

Daniel didn't bother to hide his disgust and suddenly hoped that Harry Quimby would never be released.

Almost as if reading his thoughts, the man said, his voice low and hoarse, "She had better find a new bolt hole now the earl is dead, the duplicitous little minx, because I will kill her if ever our paths cross again, and it won't be quick."

Harry Quimby turned away, his face lifted toward the sunlight, his head haloed by the light. Finding nothing further to add, Daniel turned on his heel and left. Now that he had met Harry Quimby, he could understand why his daughter was terrified. Daniel had met many a violent man in his line of work, but there was something about Harry Quimby that had completely unbalanced him. The man alternated between aggression, coyness, and an almost childlike innocence without making any noticeable effort, as if there were several personalities warring for supremacy inside his disturbed mind. But one thing was certain, Daniel decided as he stepped out into the bitterly cold morning. Harry Quimby was capable of unspeakable cruelty, and he would revenge himself on the daughter who'd outwitted him and dared to throw off the yoke of his violent control. His parting words had not been an idle threat.

Chapter 14

It was just past nine when Daniel arrived at Scotland Yard, his innards writhing with apprehension as he pulled open the door. Ransome would be waiting, expecting to hear about Daniel's progress on the investigation, but he had nothing to tell the man. He had no new leads, and the ones he'd already investigated had come to nothing. Daniel inhaled sharply when Sergeant Meadows hailed him from behind the tall counter.

"Oi, Inspector Haze. Superintendent Ransome wants to see you without delay." Sergeant Meadows smiled conspiratorially. "There's been a hullabaloo this morning," he imparted, lowering his voice almost to a whisper. "The super is beside himself."

"What? What are you talking about?" Daniel demanded.

"I reckon he'll tell you himself. I know nothing," Meadows said, tapping the side of his nose. "Not my place."

Daniel couldn't begin to imagine what Sergeant Meadows was referring to, but now was not the time to ponder his strange announcement. Daniel removed his hat as he headed toward Ransome's office but didn't bother with his coat; he likely wouldn't be staying long. The door was open as usual, so that Ransome could keep abreast of everything that went on in the building, or at least hear enough to demand an instant report should some random comment arouse his interest.

"Haze, shut the door and sit down," he commanded.

Daniel settled into the guest chair. He couldn't quite make out Ransome's expression. The man normally radiated disdain and impatience, but today he seemed calmer, his demeanor bordering on gleeful. That in itself was extremely unsettling, and all the more so after what Sergeant Meadows had just said. Daniel couldn't conceive of any development that would cause such an uncharacteristic turnabout in Ransome's mood.

"Sir?" Daniel asked, unable to bear the suspense a moment longer.

John Ransome clasped his hands on his desk and looked at Daniel, his gaze radiating amusement. "Simonds was just here."

"The earl's butler?"

"The very one. He had some news to impart," Ransome said. He was clearly enjoying himself. "Albright and Sons, undertakers to the Langley family for generations, had delivered the casket to the Park Lane residence early this morning," Ransome announced. "They had given up their Christmas to collect the body and prepare the earl's mortal remains for viewing. I do hope they charged an exorbitant fee." Ransome's lips twitched with mirth, but Daniel remained silent, waiting for the punchline to this very unfunny joke.

"The countess, who was unable to sleep, asked to see her husband right away. She had Simonds with her when she entered the room." Ransome shook his head, as if he still couldn't believe what he was about to say. "The deceased is not the earl."

"The undertakers brought the wrong body?" Daniel asked, trying to understand why Ransome was so elated.

"No, they brought the right body, except that the body is not that of the Earl of Granville."

"The countess is in shock," Daniel said quietly. "She's grieving."

"One would think, but she immediately demanded that Simonds pull down the man's trousers."

"What? Why?" Daniel cried. He hadn't expected that.

"It seems the earl was deeply interested in Jewish mysticism. He studied the Cabal, or some such nonsense. Don't ask me what that's all about," Ransome muttered, shaking his head in disbelief before continuing. "Had himself circumcised. Swore the practice enhanced sexual pleasure."

"The countess actually said that?" Daniel asked in utter disbelief. He was still trying to comprehend the significance of this.

"Pay attention, man," Ransome snapped. "The earl told the butler and his valet, apparently. Thought all men should do it. I shudder at the mere thought," Ransome said, his eyebrows lifting comically. "Anyway, the deceased was still intact, so to speak. The victim of the pitchfork murder is not the earl." Ransome released an exhalation of relief, as if he felt suddenly absolved of all responsibility for finding the man's killer.

"Just a minute," Daniel cried, staring at the superintendent as if he'd just lost his mind. "If the victim was not the earl, then who the devil is he, and how is it that he resembles the man to such a degree that he was readily identified as Damian Langley? And what on earth was he doing on the Granville estate? Who killed him, and why? And where is the real earl if he's still alive? He's certainly not in Hastings, unless his mistress is hiding him under her skirts."

John Ransome raised his hand in a placating manner. "Slow down, Haze. One thing at a time." He leaned back in his chair, looking for all the world like he was about to enjoy a brandy and a cigar. "Whoever the victim was, he's not the Earl of Granville, which means there will no longer be any pressure from the palace to solve this case quickly. Whoever the deceased is, he must have trespassed on the estate and come across someone who tried to evict him, rather forcefully, I should think."

"But he resembles the earl enough to be mistaken for him," Daniel argued.

"The groom and the butler were in shock, and it was fairly early in the morning when they found the body. The man might have resembled the earl superficially in the dim light of the stable. There are plenty of unrelated people who share certain physical attributes. Half the men in this station joke that Constable Collins could pass for my younger brother," Ransome added.

That was true. Constable Collins did look remarkably like John Ransome, but as far as anyone knew, they were not related in any way Of course, Constable Collins was young enough to be the superintendent's natural born son, but no one was foolish enough to speculate about the possibility aloud since such an insinuation could lead to instant dismissal.

Ransome took Daniel's silence for agreement and continued. "The earl left his estate in Surrey, taking his coachman and valet with him. Clearly, he had somewhere he wished to be, somewhere other than Hastings. Where the earl has gone is none of our affair, as long as he hasn't been declared missing. Therefore, our only priority is to discover who killed this vagrant and why. And if we don't—" Ransome lifted his hands in a universal gesture of *who knows*?

"Are you suggesting that we close the investigation and consign the man to a pauper's grave?"

"I'm suggesting that you do your job and investigate to the best of your ability and within the confines of our limited resources. If you fail to identify any leads by say, Wednesday, then close the case and move on."

"Yes, sir," Daniel replied. "And if the earl does not return within that timeframe? He was expected back two days ago."

"Unless the countess is prepared to declare her husband a missing person, the earl's whereabouts are of no concern to us."

"Yes, sir," Daniel said again. He stood, but Ransome lifted a finger, stopping Daniel in his tracks.

"I suggest you speak to the groom again. I think he came upon this person in the mews, became frightened, perhaps felt threatened, and used whatever was to hand to defend himself. The man was trespassing. Possibly looking for a warm place to bed down for the night. If the hapless groom killed him, then as long as it was an act of self-defense, we'll go easy on him. And let's keep this out of the papers, Haze. We don't want the press making the most of our blunder."

"It wasn't our error, sir," Daniel replied. "Both the groom and the butler had identified the victim as the Earl of Granville. We acted on the information we were given."

"Yes, but you know the facts will get twisted. Honest mistakes don't sell copies of *The Illustrated Police News*. 'Inexperienced inspector mistakes vagrant for earl' or something equally scathing will be splashed across the front page. And it will be you they'll roast, not Scotland Yard," Ransome reminded him viciously.

"Right," Daniel replied, and slapped his bowler onto his head. "Good day, sir."

"It is now," Ransome replied smugly. "And Haze, tell Meadows to bring me a cup of tea."

Chapter 15

Jason was surprised to find Daniel waiting for him when he emerged from the operating theater just before noon. He'd just performed a hysterectomy on a woman of twenty-four whose womb had been grotesquely extended, the fast-growing mass nestled within as large as a four-month fetus and most likely malignant. Jason was glad that the patient already had three children, and he hoped that the procedure would ultimately save her life, but he had his doubts. The woman had initially assumed she was pregnant and had not consulted a physician until it became obvious that her symptoms were caused by something other than a normal pregnancy.

The theater had been packed with students, as it always was when the operation was on a young woman. Aside from wishing to learn, the exclusively male students were always eager to glimpse something of the living female anatomy, since the women they practiced on were generally cadavers. To the great disappointment of the students, Jason always made sure to cover his patients for modesty's sake and only leave the area he intended to operate on exposed, unlike several surgeons of his acquaintance, who simply pushed the patient's gown out of the way.

"Do you have time for a quick meal?" Daniel asked.

"Yes. I have to be back in an hour, though," Jason replied. He needed to check on his patient, and there was a routine tonsillectomy scheduled for later in the day.

Jason retrieved his coat and hat, and the two men left the hospital, heading toward one of the chophouses frequented by doctors, hospital staff, and medical students alike. Daniel led Jason to a table in the corner, where they wouldn't be disturbed.

"Dr. Redmond," the proprietor, who hurried over to their table, greeted Jason. "It's a pleasure to see you again."

"Thank you, Mr. Pilcher. This is my friend, Inspector Haze of Scotland Yard."

"Inspector," Mr. Pilcher said, bowing from the neck. "Can I recommend today's special, fillet of beef served with roasted potatoes and buttered carrots?"

"I'll have that," Jason said. "And a glass of red wine."

"So will I," Daniel added. "Only I'll have a pint of stout."

"Very good, gentlemen." Mr. Pilcher departed, leaving them in peace.

"Daniel, is everything all right? You look—what's that word you English like to use?—peaky," Jason said, hoping to lighten the mood, but Daniel looked like a thundercloud.

"The victim is not the earl."

"Excuse me?"

"The countess is certain that the man who was murdered was not her husband. And she has proof."

"What sort of proof? Both the groom and the butler swore the man was Damian Langley," Jason said, wondering how such an error could have been made by men who'd been in the earl's employ for years.

Daniel leaned in closer and lowered his voice. "The earl was a follower of the Cabal. It's something to do with Jewish mysticism. He was circumcised. The countess checked."

"Do you mean the Kabbalah?" Jason had heard the Kabbalah mentioned by a Jewish doctor of his acquaintance while he lived in New York but knew nothing of what it actually entailed, only that its teachings were sacred and not meant to be attempted by just anyone.

"I don't know. I'd never heard of it before today. Jason, is it true that circumcision increases sexual pleasure?" Daniel asked as he lowered his voice to a near-whisper, even though the tables closest to them were unoccupied. Unfortunately for him, Mr. Pilcher approached their table at just that moment.

Jason waited until the proprietor had set their drinks on the table and departed before replying. "I really couldn't say."

"Did you ever know anyone who was circumcised?"

"Not well enough to inquire about the intensity of their climax," Jason replied, trying valiantly not to grin at Daniel's scandalized expression.

"Why would anyone—" Daniel let the sentence trail off, but it wasn't difficult to imagine what he wished to ask.

"It's a religious ritual that goes back thousands of years for both the Jews and the Muslims. There are also those who believe it's beneficial to a man's health, since the foreskin traps bacteria that can lead to infection. As far as I know, being circumcised does not diminish sexual pleasure, but I can't see from a medical perspective how it might significantly enhance it."

"And what do you know of this Kabbalah?" Daniel asked, clearly intrigued and a little put out that he had never heard of it himself.

"I'm afraid I don't know anything about its principles."

"Surely devoting oneself to its principles goes against the teachings of the Church," Daniel speculated.

"Perhaps. Perhaps not. After all, both the Jews and the Christians believe in the Old Testament."

"Yes, but that's the Bible, not some mystical claptrap."

Jason didn't feel qualified to discuss the subject intelligently, so he tried to steer the conversation back to the matter at hand. "If the victim is not the earl, then who is he, and where's Damian Langley?"

"Those are the same questions that I asked John Ransome, but he doesn't seem to care now that the palace will no longer be following the investigation. He as good as told me to have the man buried in a pauper's grave and move on."

"And who does John Ransome think killed this nameless person?"

"He thinks it was Grady, the groom. His theory is that the victim, most likely a vagrant, sneaked onto the property in search of shelter for the night, and the groom killed him as an act of self-defense."

"I suppose that's possible, but how is it that this man was mistaken for the earl, especially when both the groom and the butler knew the earl to be away from home? They were confident enough in their assumption to inform the countess her husband was dead," Jason pointed out.

"That's what troubles me. I know unrelated people can sometimes resemble each other, but even the countess needed to be sure the body in the casket wasn't that of her husband. I doubt she would have gone so far as to check his member if she knew with unwavering certainty that the man before her was someone other than the earl."

Jason leaned back in his chair. He could see why Daniel was troubled by this unexpected development. Mr. Pilcher delivered their plates and left, but Jason wasn't ready to eat. "So, if the earl had not been circumcised, the countess might have accepted the victim as her husband?"

"She clearly saw something that led her to question the man's identity, but he must resemble the earl a great deal. Jason, is it possible the man was some poor relation come to beg the earl for a handout?"

"It's possible, but why would he lurk in the stables rather than come to the door?"

"You said yourself that the man was underweight and looked unkempt. Perhaps he'd fallen on hard times. Perhaps he was ashamed. Were there any signs of syphilis?" Daniel asked.

"No."

They began to eat, each lost in his own thoughts. This was an odd case for sure.

"Does the earl have any siblings?" Jason asked after a few bites of the fillet.

"No. He's an only child."

"Perhaps this man was a cousin, or the late earl's illegitimate son," Jason mused.

Daniel stopped chewing. "Now you're on to something," he said. "An illegitimate son would not come to the door to ask for money, but he just might try to confront his half-brother in a stable in the hope that they might come to some arrangement. Perhaps he meant to blackmail Langley and threatened to cause him embarrassment if he didn't pay up."

"But as far as we know, Damian Langley was nowhere near his ancestral home at the time of the murder. And why would Thomas Grady attack the victim with a pitchfork? He could have simply asked him to leave or physically evicted him if it came to that. Grady is a strapping young man. He could hardly have felt threatened by a man who was noticeably weaker. And," Jason added triumphantly, "had Grady wielded the pitchfork, the angle of the wounds would be different. The entry points would be higher than the exit points, since Grady is at least a head taller than our victim."

"You've got a point there," Daniel agreed. "Grady is much taller, and broader. I can't see him acting out of fear when faced with that wraith of a man."

"Do you intend to carry on with the investigation?" Jason asked as he speared a potato.

"Ransome gave me until Wednesday. I do hope the earl turns up, so that I can at least question him, but I doubt he'd tell me the truth."

Jason nodded in agreement. The earl had nothing to gain by admitting to his father's past indiscretions, especially since the unidentified man was dead and no longer a threat to the earl's family.

"I think I might have reached a dead end on this one," Daniel said morosely.

"There's always someone who knows the truth," Jason replied.

"Perhaps, but that doesn't mean they're willing to divulge it."

"Not willingly, no." Jason set down his knife and fork and took a sip of wine. He had to get back to the hospital, but his mind was still on the case. He felt as if he'd let Daniel down by failing to identify any viable theories. "What now?" he asked.

"I'd like to speak to the countess again," Daniel replied.

"To what end?"

"If she's willing to declare her husband missing, then I will have leave to pursue an investigation. If she refuses, then I will no longer be permitted to question the family or staff."

"Do you honestly believe the earl is missing?" Jason asked.

"No one seems to know where he is, unless they do know and are simply not saying."

Jason considered the possibility. "If they knew where he was, they wouldn't have raised the alarm. Everyone believed the victim was Damian Langley until the unverifiable disclaimer by the countess. Unless we return to Hastings and question Miss Lillie, we won't know for certain if the earl was really circumcised."

Daniel nearly choked on his food at the prospect of putting such a question to Rosamunde Lillie. He took a gulp of his ale, swallowed hard, then set down his glass, ready to resume the discussion.

"You think it's a ruse of some kind?" Daniel asked.

"I don't know, but surely time will tell. If the earl is not dead, then he will surface eventually. Now, I really must go," Jason said with a sigh. "Please keep me abreast of any developments."

"Of course."

"Put the meal on my tab," Jason said to Mr. Pilcher as he approached the door. "I will settle up at the end of the week, as usual."

Mr. Pilcher smiled and wished Jason a pleasant afternoon.

Chapter 16

The countess was willing to receive Daniel, which was a relief. He'd thought she might refuse him admittance now that the investigation officially had nothing to do with her. Daniel was shown to the same room as before, but now the countess was dressed in a gown of emerald-green satin, her diamond-encrusted emerald teardrop earrings twinkling in the afternoon light. She smiled happily and invited Daniel to take a seat.

"Would you care for some refreshment, Inspector?" Euphemia Langley asked airily.

"No, thank you, my lady. I hope you will permit me to ask you a few more questions."

"Of course. I feel like the happiest woman on earth today," she gushed. "Not only was I snatched from the jagged jaws of widowhood, but now we won't have to postpone Lady Viola's engagement party."

"Your daughter is to marry?" Daniel asked. "I didn't realize she was out."

Daniel wasn't sure at what age the daughters of the nobility were presented to society, but sixteen seemed a bit young. Clearly the earl and his countess were in a rush to see their daughter wed.

"No young woman relishes being paraded in front of eligible bachelors like a gladiator before a crowd of bloodthirsty Romans. My husband has arranged a match with the son of the Earl of Cromartie. He has a vast estate in Scotland but spends most of his time in London and had met Viola when my husband invited him to dine. For Viola, it was love at first sight," she exclaimed, clapping her hands in delight.

"And is the feeling mutual?" Daniel asked. What did a sixteen-year-old girl know of love? Then again, Sarah had already had her eye on Daniel by the time she was sixteen, and Daniel had fallen in love with her when he was hardly more than a boy.

"Oh, yes. Francis is smitten. He is twelve years older, but a man should be older than his wife, to provide a touch of paternal influence that women require throughout their lives. And Viola will have a chance to mature before her husband attains the earldom on his father's death."

"And when is the happy event to take place?" Daniel asked, not that it mattered, but he wanted to keep the countess talking. The more at ease she felt, the more likely she was to reveal something that might be helpful.

"Viola would like a June wedding. She's mad for flowers and wants the church to be decorated with white orchids. I heartily approve. White for purity. Very fitting."

"Indeed," Daniel agreed. Having exhausted the topic of Lady Viola's engagement, he steered the conversation back to the earl. "Do you have any idea where your husband might have gone? He wasn't in Hastings."

The countess looked momentarily surprised by this piece of news but instantly rearranged her features into a mask of bland indifference. "You've been to Hastings?" she asked, keeping her voice casual.

"I have."

"So you must know."

"Know what?"

"That Lady Seton is no longer with us."

"Yes, I learned of her passing during my visit," Daniel replied politely.

"I know about my husband's mistress," the countess said. She tried to sound matter-of-fact, but Daniel could see the pain in her eyes. "He's quite enamored of her. We've never discussed the matter outright, but I'm grateful he's not keeping her in London.

That would be difficult," she added quietly. "He's a well-known figure in certain circles."

"Did you believe he was in Hastings?" Daniel asked.

"I did. I spent countless hours trying to understand why he would have come back, and in such a state, but it never occurred to me until I saw the eh…remains that the victim wasn't Damian."

"If his lordship didn't go to Hastings, where might he have gone?" Daniel asked again, hoping the countess would let something slip.

"Damian was distracted the day before he left. He hadn't been planning to go to Hastings, but then he received a letter from that woman and announced that he had to leave. I was so angry with him. He was the one who wanted to spend Christmas in Surrey, enjoying country pursuits, but then he just abandoned us. Many a man keeps a mistress, but they still put their family first."

"Are you certain the letter came from your husband's mistress?" Daniel asked.

The countess grimaced. "Well, no," she admitted. "But he said he was going to Hastings. Who else would have summoned him there if not that vile creature?"

Daniel was surprised that the countess was being so truthful with him. To someone like her, he was hardly more than a tradesman, but she was clearly angry with the earl, so perhaps she needed to vent her feelings to someone who'd have no immediate interest in her husband's affair.

"Do you have any idea what might have been on his mind?" Daniel asked.

The countess sighed, her gaze meeting Daniel's. "I thought she had written to tell him that she is with child, but if he never went to Hastings, I don't suppose that was it." The countess's eyes narrowed dangerously. "Is she with child?"

"Not that I could see," Daniel replied diplomatically, which didn't mean Miss Lillie wasn't, only that she wasn't yet showing.

"I hate to admit it, Inspector Haze, but I think Damian would have been overjoyed at the prospect of another child, especially with her. I suppose it would have been a solution of sorts," she mused.

"A solution to what?"

"Damian doesn't remember his mother. She died when he was a small boy, but he has always loved his nurse. She's a kindly old soul, but she's getting on in years, and Damian won't hear of sending her away. Nanny Briggs raised our two children, and they love her dearly, but they're no longer in need of a nurse. If Rosamunde were to have a child, we could pack Nanny Briggs off to Hastings to help with the new arrival. Damian would like that."

Daniel averted his gaze to prevent the countess from seeing his expression. It struck him as terribly odd that the woman would view her husband's mistress having a child as a means of getting rid of an old family retainer. In fact, it was so bizarre, it almost made sense.

"Do you think your husband might be missing?" Daniel asked carefully, eager to broach the real reason for his visit.

"Missing? As in gone?" Euphemia Langley seemed genuinely surprised by the question.

"Yes. If no one knows where he is…"

"I really don't think so, Inspector. Damian probably had some business to attend to and didn't want to worry me. Perhaps he's ready to move on from Miss Lillie and has found a replacement," she added bitterly.

"But you were expecting him back days ago."

"Clearly, he was delayed," the countess replied tersely.

"Will you let me know when your husband returns? I have some questions to put to him," Daniel said.

"I doubt he'll speak to you. Damian is not overly fond of the police."

Few people are, Daniel thought. *Until they have need of us.*

"Surely you don't expect him to care about the demise of some wretched tramp," the countess said angrily. Perhaps she regretted her earlier confidences and wished to reassert her dominance over the lowly policeman who was now privy to some of her innermost thoughts.

"What of the body?" Daniel asked, wondering if the nameless stranger had already been disposed of.

The countess waved her hand dismissively. "I instructed Simonds and Mrs. Frey to deal with all that."

"Who is Mrs. Frey?" Daniel asked. He hadn't met Mrs. Frey when interviewing the servants at the house in Surrey.

"The housekeeper. She had stayed behind when we went to the country. Normally, she would go on ahead to open the house, but she was ill, so I gave her a few days to recover. Besides, whatever she had might have been catching. The servants are well trained. They know what needs to be done. Anyway, Mrs. Frey seems strongly opposed to tossing that man into a pauper's grave."

"She does? Why?"

"Who knows?" the countess replied. "She can be a rigid old stick at times, but she's an excellent housekeeper. Been with the family for eons. That's another one we should put out to pasture, but Damian feels an inexplicable loyalty to old retainers. I suppose that's a quality to be admired, but it does get tiresome, Inspector Haze."

"I'm sure it does," Daniel muttered. "May I speak to Mrs. Frey and Mr. Simonds?"

"If you feel it will help. Now, if you don't mind…" It was a dismissal, so Daniel sprang to his feet and bowed to the countess before taking his leave and going in search of the butler, who was in the foyer, awaiting Daniel's reappearance.

"I trust we won't be seeing you again, Inspector?" Simonds said as he tried to usher Daniel toward the door.

"I would like to ask you a few more questions, Mr. Simonds, and I'd like a word with Mrs. Frey."

The butler looked annoyed but gestured toward the green baize door. "We'd better speak in the butler's pantry, then. Your presence will no longer be tolerated upstairs."

Daniel followed Simonds and settled in the guest chair before he was invited to do so. He was deeply annoyed and felt no need to show the butler the respect he thought was his due.

"The case is closed. Is it not?" Simonds asked as he settled behind his desk.

"We still have a murder to solve, Mr. Simonds."

"Yes, but it no longer has anything to do with his lordship."

"Where's the body?" Daniel asked.

"It was taken away by Albright and Sons this morning."

"What will happen to it?"

The butler shrugged in indifference. "The undertakers will not be paid for any additional expense incurred, so the only thing they can do under the circumstances is dispose of the body in whatever way they see fit. The lucky chap will be buried in his lordship's suit, since the clothes would be consigned to the fire if retrieved in any case."

"I doubt he would consider himself lucky," Daniel snapped. Simonds shrugged, his indifference requiring no answer.

“Mr. Simonds, you mistook the victim for the earl. As did Mr. Grady. Surely that’s an error that bears further investigation.”

Simonds bristled. “It was still dark, and we were both in shock. It’s not every day you see a corpse staring back at you.”

Having been in the army, Daniel doubted Alfred Simonds had never seen a mutilated corpse, but it was fair to say he hadn’t expected to find on in a stable. Still, it wouldn’t have taken him long to regain his wits, yet he had insisted the victim was the earl until the countess had suggested otherwise.

“The man bears an uncanny resemblance to Damian Langley. Might he have been a relative?” Daniel asked.

Simonds rolled his eyes in exasperation. “If you’re asking me if the late earl might have had an illegitimate son, then the answer is yes, he may have. Most men of his stature sire one or two by-blows in their youth. I reckon this was one of the earl’s mistakes coming to demand reparation.”

“Do you not think the son of an earl, even if illegitimate, deserves a proper burial?”

“That’s not for me to decide, Inspector. His lordship is not here to ask, and the countess instructed me to deal with the situation.”

“I hear Mrs. Frey had something to say on the subject.”

Simonds’s eyebrows rose so high, they brushed against his gray forelock. “Her ladyship told you about that?”

“She did.”

“Look, Inspector, Mrs. Frey’s father and two brothers died when their fishing boat sank during a storm. Their bodies eventually washed up, but since there was no money, they were buried in a pauper’s grave with a dozen others from a nearby workhouse. Mrs. Frey, plain Miss Frey then, was turned out of their house and sent to the workhouse. When the late earl heard of the tragedy, he took her in and gave her employment as a scullery maid. She was fourteen at the time. She never forgot his kindness, but the tragedy still haunts her, and she wishes she had graves to visit when the family goes to Surrey."

Daniel made a mental note of this, just as he did of the name. Housekeepers were referred to as Mrs. even if they had never married, and Mrs. Frey never had. This wasn't relevant, but Daniel liked to form a mental picture of the individuals he interviewed.

"I'd still like to speak to her," he insisted.

"As you wish. Come with me."

Daniel followed the butler toward the housekeeper's office, where a woman of about fifty sat behind a desk, going through the household accounts. She looked up when they entered and smiled shyly. Daniel initially thought the smile was for him but quickly realized her gaze was fixed on Simonds.

"Mrs. Frey, this is Inspector Haze. He wishes to ask you a few questions," Simonds said stiffly.

"By all means. Please, have a seat, Inspector."

Daniel sat down but didn't speak until Simonds, who looked like he planned to remain in the room, left and shut the door behind him. Daniel took the time to study Mrs. Frey. She had blue eyes and chestnut-colored hair gently silvered with gray, her face still beautiful. There was a dignity about her that Daniel found attractive, and the lines that bracketed her mouth told him she was quick to smile, not a quality normally associated with housekeepers, who had to remain stern to keep their underlings in check.

"How can I help?" Mrs. Frey asked when Daniel failed to begin.

"Mrs. Frey, the countess said you had reservations about consigning the dead man to a pauper's grave."

Now that he thought about it, it was odd that Mrs. Frey had been informed and had spoken her mind in front of her mistress, but perhaps she had simply been passing and her comment had been unwitting when she witnessed the commotion.

Mrs. Frey colored. "I never meant to—" she sputtered. "It wasn't my place."

"Why did you feel so strongly about it?" Daniel asked.

Mrs. Frey's gaze slid away, focusing on the flames in the grate, but Daniel could tell she was laboring under strong emotion.

"He doesn't deserve to be buried like a dog," she said at last.

"Do you know who he is, then?" Daniel asked.

Mrs. Frey turned to face Daniel. "He's the earl's brother."

"Yes, so I surmised."

"The earl has more money than he can spend in a lifetime," Mrs. Frey said bitterly. "It wouldn't cost much to give the man a proper burial. They are of the same blood, after all, and his lordship's father would want his son interred with the respect due him."

"But he's a bastard," Daniel replied, then winced inwardly at his crude choice of words.

Mrs. Frey looked like she was about to say something, then shook her head. "It's none of my affair, Inspector. I only felt sorry for the man, that was all. Every person who's born onto this earth deserves a bit of respect, be they a fisherman or an earl's love child. I expect the poor man no longer cares."

"Mrs. Frey, do you have any idea where the current earl might be?"

"He doesn't share his plans with me, Inspector."

"No, I don't believe he does, but a housekeeper knows everything that transpires in a household. And I expect you know more than most," Daniel added. There was something in Mrs. Frey's closed expression that told him she knew considerably more than she was saying. She'd already revealed that she knew about the late earl's love child when no one else had been willing to admit that the man had a connection to the family. Daniel just couldn't figure out if it had been a careless slip of the tongue or a calculated maneuver on her part.

"I don't know where his lordship is, but he still confides in Nanny Briggs. She was like a mother to him growing up, and he often turns to her for advice. It infuriates the countess," she added in an undertone. "She wants her gone."

So I heard, Daniel thought. What was so threatening about a harmless old lady?

"Can I speak to Nanny Briggs?"

Mrs. Frey shook her head. "The countess wouldn't like it, so unless you have her express permission, then I'd say you had better leave it alone."

"Does Nanny Briggs ever go out on her own?" Daniel asked.

Mrs. Frey tilted her head as she considered the question. "She goes to Harriman's every Monday at ten."

"Harriman's?"

"It's the apothecary shop in Mount Street. Nanny Briggs suffers from rheumatism, and Mr. Harriman makes up a tonic for her. He could give her a month's supply, but she says going to the chemist gets her out of the house."

"Thank you, Mrs. Frey. I appreciate your candor."

Daniel wasn't sure just how honest the housekeeper had been, but she had thrown Daniel a lifeline. The housekeeper knew everything that went on in the house, but a nanny usually knew her charges' deepest secrets. He'd have to wait until Monday to discover if Nanny Briggs knew anything worth learning, but Ransome had given him until Wednesday, so he had time.

Simonds was waiting for Daniel just outside Mrs. Frey's office, his gaze boring into Daniel's face, likely to gauge if he had learned anything that might be detrimental to the earl and his family. Daniel sighed as if deeply disappointed and approached the butler.

"I'll take my leave now, Mr. Simonds."

"If you feel the need to come back, which I hope you won't, use the tradesman's entrance, Inspector," Simonds said as he ushered Daniel toward the servants' entrance.

"Good day, Mr. Simonds," Daniel replied, and stepped outside, the door slamming shut behind him.

Chapter 17

Since Superintendent Ransome no longer expected a daily update, Daniel turned for home. He had no leads to follow and was relieved the pressure was off but did intend to interview the nanny come Monday. The least he could do was learn the victim's name and inform his nearest and dearest of his passing, if he'd had anyone who cared for him. How unfair it was that two children sired by the same man had faced such different circumstances the moment they were born, through no effort or fault of their own. The earl's bastard brother had clearly been down on his luck, possibly starving, while the earl enjoyed a life of untold luxury and could support a dozen siblings if he chose to. Would he have helped the man had they met?

Had they ever met? Daniel asked himself as he hurried down the street, paying little attention to passersby. Was it possible that the unnamed man had been milking Damian Langley for years and the earl's forbearance had come to an end? He couldn't have murdered the man himself, having been away at the time, but perhaps someone else had been installed in the stables, waiting for the hapless man in the earl's stead. Maybe that was the reason the earl had suddenly decided to leave, to clear the way for his brother's murder. And the obvious candidate would be Simonds, having been a soldier and owing the earl a debt of gratitude, since the earl had taken care of his batman since their India days.

Speaking to Simonds again would be fruitless at this juncture, Daniel decided. He would admit to nothing, and unless Daniel could discover a link between the earl and the dead man, no matter how tenuous, he could hardly go around making accusations and jumping to conclusions. No, he would put the case from his mind for the time being and resume his inquiries on Monday.

Daniel sighed. He had no desire to attend church again tomorrow, having just been on Christmas. Once a week was quite enough, thank you, but proprieties had to be observed, for the sake of both Charlotte and Miss Grainger. He couldn't have her think him a godless heathen, but how nice it would be to have a whole morning to himself. Not since his days as a parish constable in Birch Hill had he had a free day to spend as he wished. Daniel felt a pang of homesickness for that other life, but immediately rebuked himself. He had always wanted to be a policeman, and he wasn't just a bobby but an inspector, a senior member of the Metropolitan Police Service who had been entrusted with a case involving the highest echelons of society. Granted, the victim had turned out to be someone quite different, but still, Daniel had much to be proud of.

He only wished he had someone to share his life with. He'd never felt as anchorless as he had since Sarah's death. Perhaps that was why he longed for Rebecca's company. He'd always thought he could manage on his own, but in truth, he was desperately lonely and felt woefully inadequate as a single parent. Charlotte needed a mother, and he needed a partner. Daniel gazed over the rooftops, awed by the lavender glory of the December twilight, suddenly seeing nothing but the romance of the great metropolis and the promise the future held.

Hastening his steps, Daniel arrived at home just in time for tea and joined Miss Grainger in the parlor. Charlotte was in the kitchen, helping Grace with dinner preparations. This likely meant that Charlotte was up to her little ears in flour or stealing pieces of carrot from the chopping board, but she loved to spend time in the kitchen, and Daniel saw no reason to forbid it unless Grace found her presence disruptive.

Miss Grainger smiled warmly when Daniel settled across from her. "Shall I make you a cup of tea, Inspector?"

"Please," Daniel replied, smiling back. "It's frigid out there. Did you and Charlotte go out today?"

"Very briefly. I was afraid she'd catch a chill. We returned home and read by the fire."

"Very wise," Daniel replied, accepting the tea. Miss Grainger made it just the way he liked it, with a splash of milk and two sugar cubes.

Without asking, Miss Grainger served Daniel a slice of sponge and handed it to him. "You don't look happy, if you don't mind me saying so, Inspector."

"Please, call me Daniel," he blurted out, and instantly regretted it. Referring to each other as Inspector Haze and Miss Grainger erected a barrier of propriety, but if Miss Grainger were to call him by his Christian name, then he would be tempted to refer to her as Rebecca.

Miss Grainger smiled politely, but Daniel could see he'd made her uncomfortable with his request.

"I'm sorry," he rushed to add. "That was inappropriate."

"It wasn't," Miss Grainger replied. "It's just that addressing you by your rank helps to foster an emotional distance, which I must maintain," she added, coloring at such a personal admission.

"Must you?"

The words were out before Daniel could stop himself. He knew he was taking a great risk but couldn't bear to pass up this opportunity. Perhaps it was too soon to make his regard known, but Daniel had learned to listen to his instincts. Had he done so in the past, perhaps his marriage would not have had such a catastrophic ending.

Rebecca looked down, her lashes fanning across her cheeks. She was still holding her teacup on a pretty china saucer, and Daniel noticed that her hand was shaking. She set the saucer down, then faced him, her chin set at a defiant angle.

"Inspector Haze, I love Charlotte as if she were my own, and I will admit that I enjoy your company and look forward to our talks, but I'm not prepared to enter into an inappropriate relationship with my employer. If that is what you had in mind, then please accept my resignation."

Daniel nearly spilled the hot tea all over his trousers. "Miss Grainger, please," he sputtered. "You've misunderstood my intentions."

"What *are* your intentions, Inspector? Except for Grace, who's hardly ever within hearing distance, we're alone in this house. A man and a woman. Unchaperoned. If there's even a whiff of scandal attached to my name, I will never be able to find a position in a respectable household again. I will be reduced to hiring myself out as a servant in order to survive. Or worse," she whispered, unable to put her fears into words.

A silent tear slid down her cheek, but she refused to look away, her blue gaze fixed on his face. Daniel could understand her position only too well. As a nursemaid, she wasn't precisely a servant, nor was she on par with the family, which in this case included only Daniel. She could either retire to her room every evening and take her supper on a tray, or she could go downstairs and join Grace, but the two women had little in common and were not social equals.

After the first few weeks in his employ, Rebecca had reluctantly agreed to join Daniel for the evening meal, partly because by her own admission she was lonely and starved for conversation after a day spent with a small child, and partly because he had behaved in a way that reassured her they were nothing more than friends. And he was still in mourning for his wife. But now Daniel had altered the balance of power and put Rebecca in an untenable position. His obvious interest had changed the nature of their relationship irrevocably, and nothing he said would bring it back to what it had been only a few minutes ago, at least to an outside observer. Daniel wasn't sure how Miss Grainger felt about him, in the privacy of her thoughts, but he knew precisely how he felt about her, and there was nothing platonic in his desires. Daniel wished the floor would open up and swallow him whole, but he had started this and had no choice but to see it through.

"Miss Grainger, I apologize if I have offended you in any way or allowed you to think that my intentions are anything but honorable. I completely understand how vulnerable you must feel, especially since you have no family to turn to should you require emotional or financial support." Daniel sucked in a shuddering breath.

"The truth is that I find myself thinking about you all the time and looking forward to spending a quiet hour with you when Charlotte is asleep or downstairs with Grace. I had hoped you felt the same and might permit me to court you in a proper and respectful way, but if that is not your wish, then we will never speak of this again. Please forgive my gross miscalculation and don't leave us," Daniel pleaded.

Miss Grainger's expression was inscrutable as she considered his heartfelt plea, but Daniel noticed that her lip trembled ever so slightly. "Do you really think about me?" she asked softly.

"Endlessly. I think of all the things I'd like to tell you, and I look forward to hearing your views on the subjects we discuss. Whenever I hear something amusing or see something wondrous, I immediately wish I could share it with you so that you could enjoy it as much as I did." She looked disappointed, so Daniel blundered on. "And I think you're very beautiful."

Miss Grainger smiled at that. "No one has ever called me beautiful," she said, her eyes filling with tears.

"Then let me be the first," Daniel said.

He wanted to take her hand but thought better of it. Whatever followed had to progress at Rebecca's pace. She nodded and stood. Daniel sprang to his feet but made no move to close the space between them.

"If you will excuse me, Inspector, I think I need a few moments on my own."

"Of course," Daniel said, thinking this didn't bode well and the next time he'd see her would be the last.

Miss Grainger turned to leave, but then stopped and looked back. "I'll see you at dinner, Daniel," she said softly, and was gone.

Daniel thought that his name hadn't sounded this sweet since the last time Sarah had uttered it in a moment of passion. It was a long time ago now, and all he could recall were the times she'd addressed him with impatience or indifference.

Rebecca, Daniel thought dizzily as he sat back down. *Rebecca.*

Chapter 18

Monday, December 28

Having left the house early, Daniel took himself off to a nearby coffeehouse and ordered breakfast. Now that the cat was out of the bag and Rebecca knew of his regard for her, he felt much like a trapeze artist, the kind he'd once seen at a carnival and thought the silly fool would lose his balance for sure and wind up splattered on the ground beneath. Sunday had been a trial, with both of them walking on eggshells around each other and carefully feeling their way around this new and uncertain reality.

Daniel poured the last of the coffee, which he'd come to enjoy thanks to Jason's endless devotion to the bitter brew, added a splash of cream and two sugar cubes, and took a slow sip. Now that he'd taken the plunge, he had to let the relationship with Rebecca develop naturally. It was Monday, and he had a job to do. His personal life would have to wait until the case was solved. Or so he told himself in order to stop obsessing about the possibility of kissing those pink, pouty lips. Daniel finished his Welsh rarebit, drained the last of the coffee, and headed to Park Lane.

He positioned himself behind a tree that gave him a clear view of the servants' entrance and hoped that Nanny Briggs wouldn't miraculously recover from her rheumatism and choose this day to skip her weekly trip to the chemist. It was bitterly cold, a chill wind penetrating Daniel's coat and tugging at his muffler. His feet were beginning to feel numb, and his glasses were fogging up from his warm breath. Instead of cleaning them every few minutes, Daniel allowed the specs to perch on the end of his nose and gazed over the lenses. The world around him blurred, but his vision wasn't so impaired that he wouldn't be able to spot a person.

Somewhere, a clock chimed the hour. Ten o'clock. And then a quarter past, but there was no sign of Nanny Briggs. Daniel briefly wondered if the housekeeper had intentionally misled him but then saw the door open and an elderly woman carefully navigate the icy steps. She had to be at least sixty-five and wore a drab woolen coat and a matching bonnet in a shade of brown that few women would think becoming. Her only nod to adornment was the scarlet cherries with dark green leaves on the brim that bounced merrily as she waddled from side to side.

Nanny Briggs wasn't stout but walked like a woman who was accustomed to being in pain and would rather have sat by a warm fire than tread the few streets to the chemist's shop. Daniel left his post and walked behind her, keeping a respectful distance. He had no wish to accost her too soon, or she might hurry back and complain to Simonds or Mrs. Frey. She might even tell the earl, if he ever came back, Daniel thought sourly. It really was odd that the countess wasn't more worried about her husband's whereabouts, but perhaps she had no wish to give Daniel more ammunition for his investigation.

Daniel loitered in the street until Nanny Briggs exited the chemist's shop, then made his approach. "Mrs. Briggs, my name is Inspector Haze of Scotland Yard, and I would like to ask you a few questions." He held up his warrant card, giving the woman a chance to verify his credentials. She nodded, looking up at him in a way that made him think she wasn't all that surprised to see him.

Up close, Nanny Briggs appeared older than Daniel had first assumed. She had to be seventy at the very least, but her dark gaze was still sharp and her expression somewhat puzzling since she seemed to be pondering something.

"We can hardly talk in the street, Inspector," she said at last.

"Where would you prefer to have this conversation?" he asked, hoping she wasn't trying to fob him off.

"I'm cold," Nanny Briggs replied. "And tired."

"Perhaps a cup of tea and a scone would revive you," Daniel suggested.

"Yes, perhaps they would," Nanny Briggs mused. "Or a pot of chocolate. I do like chocolate."

"It would be my pleasure to treat you to a pot of chocolate. And perhaps a slice of cake?"

"I've always had a sweet tooth, me," Nanny Briggs said. "Could never say no to a treat." Daniel could practically feel her salivating. "There's a lovely tearoom just up the street," she said, pointing toward a building on the corner.

"Then let us go there," Daniel said, relieved that Nanny Briggs hadn't sent him away.

The establishment on the ground floor boasted a striped pink-and-white awning, and the windows were fogged up, promising the shop to be pleasantly warm inside. Daniel offered Nanny Briggs his arm, and they walked toward the tearoom, looking for all the world like a mother and son. The interior smelled of freshly brewed tea and the sweet scent of melted sugar that emanated from the counter, where beautiful pastries and colorful marzipan sat beneath glass domes. Daniel thought it would be nice to sit by the window, but Nanny Briggs shook her head and headed toward a table in the corner.

"Wouldn't do to be seen talking to you," she explained once they sat down and she pulled off her gloves and set them atop her rather tatty reticule.

Daniel ordered a pot of chocolate and an assortment of pastries from the spotty youth who had materialized at his elbow, then turned his attention back to the older woman.

"Has there been word from the earl?" Daniel asked.

"He returned on Saturday night, as it happens."

"Did he? And did he say where he had been?"

Mrs. Briggs was prevented from replying by the return of the young waiter, who approached their table with a tray bearing their order. Daniel hadn't expected such quick service, but then he supposed a place like this had everything ready and had only to fill the pot and arrange the pastries on a plate. Once the tray was unloaded, the chocolate poured, and a pastry selected, Mrs. Briggs took a dainty sip, then a forkful of cake. She grinned like a little girl.

"It's been many years since I've been taken out like this. No one pays attention to old people, even less when they're in service."

"Then I hope you enjoy it," Daniel replied. He'd ply her with chocolate until she was ready to float away, as long as she shared something useful with him.

"I do love marzipan," Nanny Briggs said wistfully as another waiter passed by, colorful squares of marzipan candy artfully displayed on a dainty dish.

"Then permit me to buy you some," Daniel said, signaling to the waiter. "You can take it back with you."

Daniel ordered a small box of marzipan and asked for it to be wrapped, then fixed his gaze on Nanny Briggs once more.

"Where had the earl been these past few days?" he asked again.

Mrs. Briggs took another bite of cake, then set her fork down on the plate. Her face was tense, her eyes betraying her concern.

"Inspector, I'm an old woman and have guarded Langley family secrets for a long time. Talking to you might cost me not only my job but my home. I fear I'll find myself at the workhouse if I reveal what I know."

Daniel nodded. He could understand the woman's fears. No family looked kindly on betrayal, especially from someone they'd trusted for decades. "I will keep whatever you tell me in the strictest confidence."

"No you won't, not once you hear what I have to say," Nanny Briggs replied. "And believe me, Inspector Haze, I would never betray a confidence, but my conscience is troubling me more than my aching bones, and I need to make amends before the good Lord calls me to His side."

"What is it that you need to make amends for?" Daniel asked, his pulse quickening. He was certain that whatever Nanny Briggs had to say would change the course of the investigation.

"For my silence."

Daniel was desperate to ask all the questions that were teeming in his mind, but he forced himself to remain quiet and still. The nanny was clearly conflicted about telling him what she knew. Clearing one's conscience was all well and good, but being thrown out on the street was a real threat, one Nanny Briggs was all too aware of. Daniel could understand her hesitation. She was too old to find new employment and too frightened to find herself living in abject poverty at the end of her days.

The silence stretched on. Just when Daniel thought the woman had changed her mind, she began to speak, her voice so low, Daniel could barely hear her. "The earl went to the Rothman Institute. That's in Sevenoaks, Kent," she added.

"Why?" Daniel asked.

Nanny Briggs sighed heavily. "Because he'd been summoned."

Daniel waited for her to take another sip of her cooling chocolate. She was going to tell him the story; he knew that now, but she would do so in her own time, and he had to be patient.

"Before the current earl made an appearance, another child was born to Martin Langley. He was thrilled to have a son, and so proud of his boy. He'd named him Damian, after his own father."

"There were two Damians?" Daniel asked, and wished he'd kept quiet. It wouldn't do to interrupt.

Nanny Briggs shook her head. "Not exactly." She sighed heavily again and continued. "As the boy grew out of babyhood, the earl started to notice flaws in his son. Damian had difficulty walking when other little boys were running, and was so thin, a strong wind could have blown him over. And his speech was slow and labored. It took him too long to think up the words, you see."

Daniel pinched himself under the table to keep quiet, even though he was raring to jump ahead of this story.

"By the time Damian was four, it was clear he was slow-witted. Lady Cecily had failed to produce another child and was sinking deeper and deeper into melancholia, fearful for her only son's future. Oh, Damian was a sweet boy, but he wasn't the son the earl wanted to present to the world, nor did he trust Damian to perpetuate the bloodline."

"So he packed him off to this Rothman Institute?" Daniel asked, unable to keep silent any longer.

"Yes, but it wasn't as simple as that. The earl could hardly tell the world that his son was mentally deficient and had been placed in an asylum, so he came up with a plan."

Daniel stared at the old woman. If the true heir had been incarcerated at an asylum in Kent for the past several decades and the countess never bore another son, then who was the man the world knew as Damian Langley?

Nanny Briggs nodded when she must have seen in Daniel's face that the penny had finally dropped.

"The current earl is illegitimate," Daniel said.

"He's the earl's son all right, but he was born on the wrong side of the blanket, so to speak."

"So the earl took him from his mother and presented him to the world as his son with the countess?"

"That's right. The child was born to Lucille Frey," Nanny Briggs said.

"The earl is the housekeeper's son?" Daniel exclaimed.

"Lucille was the upstairs maid then. And she spent her time upstairs most productively," the nanny said with a sneer.

"Did no one suspect?"

Nanny Briggs shook her head. "Lucille's boy, Edward, had been sent to live with a family in Ripley, so no one had ever seen him. And they hardly ever saw Damian, since he was kept in the nursery and allowed only an hour's walk in the garden during the staff's dinner break. And the two boys looked very much alike, having both taken after their father. Edward was a year younger, but he was a sturdy boy, and clever, so could easily pass for a child of four. Once the earl was sure Damian wouldn't improve, he packed him off to the Rothman Institute and installed Edward in his place."

"And the countess?" Daniel asked, horrified by the earl's heartless solution.

"Lady Cecily never had any say in the matter. She was heartbroken but wasn't allowed to either speak of her son or visit him, even in secret. She took her own life not long after Damian was taken from her."

"What about the couple that cared for Edward Frey?"

"They were told that he was going to live with his mother," Nanny Briggs replied. "It was all frighteningly simple, Inspector. Substitute one boy for another and get rid of the unwanted son once and for all. I assure you, no one noticed or cared, except for Lady Cecily and myself. She'd loved the boy despite his flaws. Or maybe because of them. A child like that needs a champion."

"Did you ever tell anyone?" Daniel asked, wondering how Nanny Briggs had managed to keep such a secret for nearly forty years.

"People in my position don't have the luxury of questioning their employers. Oh, I cried for Damian and prayed for him every night, but if I wanted to retain my position, I had to keep my own counsel and pretend that Edward was Damian. Had I given even the slightest indication that something was amiss, Martin Langley would have dismissed me without a character and possibly even had me taken up for some imaginary crime, so as to silence me for good."

"So, the man who was found in the stables was the earl's true heir?"

"That he was. That was why Lucille Frey thought he should be properly buried. Her son owes the poor man that much, having stolen his identity."

"Does Euphemia Langley know who the victim was?"

"Oh, no," Nanny Briggs said. "No one knows. Even the earl himself had no idea until quite recently. He had never met his brother, and his natural mother wasn't allowed anywhere near him under the threat that she would be instantly dismissed if she ever approached the boy. I wager a stronger incentive had been issued, if I knew Martin Langley. Probably threatened to accuse her of theft and have her sent to Botany Bay on a convict ship," Nanny Briggs said, shaking her head.

"So, what happened this past week?" Daniel asked as he tried to piece together the disparate bits of the story.

"His lordship received a letter from his solicitor, advising him that his brother had escaped from the Rothman Institute. The staff had searched and searched but found no trace of the real Damian, and the institute needed instructions on how to proceed. The earl was shocked to the core; I'll tell you that much, Inspector. He came to see me that night and demanded to know the truth of the matter. He'd correctly assumed that I was the only person who might know what had transpired the summer he was brought to live at Langley Hall. So I told him. He wept when he found out, most of all because his own mother had been there all along and not permitted to so much as speak to him. He left the very next morning. Went in person to find out as much as he could about his older brother and see if he could be located safe and sound."

"But if the earl was in Kent, who killed the real Damian Langley, and why?" Daniel asked.

"That I can't tell you, Inspector, because no one else knew of the switch. Even if he had made his claim to the earldom, no one would believe the poor wretch."

Daniel gulped some chocolate. It had cooled, but his mouth had gone dry, and his mind was spinning like a top. If what Nanny Briggs was saying was true, then there was a list of suspects, none of whom Daniel could openly approach without evoking Superintendent Ransome's ire. He'd have Daniel's head on a silver platter if Daniel so much as breathed a word of what Nanny Briggs had just told him, especially now that the escapee was dead and no good would come from raking over the past.

"You do what you must, Inspector Haze, but remember, the current earl is not to blame. He knew nothing of his brother growing up."

Daniel settled the bill, handed the box of marzipan to Nanny Briggs, and helped her to her feet. "Thank you for putting your trust in me, Mrs. Briggs."

"You seem like an earnest young man. I hope you'll do what's right with the information I have shared with you. Although, at this point, I don't rightly know what that might be. Perhaps it's best that no one learns the truth, but someone is guilty of murder, and I won't cover for them, be they a nobleman or a groom."

Daniel stood beneath the cheerful awning, watching Nanny Briggs as she walked away, the box of marzipan safely stowed in her reticule. He now knew the truth, but he wasn't any happier for it.

Chapter 19

“A word, sir,” Daniel said as he strode into Ransome’s office without knocking.

“I’m rather busy, Haze.”

“Not for this, you’re not,” Daniel replied.

He was being needlessly rude and aggressive, but the newfound knowledge was simmering inside him, his outrage threatening to boil over. Ransome set aside the document he’d been perusing and gestured toward the guest chair, clearly intrigued.

“Let’s hear it, then.”

Daniel laid out the facts as succinctly as possible, watching Ransome for a reaction. He thought he knew how the superintendent would react but hoped Ransome’s sense of fair play would prevail. John Ransome was a political animal, focused on his own professional success and upward mobility, but deep down, he believed in justice and the rule of law, and it was that quality that had earned Daniel’s grudging respect.

Superintendent Ransome’s expression didn’t change, but a nervous tic appeared to be pulsing in his tightly clenched jaw as his gaze slid away from Daniel, going to the photograph mounted on the wall. It was a picture of John Ransome as a young peeler, posing with a group of new recruits. His face shone with pride and his shoulders were set back, his feet planted slightly apart. This was a young man who felt confident in his choices and knew right from wrong.

“Well, sir?” Daniel asked when Ransome remained silent for far too long.

“Well what?”

“How shall we proceed?”

Ransome's eyes widened in disbelief. "How shall we proceed?" he echoed.

"Surely you don't expect me to ignore what I've learned."

"What you've learned came from a batty old woman who offered no tangible proof of this fairy tale she told you in exchange for a pot of chocolate and a box of sweeties."

"This was hardly a fairy tale for the earl's son," Daniel snapped. "Surely someone should be held accountable for what happened to that poor man."

"We don't know what happened," Ransome retorted. "All we know is that a stranger trespassed on private property and found himself at the end of a pitchfork."

Daniel stared at his superior, not bothering to hide his disappointment and disgust. "Are you suggesting that because the victim was said to be mentally deficient, he deserved to be obliterated, first by his own parents, and then by a pitchfork-wielding killer? Doesn't every human being deserve the same justice?"

Ransome's expression softened. "Haze, it's commendable that you care so deeply and want to see justice done, but think of the long-term ramifications. The man is dead. Whether he was the true earl or an impostor we may never know, but imagine what this sort of accusation will do to the current earl's family and reputation."

"Don't you mean what this sort of accusation will do to the police service and its future?"

"Yes, that too," Ransome replied calmly. "If we get this wrong, we'll get crucified, and the nobility will never put their trust in us again, fearing that we will try to tear them down rather than protect their interests."

"So this organization's only goal is to protect the interests of the wealthy and titled?" Daniel exclaimed.

"No, but it's those who have a voice that keep us afloat. Their contributions and support ensure our survival."

"Are you seriously asking me to close this investigation?" Daniel demanded. "I need to hear you say the words, *sir*." He put undue emphasis on the word, because at the moment, all he felt for Ransome was derision, not the respect due a superior officer.

Ransome sighed wearily. "No. You are right, the man deserves justice after his life was stolen from him, not once but twice. But you can't go charging in and damn the consequences, Haze."

"What would you have me do?" Daniel asked, a tad calmer now.

"You may investigate discreetly, without involving the family until you absolutely must. And what I mean by that is that you have to have concrete, indisputable proof to back up your insinuations. The word of Nanny Briggs is not enough to challenge an earl's right to his title and estate." Ransome nailed Daniel with an anxious stare. "I want daily reports. Is that understood? Nothing happens without my say-so."

"Do I need your permission to interview suspects and witnesses?" Daniel asked, feeling as if he'd just been handcuffed.

"You may interview persons of interest. Discreetly," Ransome reiterated. "But you are not to charge into the earl's residence and make accusations. Nor are you to make an arrest without informing me first."

"Understood, sir."

Daniel supposed he could see Ransome's point of view. In this case, it would be Ransome who would get the blame, not Daniel, since Ransome was the one to authorize an investigation. When it came to individuals who wielded the kind of power the Earl of Granville did, Daniel was no more than a tadpole. The earl would come after a bigger fish, someone he could destroy both personally and professionally in his quest for retribution. Ransome would be first in line, followed by Commissioner Hawkins, who just happened to be Ransome's father-in-law.

"Do I have your word that you will not make any rash judgments?" Ransome demanded.

"You have my word."

Daniel stood to leave, but Ransome called after him, "Are you consulting with Lord Redmond on this?"

"Unofficially," Daniel replied.

"Make it official. I want his input on this case. He might be American, but he's still a member of the nobility, and we will need all the guidance we can get when dealing with individuals of the earl's standing."

"Yes, sir."

"I authorize you to offer him whatever monetary compensation you think is appropriate."

"Jason Redmond is not in it for the money, sir."

"I know that, but I can't demand his help without offering him something in return. If he chooses to decline, then that's his decision."

Daniel nodded and left Ransome's office, going directly outside, where he trotted toward the nearest hansom stand.

"St. George's Hospital," he barked as soon as he'd climbed into an empty cab.

Chapter 20

Jason wasn't at the hospital, so Daniel directed the cabbie to take him to Kensington in the hope that he'd find Jason at home. The house in Hyde Park Gate was a far cry from Daniel's own modest dwelling, but the property had not been chosen by Jason but by his late grandfather, who'd used it as his London base until he became too ill to travel to the city. Jason had updated the plumbing, and Katherine had disposed of the fussy, old-fashioned furniture, creating a home that was both modern and comfortable.

"Daniel, how lovely to see you," Katherine exclaimed when he was shown into the drawing room by the ever-dour Dodson.

Katherine was on her knees, her skirt spreading out from her waist like a giant umbrella. Lily was beside her, carefully constructing a tower with large wooden blocks. Lily's dark curls escaped from her frilly bonnet, her rounded cheeks rosy from the heat of the fire that burned bright behind an ornamental fireguard. Lily's look of intense concentration resembled Katherine, but her little hands were delicate, the fingers long and nimble, just like Jason's. Katherine scrambled to her feet and scooped up the child, who wailed in protest.

"Come on, my darling," Katherine said in a soothing tone. "Let's go find Papa and tell him he has a visitor." Lily instantly quieted at the mention of her father.

"Please, make yourself comfortable, Daniel," Katherine said. "I'll ask Fanny to bring some tea. Jason won't be a moment."

Daniel was on his second cup of tea by the time Jason appeared. "I'm sorry to have kept you waiting. I was at the hospital until the small hours."

"Katherine should have said. I could have come back later," Daniel said, but he didn't really mean that. He needed to speak to Jason now and was glad Katherine had taken it upon herself to wake him.

Jason glanced longingly toward the door, where Fanny appeared as if by magic, carrying a silver pot whose contents filled the drawing room with a delicious aroma.

"I'm afraid I need my coffee. My mind is still a bit sluggish."

Fanny poured Jason a cup of steaming coffee, added cream, and handed Jason the cup. He ignored the tiny cucumber sandwiches and helped himself to a thick slice of raisin cake.

"I thought you were off baked goods," Daniel remarked, concerned for Jason's well-being.

"I'm hungry, and this has eggs."

Daniel nodded, although he didn't quite understand what difference eggs made to Jason's condition.

"What happened, Daniel? You look like you've seen a ghost," Jason said as he eyed Daniel over the rim of his coffee cup.

Daniel filled Jason in on his conversation with Nanny Briggs and then the meeting with John Ransome.

Jason didn't interrupt, but his thunderous expression reflected his emotion. "A parent really should be held accountable for such cruelty," Jason said once Daniel had finished.

"It seems no one was held accountable for anything and likely won't be if Ransome has his way. What are the odds of obtaining irrefutable proof at this stage?"

"Not high, but not completely impossible," Jason replied, and refilled his cup.

"Oh, and Ransome wants to pay you a fee in return for your help."

"I don't want his money," Jason retorted.

"Then take it and give it to a charity of your choice," Daniel said. "You shouldn't offer your time and services for free. Ransome doesn't deserve such generosity, given that he profits handsomely from it."

"That's a good idea. Katherine belongs to an organization that works for the improvement of conditions for London's orphans. I'd like to say they're making headway, but sadly, all the members seem to do is vent their outrage at the cruel indifference the poor children are subjected to by those who are in a position to help them," Jason said.

"How do you know?"

"I've had the pleasure of dining with its most vocal member," Jason said, grinning. "Adelaide Powell is a force to be reckoned with, at least in the dining room."

"Lord save us from do-gooders," Daniel said with a sigh.

"Change has to start somewhere, and it's the do-gooders that bring society's attention to grave social injustices."

"Right," Daniel said, not really interested in the fate of London's orphans just then. "Let's get back to the case, shall we? Where do we begin?"

"First, we need to identify all the potential suspects, since we now have a possible motive for the murder."

"*Possible* motive?"

"It's too soon to rule out Thomas Grady as a suspect. He might have been startled or felt threatened by the victim and charged him with a pitchfork, belatedly realizing that he might have just killed the earl. The most logical thing to do would be to claim that it was murder by persons unknown. And, for clarity's sake, let's call the victim Damian Langley and the current earl Edward Frey or we will get thoroughly confused."

"Agreed. So, besides Thomas Grady, we have Edward Frey, who had the most to lose by the reappearance of his father's legitimate heir. If he suspected that Damian Langley was headed for Langley Hall, he might have staged his departure and then returned and murdered the man who had the power to destroy the life he'd always believed to be legitimately his."

Jason nodded. "We also can't discount the countess. Edward Frey might have told his wife the truth of what happened, and she then simply played along, pretending for a few days that the victim was her husband and hoping that once she pronounced the man to be an imposter, he'd simply be disposed of, never to be mentioned again."

"But why go to all the trouble?" Daniel asked. "If Edward Frey was aware of his brother's imminent arrival and killed him, whether by design or in the heat of the moment, he could have simply disposed of the body. Why leave him there for Grady to find?"

"Perhaps he didn't have time to hide the body and didn't expect Simonds to send for the police right away," Jason suggested, then shook his head. "No, that doesn't add up, does it? Damian Langley was murdered sometime in the evening, and the body wasn't found until early the following morning. There was plenty of time to dispose of the corpse."

"That's true, but perhaps he had a reason for wishing the corpse found," Daniel mused. "The death of the legitimate earl would secure Edward Frey's position once and for all, so perhaps he needed those who were aware of Damian Langley's identity to know for certain that he was dead."

"Or perhaps he was more concerned with his own alibi and needed to get back to wherever he was staying in order to be conveniently seen. But there's also Mrs. Frey," Jason said excitedly. "She'd given up all rights to her only son to see him take his place as the legitimate earl. If she discovered that her son's position was at stake, she could have very easily tried to dispose of the true heir."

"And then there's Simonds," Daniel added. "He seems devoted to his master and might have taken matters into his own hands. If Damian Langley came to the door and informed Simonds that he was the late earl's son, Simonds might have somehow convinced him to go wait in the stables while he broke the news to his master, then gone to the stables himself and killed the man. Perhaps he left the body there intentionally, so he'd have future leverage over Edward Frey."

"Yes, that's certainly a possibility," Jason agreed.

"So, how do we go about narrowing down the list of suspects and obtaining solid proof without involving the family?"

"I think we must begin at the beginning," Jason proposed.

"Which is?"

"Which is the disability that had led to the fateful switch in the first place. We must ascertain the severity of Damian Langley's condition and determine whether he was even capable of trying to reclaim his rightful place. We must also obtain a record of Damian Langley's incarceration at the Rothman Institute and a history of treatment administered, if he had received any. It would be helpful to know if he'd suffered from violent outbursts or if he'd given any indication that he was aware of what had been done to him by his father. We should also check if Edward Frey had ever arrived at the asylum, and precisely when."

Jason glanced toward the carriage clock on the mantel. It was just past noon. "How far is Sevenoaks?"

"We can get there in a matter of several hours if we leave right away."

"I'll tell Joe to bring the brougham around," Jason said, already on his feet. Daniel followed him out into the foyer.

"Katie, if I'm not back in time for dinner, don't wait for me," Jason said when Katherine swept into the foyer, sans Lily.

"Where are you going?" Katherine asked, her brow creasing with worry.

"Kent," Jason replied, and smiled at her gently. "Don't worry, sweetheart. Just a routine visit to an asylum."

"Right," Katherine mumbled under her breath, knowing she had no say in the matter. "Nothing with you two is ever routine." Her attitude turned brisk. "Jason, don't forget your muffler, and make sure Joe has a warm rug in the carriage. The temperature is dropping. Should I ask Mrs. Dodson to prepare some sandwiches? You haven't had breakfast, and you're about to miss lunch. You need to eat, my dear."

Daniel felt a slight pang of envy. He missed the days when there had been someone besides Grace to worry about his well-being.

"Why not?" Jason agreed, seemingly to pacify his wife.

Katherine returned about ten minutes later with a small wicker basket and handed it to Jason. "Make sure you eat. You know how you get if you don't."

"Yes, dear."

"Daniel, look after him," Katherine said sternly.

Daniel almost blurted out *yes dear* but stopped himself just in time.

Chapter 21

Once they had arrived in Sevenoaks, the Rothman Institute wasn't difficult to find. It was a few miles west of the town, well past Knole Park, an estate held for centuries by the Sackvilles, the family name of the Dukes of Dorset. The institute was a forbidding redbrick building with truncated turrets, narrow mullioned windows, and countless chimney pots, only some of which were in use, the smoke curling into the pristine blue of the winter sky.

The gate was locked, and there was a watchman, or more accurately a guard, posted in a small wooden booth discreetly situated next to a stone pillar. When Jason and Daniel alighted from the carriage and approached the gates, he emerged, and Jason noticed with some surprise that the man was armed with a revolver.

"Are ye lost, gentlemen?" the guard asked in a distinctly unfriendly manner, his left arm pressed to his side to hide the weapon from view. He didn't unlock the gate and spoke to them through the wrought-iron bars.

"We are here to see the director of the institute," Daniel replied, undaunted.

"Do ye have an appointment, then?"

"We do not."

"Then I'm afraid ye've had yerselves a wasted journey."

Daniel produced his warrant card and held it between two bars so the man could see it clearly. "I can always come back with reinforcements."

The man chuckled. "What, a bunch of clueless yokels with wooden sticks? I quiver in me boots, yer worship."

Daniel's nostrils flared at the insolence of the man, but he was too much the professional to allow his anger to get the better of him. Instead, he chuckled, his reaction taking the guard by surprise. His eyebrows lifted in astonishment as he fixed Daniel with a baleful stare.

"You might not be aware, dwelling in the backwoods of Kent as you do," Daniel replied calmly, "but we do have firearms at our disposal these days. However, I highly doubt your employer would prefer that we shoot our way into this facility instead of simply speaking to us for a few minutes. Of course, if you take it upon yourself to decide who can and cannot speak to the director without consulting him first, then the blame will lie squarely with you, my good man."

That put the guard firmly in his place, and he nodded, his gaze sliding away from Daniel. "Fine. Ye win, Inspector. I'll ask Mr. Rothman if he'll see ye." Not prepared to forsake his position of power entirely, he turned to Jason. "And who might ye be?" he growled. "If ye're not a policeman, ye'll have to wait outside."

"Jason Redmond, Esquire," Jason replied haughtily. "I represent one of your clients, and it is my legal right to consult with the patient in question."

Daniel didn't bat an eyelash at this outrageous lie and kept his gaze trained on the guard, who looked even more abashed at this pronouncement.

"Well, well," he muttered under his breath. He appeared poised to say something more but changed his mind. "Ye wait right 'ere," he said grudgingly, and walked off.

Since the building was set a good distance from the gates, it would take him some considerable time to return. The men climbed into the brougham to wait. It was too cold and windy to stand by the locked gate for any length of time, and Jason was glad that Joe, who'd been exposed to the elements for the past few hours, was ensconced in a thick sheepskin coat and hat with earflaps. He would be freezing otherwise.

The guard returned quicker than Jason had expected, trotting toward the gates with surprising speed for a man of his bulk. He unlocked the gates and waved to them to step out of the carriage.

"He stays here," he said, jutting his chin belligerently toward the carriage and Joe. "I'll escort you to the door." He locked the gate behind them and strode on ahead down the gravel path.

Jason supposed there was some concern about them liberating an inmate, but an escape from the Rothman Institute would require some planning, something Damian Langley had obviously understood. The grounds were vast, but the land surrounding the building was flat, uninterrupted by bushes or trees, the view unobstructed in all directions, leaving whoever was abroad completely exposed. The high iron fence that surrounded the property had nothing to use as a foothold should someone hope to get over. As they approached the building, Jason noted the narrow iron bars on all the ground floor windows. It seemed that the Rothman Institute either took the security of their patients very seriously or was single-mindedly focused on their continued incarceration.

How had Damian Langley got out? And how in the world had he escaped without getting caught?

The guard used the knocker to announce their presence and waited until the door was opened by a matronly woman in a severe black gown and matching lace cap. She didn't appear to be a servant but someone in a position of authority.

"These are the *gentlemen* who are here to see Dr. Rothman," the guard said with obvious contempt.

The woman nodded and stepped aside. "This way, gentlemen," she said curtly.

They were led along a white-painted corridor punctuated by a number of closed doors. The dark-wood floor was highly polished, and the smell of beeswax pervaded the air. Jason strained his ears but heard nothing besides their footsteps. He wondered where the patients might be. It was nearly three in the afternoon. Surely they were awake and occupied in some fashion.

The woman led them to a door at the very end of the corridor and knocked gently.

"Come," a reedy voice called.

"Wait here, please," the woman said.

She opened the door and approached the desk, leaning down to say something to the man seated in a high-back chair. He nodded, smiled at her kindly, then beckoned Jason and Daniel to enter. There was a certain intimacy in their interaction, and Jason deduced that the woman must be his wife.

"Do sit down. I'm Dr. Elias Rothman," the man said as soon as they were alone. "May I examine your credentials?"

Elias Rothman was around sixty, with a pale, narrow face bracketed by bushy muttonchops and thinning gray hair. A pair of rimless spectacles magnified his pale blue eyes, and he had the thin lips of someone who always looked disapproving. He wore a black suit and a white shirt whose high, starched collar seemed to be chafing his reddened neck, the tie more a noose than an accessory. He had long, bony fingers, and the bare desk of a man who liked to maintain complete control over his surroundings.

Daniel produced his warrant card, and Jason tossed a calling card on the pristine surface of the desk.

"So, what can I do for you, gentlemen?" Dr. Rothman asked once he had studied Daniel's identification and glanced at Jason's card.

"We are investigating the murder of one of your patients," Daniel said.

"Oh?"

"Damian Langley," Jason interjected.

"We have never had a patient by that name," Dr. Rothman replied, but he couldn't quite hide his shock at the news that the man had been murdered. His gaze slid to a portrait that hung above the mantel, and his right hand shook slightly. The portrait was of a severe-looking older gentleman who bore a strong resemblance to Dr. Rothman.

"No, but you had a visit from a man of that name only a few days ago," Daniel pressed.

There was a flicker of surprise in the doctor's gaze that was quickly extinguished. Dr. Rothman clasped his hands on the desk, fixing Daniel with a defiant stare.

"And how would you know that?" he asked.

"Because the earl told us," Jason supplied smoothly.

Daniel could be held accountable for fabricating events if Dr. Rothman chose to make a complaint, but Jason was a free agent. Superintendent Ransome held no sway over him, and he meant to get the answers they'd come for.

"And what exactly is *your* interest in this, my lord?" Dr. Rothman demanded. He was clearly unnerved by Jason's presence and rank, and Jason meant to press his advantage.

"I'm a solicitor, representing the interests of your patient."

"Hired by whom?"

"An interested party who wishes to remain anonymous."

"How convenient," Dr. Rothman snapped.

"When did you discover the earl's brother had escaped?" Daniel asked. Dr. Rothman did not reply.

"I can arrest you for obstruction," Daniel said, producing a pair of iron handcuffs from inside his coat and placing them on the desk.

"You have no jurisdiction here, Inspector," Dr. Rothman said nastily. "We're a long way from London."

"Dr. Rothman, given that you had been charged with the care of an earl's firstborn son, I can only assume that you cater to an elite and wealthy clientele, not just the usual deranged riffraff you find in most lunatic asylums," Jason drawled, keeping his gaze fixed on Dr. Rothman's face.

It was obvious that Dr. Rothman was thrown off balance by Jason's American accent and was scrambling to figure out who Jason really was and if he should feel genuinely threatened or brazen out this ambush.

Jason pressed on. "Imagine how your clients' families might react if the name of your establishment was to find itself splashed across the papers, detailing how you permitted a patient to escape, an oversight that led to the man's brutal killing on the grounds of his family estate. Would they feel able to trust you with their secrets?" Jason asked, lowering his voice so that Dr. Rothman was forced to lean forward to hear him. "Imagine the embarrassment that would cause to those individuals who wish to keep their less-than-sane family members safely locked up."

"He wasn't mad," Dr. Rothman exclaimed, and instantly winced at his slip-up. He had now committed himself.

"What was he, then?" Jason demanded. "I would like to see his file. What name is he listed under in your records?"

Dr. Rothman resembled a cornered animal that knew it wasn't escaping unscathed. "That information is confidential, and I can only share it with another medical professional," he retorted, trying valiantly to find a way out of his predicament.

"Lucky for you, then, that I also happen to be a doctor," Jason replied smugly. He extracted an identification card issued to him by St. George's Hospital when he first began to volunteer his services and passed it to Dr. Rothman.

The man looked positively ill. “So, you are an American who possesses a British title and who just happens to be a doctor as well as a solicitor?” he demanded angrily.

“Exactly so. You got it in one,” Jason said, smiling at Dr. Rothman as if he were a particularly gifted pupil. “It would seem that a medical man is uniquely positioned to defend the rights of those who have suffered at the hands of medical professionals who are less than qualified to undertake their care and resort to unscrupulous practices to mask their gross incompetence.”

“Damian Langley did not suffer,” Dr. Rothman exclaimed, giving up all pretense. “He was well treated here.”

“He was incarcerated against his will,” Jason reminded the man.

“He needed to be.”

“What was the diagnosis?”

All fight seemed to have gone out of Dr. Rothman. He was astute enough to realize that the only way to protect his reputation and that of his asylum was to cooperate and refute any wrongdoing. He sighed heavily. “Damian Long, as he was known, was brought to us as a small boy. His father had serious concerns about his cognitive development.”

“And were those concerns valid?” Jason asked.

Daniel remained silent, allowing Jason to take the lead on this line of inquiry, since he was better qualified to pose the right questions and extract useful answers.

“Yes, they were, but the issues weren’t as severe as his father had intimated. The boy was slow to learn and had difficulty engaging with other people, but he certainly wasn’t mentally deficient. He rarely made eye contact and often repeated the same phrases over and over again, especially songs he’d heard while in the care of his nanny. He preferred to be alone, sometimes staring out the window for hours on end or drawing pictures of the same scene, but he was acutely aware of everything and everyone around him and cognizant of the fact that his family had abandoned him."

"Was he ever violent?" Daniel asked.

"No. Never."

"Did he ever express a desire to leave?" Jason asked.

"He asked to go home, especially at the beginning. He never cried, just repeated his request like a chant."

"What was he told about his family?" Daniel asked. It was clear he felt deep sympathy for the lonely boy who'd been so cruelly discarded.

"My father, who founded the institute, told him that he was ill and needed to remain at the institute in order to get better."

"Did he get better?" Jason asked.

"He was capable of absorbing new information, but his social behavior did not improve. He grew silent and detached and rarely spoke to anyone. He seemed to retreat into a world of his own. The only things he ever asked for were books. He liked to read and would often read the same book over and over until he could recite the entire manuscript from memory."

"Was he ever subdued by any means?"

"He didn't need to be. He accepted that this was his home and went from day to day quietly and stoically."

"So, what prompted his escape, if he was so accepting of his fate?" Daniel asked rather sarcastically.

"He'd read *The Ring and The Book* by Robert Browning. One of our doctors gave it to him after he'd finished with it. I saw no harm in him reading the book. I didn't think he'd even understand the gist of the plot, but something about an impoverished nobleman on trial for murder triggered memories of his childhood home. He started asking about Langley Hall and who lived there now. I suppose he saw himself in that poor, imprisoned nobleman. I think something inside him had finally snapped."

"What was he told of his family?" Jason asked again, since Dr. Rothman had never really answered Daniel's inquiry.

"Nothing." Dr. Rothman sighed. "I led him to believe that his memories were inaccurate, and he had never lived at Langley Hall or was, indeed, of noble birth. It was a kindness," Dr. Rothman cried defensively, even though neither man had claimed otherwise. "What was the point of telling him he was the true Earl of Granville, condemned to this pathetic half-life by his own father?"

"You sound as if you sympathized with him," Jason said.

"I did. Damian Langley did not belong here. He was different, yes, but not incapable of living a normal life. What his father did to him was unnecessarily cruel, his need to get rid of the child based on nothing more than sinful pride and a fear of being judged by his cronies."

"Did you ever tell the earl that you believed his son needed extra tutelage rather than an asylum?" Jason demanded.

"Yes. Once," Dr. Rothman said bitterly. "The earl became very angry and said that if I couldn't do what I was paid to do, then he would find another place for the boy. I was afraid Damian would be horribly mistreated, so I agreed to keep him on. I did my best for him, as did my father before me."

"How very kind of you," Daniel spat out. "I wager the monies you have received since then didn't hurt this place too badly either. So, I take it Damian Langley didn't believe you when you told him he was a deluded commoner?"

"Damian had a very good memory. Nothing I said would dissuade him."

"How did he manage to escape?" Daniel asked. "This place is a virtual fortress."

"No one really knows. Damian had the run of the place, since there was no possibility of him doing any harm to himself or others. We simply realized that he was missing one morning when he failed to turn up for breakfast. He was a creature of routine and always presented himself at the same time."

"Did Damian Langley have enough wherewithal to find his way to his childhood home?" Jason asked.

"I wouldn't have said so, given that he'd been here since the age of four, but I suppose some memories never fade."

"Did he have any money of his own? He would have had to have taken the train."

"He did not," Dr. Rothman replied. "He took some money out of my wife's purse. She only realized it once we started searching for Damian."

"Did he take anything else?" Daniel asked.

"He took a train timetable from Mr. Potter, one of the orderlies. Mr. Potter takes the train to visit his mother on his days off and had spoken to Damian about trains in the past."

"Had Damian Langley ever been on a train before last week?"

"Not that I know of, but he'd read about trains in his books, and he was interested in maps."

"Who had administered the funds for Damian Langley's upkeep to your establishment?" Jason asked.

"Horace Quinlan, Esquire. Perhaps you've heard of him, Lord Redmond," Dr. Rothman suggested.

"The name is vaguely familiar," Jason replied with a dismissive gesture. "We may have crossed paths at one time or another." He fixed Dr. Rothman with an accusing stare. "When the postmortem was performed, Damian Langley presented as underweight, borderline malnourished," he stated. "Did you starve him?"

"What? No!" Dr. Rothman cried. "You don't understand. Damian had an aversion to most foods. He said the meat smelled dead. He only ate vegetables and bread, and even then, in very small quantities. If he ate too much, he felt ill."

"Why don't I believe you?" Jason demanded angrily. "Underfeeding a patient for decades would considerably reduce the cost of their upkeep. Perhaps your other inmates are half-starved as well. Shall we have a look?"

"This is not Bedlam," Dr. Rothman cried, visibly distressed. "We don't treat the incurably insane. And it is not our goal to cause anyone unnecessary suffering. What we offer here is a genteel environment for those who need special care."

"And whose families are willing to pay a pretty penny to dispose of their embarrassments," Jason finished for him.

"Yes, if you like. But they don't wish to see their children or spouses suffer needlessly. We treat them with kindness and make sure they're happy and calm."

"In other words, you keep them sedated," Jason inferred.

"When the situation calls for it, yes. Isn't it kinder to allow them to sleep rather than rant and rage against the unfairness of their situation? It's not as if they have any recourse. Their families have committed them to this institution quite legally. There's no way back."

"But Damian Langley found his way back and was murdered as soon as he arrived," Daniel pointed out.

"I'm genuinely sorry Damian is dead. He was a gentle soul, and his father likely wouldn't have committed him had he not been born to an earldom, but we all have a duty to future generations.

The late earl ensured that his line continued uninterrupted by passing the torch to his younger son."

"At the expense of a man's freedom," Daniel exclaimed.

Dr. Rothman nodded in agreement. "It's not for me to judge the man's actions, Inspector. I'm paid to look after those who can't look after themselves, and I do it to the best of my ability."

"You will pen a statement detailing everything you have just shared with us," Jason said.

"I will do no such thing. You can arrest me if you so wish, but I will not disclose that which I have sworn not to reveal. If I do that, no one will ever put their trust in me again."

Daniel gave Jason a sidelong glance, then held up his hand in a placating gesture. "I can understand your reservations, Dr. Rothman, but a man is dead, and we must discover who murdered him."

"And I hope that you do, but whatever befell Damian Langley did not happen here. I have confirmed your assumptions about his identity and have explained the nature of his disability and his emotional state at length. That's all I'm prepared to do."

"Did you meet with the earl?" Daniel asked, moving on.

"Yes. His lordship came here last Tuesday, demanding to know the whereabouts of his brother. In his defense, I must say that he didn't know of Damian's situation until he was contacted by Mr. Quinlan at my behest."

"How can you be certain?" Jason asked.

"Martin Langley set up a trust to cover Damian's upkeep for the duration of his lifetime. He did not wish to burden his heir needlessly so never made him privy to the arrangement."

"But you informed Mr. Quinlan that Damian Langley was missing," Jason said. "What did you hope to accomplish?"

"Mr. Quinlan is the only point of contact I've had all these years. I sent an urgent message asking him to either resolve the situation himself or involve the earl."

"How did you expect him to resolve it?" Daniel asked.

"I honestly don't know, Inspector. This was the first time anything like this has ever happened since the Rothman Institute opened its doors. I felt it my duty to inform Mr. Quinlan of Damian's escape rather than take it upon myself to keep it secret and hope he eventually turned up."

"I will need an address for Mr. Quinlan," Daniel said.

Dr. Rothman silently pulled out an address book and copied out the address, then pushed the paper across the desk.

"Thank you. How long did the Earl of Granville remain in Sevenoaks?"

"I believe he only stayed for one night. He'd considered calling on the Sackvilles, but I told him they were in London for the Season, so he asked for a name of a respectable inn. I recommended the Red Lion in town."

"Did he tell you how he intended to proceed?" Daniel asked.

"No. He was angry and upset, and frightened, I think. This came as quite a shock."

"Which part?" Jason asked, unable to mask his sarcasm.

"All of it," Dr. Rothman replied. "He never knew he had an older brother, and the fact that his father had made such a drastic decision when Damian was so young was obviously something of a revelation. It cast a whole new light on a man he'd both trusted and respected."

"Do you think he could have murdered his brother if their paths crossed?" Daniel asked.

"How can I make such a determination?" Dr. Rothman exclaimed. "I met the man once, and he was presented with an unprecedented dilemma. You must see it from his point of view."

"Oh, but we do," Jason said. "He had everything to lose and nothing to gain by acknowledging the legitimate earl."

"No one would have believed Damian, even if he had intended to challenge his brother's position. There was no need to kill him," Dr. Rothman said.

"No, there wasn't," Jason agreed, recalling the pitiful remains of a man whose life had been so cruelly stolen from him by those meant to protect him. "But if apprehended, he might not have been willing to return to the institute. Perhaps he had made it clear that he'd put up a fight."

"Perhaps. And who could blame him?" Dr. Rothman asked. "What do you intend to do?" He was clearly worried for his own reputation and afraid to be publicly accused of negligence.

"We intend to find out who killed Damian Langley and why," Daniel replied as he pushed to his feet. "And when we do, you might need to take the stand, Doctor. There'll be no escaping culpability then."

"You do your job, and I'll do mine, Inspector," Dr. Rothman replied smugly. "From what I hear, the majority of murders go unsolved, so we have yet to see if this case goes to trial."

"Oh, I will solve this," Daniel replied vengefully. "If only to see those responsible held to account."

Jason stood and followed Daniel out the door

"Where to, m'lord?" Joe asked once they returned to the carriage.

"The Red Lion in town," Jason replied, and climbed in after Daniel. Neither man spoke as the carriage pulled away from the gates.

Chapter 22

The Red Lion was much like any other tavern, with a polished bar, an outdated and less-than-pleasant-smelling taproom, and a slightly more welcoming dining area. Several tables were already occupied, mostly by men, and there were at least a dozen patrons milling by the bar, enjoying their pints and exchanging news and gossip. They were loud and boisterous and clearly annoying the publican, who cast angry looks in their direction, probably for the benefit of Jason and Daniel, who were potential customers the regulars might frighten away.

Having surrendered the horses and carriage to the adjacent livery, Joe took a table in the corner at Jason's bidding. He had to be tired, hungry, and cold after driving all that way and then waiting for Daniel and Jason outside the Rothman Institute, and Jason wanted to ensure that Joe had time to eat his fill and warm up before starting on the return journey to London.

"How can I assist you, sirs?" the publican asked politely.

He was a thickset man in his fifties or early sixties, with thinning ginger hair liberally threaded with gray, clean-shaven cheeks that were as round and rosy as ripe apples, and a sizeable belly that strained against the buttons of his waistcoat. His smile was ingratiating, since he'd probably seen the brougham and pair through the window and correctly assumed that he was dealing with men who had coin to spare.

"A pint of bitter," Daniel said. "What would you prefer, my lord?"

Jason tried to hide his amusement. Daniel had grown quite accustomed to using Jason's rank at his discretion, whipping out his noble title whenever he needed to impress or intimidate.

The publican's smile of welcome grew even wider. "What can I get you, your lordship?"

"Would you have any coffee?" Jason asked, clearly taking the man by surprise.

"None that's ready, but if you would like to take a table in the dining room, I'll ask Missy to brew a pot straight away."

"I would appreciate that, Mr.—?"

"Potter. Bert Potter."

"Thank you, Mr. Potter. Do you have rooms to let, by any chance?" Jason asked with feigned casualness.

"Oh, yes, sir. We have four rooms upstairs, two currently unoccupied, on account of the festive season," Mr. Potter rushed to explain. "The rooms are clean and comfortable, and we provide a hot bath upon request. Breakfast is included."

Jason nodded. "Do you happen to have the Earl of Granville staying with you at present? We'd made a plan to meet here in Sevenoaks, but I didn't see his carriage in the livery."

"The Earl of Granville?" Mr. Potter exclaimed. "Why, no, sir."

"Are you certain?"

"I'd be sure to know if such an elevated personage graced us with his presence."

Jason did his best to look sheepish. "He sometimes travels under an assumed name. He's a shy fellow and likes his anonymity."

"What name would that be?" Mr. Potter asked, clearly unsettled by the suggestion that he might have had an earl under his roof and treated him as a regular so-and-so.

"Damian Langley. Or Edward Frey," Jason said, lowering his voice confidentially. "Can you kindly check if he's been and gone?"

"Of course, my lord." Mr. Potter pulled out a stained leather-bound ledger from behind the bar and laid it on the counter, running his stubby finger along the latest entries.

"Ha! Here we are. Edward Frey. He stayed with us for two nights and requested two rooms." The publican looked stricken. "I should have realized," he muttered to himself. "He had servants traveling with him. I should have known he was someone of consequence."

"I feel just terrible," Jason lamented. "I was unavoidably detained, and he waited for me all that time. When exactly did he arrive, Mr. Potter?"

"Tuesday afternoon. Don't worry; he received your message, my lord," Mr. Potter rushed to assure Jason.

"Did he? When?"

"Wednesday. Late afternoon. A lad arrived, asking after Mr. Frey. Said he had an urgent message for him."

Jason nodded in relief. "I'm glad he didn't think I'd let him down. I do hope I didn't ruin his Christmas."

"No, sir. I think he enjoyed his anonymity, as you say," Mr. Potter said, having seemingly decided that he'd done the best he could for the sneaky earl. "He took walks around the town and drove out into the countryside. It can be quite peaceful at this time of year."

"Indeed, it can."

"And we did serve Mr. Frey Christmas dinner in our private parlor, and a fine dinner it was too," the publican reminisced. "My Missy is an excellent cook. Her roast goose fair melts in your mouth, and the Christmas pudding is unrivaled. Mr. Frey did say so when he asked for a second helping."

Jason smiled wistfully. "Yes, the earl is rather fond of sweets."

“That he is, sir. Cleared his plate in no time.”

“I don’t suppose you have any Christmas pudding left?”

“I’m sorry, no. But Missy did make an extra batch of mince pies. And today’s supper is fried liver with bacon and onions served with a generous helping of mash,” he imparted eagerly.

“Shall we sup here then, Mr. Haze?” Jason asked. “I can never say no to fried liver.”

“Of course, my lord. As you wish.”

“If you would bring that coffee after our meal, Mr. Potter,” Jason said. “And a couple of mince pies.”

“Of course, my lord. It would be my pleasure.”

Jason and Daniel adjourned to the dining room and settled in the furthest corner to await their meal.

“I didn’t figure you for a liver lover,” Daniel said, eyeing Jason with suspicion. He was well aware of Jason’s intense dislike of certain traditional favorites, such as kidney pie and kippers.

“It was one of my father’s favorite dishes, so we had it quite often,” Jason said, trying to swallow the lump in his throat. As his parents’ beloved faces swam before his eyes, he wondered if the pain of losing them would ever fade. “Katherine can’t abide it, so Mrs. Dodson never makes it,” he said, intentionally recalling Katherine’s very vocal disgust in order to combat his sudden sadness.

“I wager Micah is not a liver enthusiast either,” Daniel said.

“Micah will eat anything that’s put in front of him. Once you’ve known hunger, you are not so quick to refuse any food.”

“I’m sorry. That was rather tactless of me.”

“Not at all. I don’t expect you to walk on eggshells around me. All that is in the past. Right now, we have a murder to solve,”

Jason said just as a plump middle-aged woman, presumably Missy herself, delivered the plates to their table. A girl of about fifteen placed a basket of bread, a dish of butter, and a pitcher of beer on the table, then smiled shyly and hurried away.

"Enjoy your meal, my lord," Mrs. Potter said, addressing Jason exclusively, her wide back to Daniel.

"I'm sure we will," Jason assured her. The woman performed something resembling an awkward curtsey and waddled back toward the kitchen.

"Edward Frey's alibi checks out," Daniel said sourly as he buttered a piece of bread. "I was hoping he was our killer, having the most compelling reason to want his brother out of the way."

"Yes, it does, but we now know that he'd been warned to stay away, presumably by a member of his household, who sent a message to the Red Lion."

Daniel nodded and swallowed the bread before replying. "So, someone knew where he was and that he wasn't the victim all along."

"Precisely. And I think it was his wife."

"Or Simonds. I doubt the earl would have confided in Mrs. Frey, unless he'd known all along that she was his mother and felt he could trust her," Daniel theorized.

"There's really no telling what he knew, or whom he'd shared it with, but someone had a fairly good idea of who the man in the stables was," Jason said. "They also knew that the earl was going by his true name when they sent the message telling him to stay away."

"Shows utter lack of imagination, if you ask me."

"I don't agree. The fact that the earl opted to use his real name shows that he felt no shame at being born to a housekeeper, nor that he believed he was in any danger of being exposed. Had he felt genuinely threatened, he would have made up another alias."

"So where did Edward Frey go after leaving Sevenoaks?" Daniel asked.

"He did not use the carriage with the family crest in order to preserve his anonymity, a wise decision, given the nature of his errand. Once informed that his brother was dead, he might have gone to London but stayed away from the house until he felt it was safe to return."

"Which it would be once the countess declared the deceased to be a tramp."

"Precisely. Except she never bet on you continuing with the investigation."

"Had Nanny Briggs not enlightened me about the relationship between Edward Frey and Damian Langley, I would have quickly reached a dead end in my inquiries," Daniel observed. "This would have been the perfect murder."

"It still might be, since we don't know who actually killed the poor man."

"It has to be someone who was at the house that night, which narrows it down." Daniel smiled humorlessly. "Ransome forbade me to question the family, but he never said anything about the servants."

"But first, we should speak to Mr. Quinlan and obtain his version of events," Jason suggested. "It's entirely possible that the earl knew more of the arrangement than Dr. Rothman was led to believe."

"It will be too late to call on Quinlan tonight, but I intend to speak to him first thing tomorrow morning," Daniel promised.

"I'll come with you. I don't have anything on the agenda tomorrow."

"I plan to call at the Yard first, to give Ransome an update and inform him that I intend to question Edward Frey," Daniel said determinedly.

"Ransome will have something to say about that," Jason warned.

"Yes, he will, but I'm investigating the murder of the rightful earl. It would be remiss of me not to question the man who had stepped into his shoes, even if he hadn't done so intentionally."

"The first time."

Daniel nodded. "The second time he would have known precisely what he was about, which is why I need to speak to him. He might have a rock-solid alibi for the murder, but that doesn't mean he didn't have a hand in it."

Jason pushed away his empty plate and grinned. "Ransome can raise no objections to me questioning the current earl."

"What an excellent notion," Daniel said, grinning back. "Glad to see you're finally earning your keep."

Chapter 23

Tuesday, December 29

The vestibule of Scotland Yard was unusually crowded when Daniel arrived just before nine o'clock. Several constables were talking excitedly but paused when they spotted Daniel, watching him with something akin to sympathy. Daniel nodded in greeting and was about to make a beeline for the superintendent's office when John Ransome emerged into the corridor, looking entirely too harassed for a man who must have just arrived.

"Ah, Haze," he exclaimed. "Just the man I want to see. My office, please."

Ransome turned on his heel and strode back into his office, waited for Daniel to enter, then shut the door with considerable force.

"Sit," Ransome barked, and came around the desk, dropping into his chair as if he were exhausted beyond words.

"What happened?" Daniel asked. Try as he might, he couldn't come up with a scenario that would cause such consternation in the normally smug superintendent.

"I've just sent Constable Napier to fetch Lord Redmond. I hope he's an early riser."

"Why?"

"The Earl of Granville has been murdered. Grady found his body in the stables this morning."

"What?" Daniel cried.

Ransome skewered Daniel with an angry stare. "Had you investigated this case properly, his death might have been avoided."

"And had you not tied my hands, I might have had a chance of solving this case before another murder occurred," Daniel snapped. "So don't you dare try to pin this murder on me, Superintendent."

He was crossing the line; he knew it, but he was so angry, he couldn't bear to remain silent. Ransome was worried about his reputation and upward trajectory and was setting Daniel up as a convenient scapegoat to offer up to Commissioner Hawkins. Well, Daniel wouldn't go down without a fight, not now, not ever. He was made of sterner stuff, he decided, enjoying the heady sense of defiance coursing through his veins.

"I won't be spoken to this way," Ransome retorted, angry color rising in his cheeks.

"Neither will I," Daniel countered. "Nor will I accept responsibility for something that's none of my doing."

He expected Ransome to sack him on the spot and assign another detective to the case—Eugene Yates, perhaps, who was a friend of the superintendent—but Ransome exhaled loudly, his shoulders slumping, his head dipping forward. He reminded Daniel of a marionette whose master had let go of the strings, allowing the puppet to hang until the next performance, when he would bring it back to life.

Daniel wasn't sure what to make of this, so he remained where he was, refusing to leave until he received clear instructions. Ransome finally looked up, met Daniel's gaze squarely, and planted his hands on the desk, as if bracing himself against some unseen threat.

"You are right, Haze," he said at last. "I admit it, and I apologize for not trusting your instincts." Ransome looked like he was about to say something else, then seemed to think better of it. The apology was clearly at an end.

"What will you have me do, sir?" Daniel asked, trying to keep his voice level. He felt elated, not only to still have his place on the police service but also because he had stood his ground and won. It was a small victory but a victory, nonetheless, and he'd had so few gratifying moments since Sarah's death.

"I've sent two constables to the earl's residence to secure the crime scene and begin questioning the staff. I want you to head over to Park Lane immediately. Lord Redmond will meet you there."

"Yes, sir."

"And Haze?"

Daniel waited patiently to hear what Ransome had to say. The super was in an unenviable position, and they both knew it.

"You have my full support on this."

"Thank you, sir."

"You may use my carriage," Ransome added.

"I appreciate that, sir."

By the time Daniel stepped outside, Ransome's maroon brougham was already waiting, the young coachman perched on the high bench, smartly dressed in a caped black coat and top hat. He tipped his hat to Daniel and waited for him to get in before setting off at a good clip. Daniel briefly wondered if the conveyance belonged to John Ransome outright or if it was provided by the police service for his use. Either way, the fact that Ransome had offered the use of his carriage showed the depth of his disquiet. Now that the man everyone believed to be the real earl was dead, there'd be no more pussyfooting around the family or keeping the murder out of the papers. The hunt for the killer was truly on.

Jason was already in place when Daniel arrived, his Gladstone bag on a bale of hay to keep it from getting smeared with muck and blood. Jason stood still, his head tilted to the side as he studied the scene. He nodded to Daniel wordlessly and turned his attention back to the victim, who was suddenly illuminated by a flash from Mr. Gillespie's camera. Gillespie was a taciturn fellow and didn't bother with greetings or comments. He simply did his job, but he was good at it, and the images were usually sharp and well-framed, all the pertinent details visible in the shot, unlike Gillespie's face, which was shadowed by the brim of his hat and further obscured by the camera.

"One more from this angle, Mr. Gillespie," Jason finally said, having spotted something he deemed important.

"As you say, sir," Gillespie muttered. He lifted the tripod with his left hand while supporting the sizeable camera with his right to shift it to the new position. Another flash exploded in the dim space, giving the scene a surreal quality.

Edward Frey was slumped against a wooden partition, the shaft of a pitchfork protruding from his lean belly and keeping him upright. His head had lolled to the side, but his eyes were wide open, a look of surprise etched into his frozen features. He wore only trousers, a white shirt and a satin waistcoat in deep blue with a design of delicate silver birds suspended in flight. The lower half of the garment was soaked with blood, the birds reminiscent of the hapless creatures so often shot for someone's entertainment and collected by dogs, their teeth stained crimson as they brought the offerings to their masters. Edward Frey's arms hung limply at his sides, but the right hand was bloodied. The horses that occupied the stalls paid little mind to the commotion, their attention fixed on their oats. Only the snow-white Arabian was glaring at them, its nostrils flaring, its ears pressed back.

Jason turned to the two constables hovering in the doorway. "Please take down the body and take it to the mortuary. Thank you," he added politely.

Daniel leaned wearily against the opposite wall and shook his head in disbelief. "We have two bodies in the space of a week. Both men were believed to be the Earl of Granville at the time of their death. Both killed in a stable, either by coincidence or more likely by design. My initial hypothesis was that Damian Langley was killed because he posed a threat to the current earl and his family, but now that both men are dead, we have to assume that the first murder was a case of mistaken identity, and the killer came back to finish the job. Edward Frey must have been the target from the start."

"Yes, that would seem to be the case," Jason agreed as he picked up his bag.

"Do you think the postmortem will shed any light?"

"I doubt it. The cause of death is obvious," Jason replied as they emerged from the stable.

"In that case, I would like to start by questioning the family and members of the household staff right away. The postmortem can wait."

"I agree," Jason said. "We must get their impressions while they're still fresh in their minds."

"Let's begin, then."

Chapter 24

Jason and Daniel were allocated the back parlor, compliments of Simonds, to conduct their inquiries. A parlormaid brought in a pot of coffee and set it on the low table, but no other refreshments were offered, probably in the hope that they wouldn't linger. The countess was in the withdrawing room, recovering from the news of her husband's death for the second time within a week.

According to Adams, her lady's maid, her ladyship was conscious but not fully coherent, which was just as well, since Daniel intended to start with the members of staff that were of interest. There were thirty underlings in total, but most of them were accounted for and had been in the presence of others at all times since before the earl had arrived at Park Lane, according to both Simonds and the constables, who had questioned each member of staff.

First up was Thomas Grady, who was pale and perspiring noticeably despite having just come in from the outside. He advanced into the room, his step faltering as he neared the two leather club chairs occupied by Jason and Daniel. He held his tweed cap in his hands and twisted it so violently, he'd probably never wear it again.

"I didn't do it," he cried, his desperation obvious. "I swear, I didn't do it."

"No one says you did, lad," Daniel replied in his most soothing tone. "Just tell us what happened."

Grady inhaled sharply, as if in pain, and began. "I arrived at the stables at six, like I do every day. I saw im as soon as I pushed open the door. It were just like last time. I didn't touch 'im, just ran for Mr. Simonds. I were that scared," Grady cried. "I'd never seen no one murdered afore all this. It's 'orrible, it is."

"Why would we think you did it, Thomas?" Jason asked conversationally. "You held no grudge against the earl. Did you?"

"No, sir. The earl were a good master, kind and undemanding. But I were the one to find both bodies, and I were the last to leave the mews the night afore."

"Did you see anything when you arrived at the stables this morning?" Daniel asked. "Footprints? Any articles of clothing that didn't belong there?"

"No, Inspector. The ground were dry, and I saw nothin' out of the ordinary."

"Was the door to the stables open or shut?" Jason asked.

"It were shut. Like always."

"What about the earl's coat?" Daniel asked.

Thomas shook his head. "It weren't there, Inspector. 'E must'a come out without it."

"And the horses? Were they all accounted for?"

"Why, yes. Even the Arabian, and she's the most valuable. Ye think it were a theft gone wrong?" Thomas asked, a spark of hope lighting his young face.

Daniel shook his head. "I don't. Had whoever did this wanted the horses, they'd have taken them when no one was about."

"They'd fetch a fair price," Thomas said, his expression growing dreamy. "Why, the Arabian alone is worth…" His face turned red, and he went quiet, likely realizing he wasn't helping his case by betraying that he'd considered the value of the horses on the open market. The young man stepped from foot to foot and stared down at the mangled cap in his hands. "Can I go?" he whined pitifully.

"Yes. Please ask Mr. Simonds to join us," Daniel instructed. Grady practically ran for the door.

The butler walked in briskly and positioned himself before the two men, standing as if on parade, but his annoyance was obvious. He clearly had no faith in their efforts to find the killer and wanted them to know that. Daniel supposed he'd feel much the same in the butler's shoes. They'd had a week to apprehend whoever had killed the real Damian Langley and to save the life of his half-brother, but now both men were dead, killed in precisely the same manner.

Daniel tried to marshal his thoughts. Was there a message in the method of the killing? What role did the stables play, if any?

"Mr. Simonds, tell us what occurred this morning," Jason said when Daniel failed to begin.

"As I told the duty sergeant when I reported the murder this morning, Grady came running to the servants' hall, screaming and crying. The poor lad was beside himself. I hurried out to the stables, hoping I might still be of some help, but his lordship was dead. Had been for hours, by the looks of him. I asked Mrs. Frey to fetch Grady a cup of tea and add a dollop of spirits. I keep a bottle of whisky in the butler's pantry for emergencies," Simonds added. "I instructed Mrs. Frey to keep everyone inside, so as not to muddle the investigation, and asked Stills, that's the other groom, to take me to Scotland Yard."

"Why did you go yourself," Daniel asked, "instead of sending a message with Stills?"

"Because I wanted to speak to whoever was in charge, and Stills would get fobbed off." A lock of gray hair fell into Simonds's face, and he brushed it back irritably. He instantly brought his arm back to his side, standing like a tin soldier, but not before Daniel noticed that his shirt cuff was smeared with blood.

"There's blood on your shirt, Mr. Simonds," Daniel pointed out.

Simonds lifted his arm and turned it over, then winced when he noticed the stain. “Yes. I touched his lordship’s neck to check for a pulse. I didn’t realize I’d soiled my shirt.”

“There was no blood on the earl’s face,” Jason said.

Simonds looked uncomfortable. “I laid my hand on his chest. My cuff must have brushed against the bloodied waistcoat.”

“Why did you touch his chest?”

“I only wanted to make sure his heart was no longer beating. And to say goodbye,” Simonds said, showing grief for the first time. “I cared for him. Deeply.”

“When was the last time you saw the earl alive?” Daniel asked. It was imperative that they establish a timeframe for the killing.

“Last night. His lordship had dinner with the family, then retired to the library for an after-dinner brandy and cigar, as was his habit. He was still in the library when I locked up at ten.”

“Are you certain?” Daniel asked.

“Yes. I stopped in to ask if he required anything and then wished him a good night when he said he had everything he needed.”

“Were the doors locked when you came down this morning?” Jason inquired.

“Yes, sir. The front and servants’ entrance doors were locked, but there’s a door in the orangery that leads to the terrace. He must have gone out that way.”

“So, you’re suggesting that the earl went to the stables willingly.”

“I saw no evidence of a struggle. He must have fancied a walk.”

"Did his lordship take many evening walks?" Daniel asked.

"He did sometimes, when there was something on his mind. He was a great one for exercise."

"And did he normally use the orangery to exit the house?" Jason asked.

"He didn't keep a key to the front door on him, but the orangery door key is left in the lock, as a rule."

"And was the key still there this morning?" Daniel inquired.

"Yes, and the door was unlocked," Simonds replied. "I checked after I got back from Scotland Yard."

"How was the earl when he returned from his trip? What was his reaction to the news of the vagrant's murder?"

They had not released the identity of the first victim, so Simonds wouldn't know that the man was the true Earl of Granville rather than the late earl's illegitimate son. It suited Daniel's purpose to keep both the family and the staff in the dark for the time being.

"His lordship was outraged that his family should be subjected to such an awful and frightening thing. And relieved that the matter had been dealt with. The undertaker had collected the eh…remains and disposed of them."

"And what did the earl think happened?" Jason asked.

Simonds looked truly ill at ease now, loyalty to the family clearly warring with the need to assist with the inquiries into the death of his master and friend. His gaze slid toward a silver-framed portrait of the earl displayed on the mantelpiece.

"He thought the man might be his father's natural son, given the obvious resemblance," he said at last.

"Did he know for certain that his father had sired other children?" Jason asked.

"If he did, he didn't tell me."

"Mr. Simonds, can anyone account for Grady's whereabouts from the time he left the stables last night to the time he returned this morning?" Daniel asked.

"Yes, they can," Simonds said rather defensively. "Grady came in a few minutes before six, cleaned up, and had supper in the servants' hall with the rest of the household staff. He remained there until just before ten, in the company of the two footmen, Walter Reedy and John Mulch. Everyone had retired to their rooms before I locked up. Grady shares a room with Stills, who swears Grady never left his bed during the night."

"And how would Stills know if he was asleep?" Jason asked.

"He's a light sleeper," Simonds replied.

"How convenient," Daniel said. "Mr. Simonds, did Thomas Grady have any grievances against the earl?"

"No, Inspector. Tom is a good boy and was glad of the job. He rarely came in contact with his lordship."

"But the earl was fond of his horses. You said so yourself," Jason interjected. "Certainly he came in contact with the grooms who looked after them."

"He did, your lordship, but very briefly. Not to talk to, at any rate."

"How is it that Grady was first at the scene both times? What of Stills?"

"As I said, Stills is a light sleeper, so he often has a hard time getting up in the morning, on account of not getting to sleep until the early hours. Tom goes out to the stables first to give Stills a few extra minutes. He's a kind-hearted boy and covers for his friend," Simonds admitted.

"And you turn a blind eye?" Daniel asked, surprised that the butler would allow someone to remain abed when the rest of the staff was up and ready to begin their day.

Simonds blushed. "It doesn't take two men to fill a few buckets with oats or add water to the trough. No need to be unkind."

"Mr. Simonds, what is your theory on what happened?" Jason asked.

Simonds replied immediately, having clearly given the matter some thought. "I think someone intended to kill his lordship and returned when they realized they got the wrong man."

"And who would wish to kill the earl?" Daniel asked.

"I don't know of anyone who wished him harm."

"Is it that easy to get into the stables?" Jason asked.

"Easy enough. They're not a fortress."

"And you said you saw no signs of a struggle, either in the house or in the stables. So, it is your belief that the earl met with whoever it was that killed him of his own accord?"

"I do, yes."

"So, not an obvious enemy, then?"

"I wouldn't know," Simonds replied.

"You've known the earl since your army days. Is he the sort of man to make enemies?" Jason asked.

"His lordship was a good man, one that inspired loyalty and respect, but there's no accounting for who someone blames for the death of their husband or son, or brother."

"You think this killing goes back to something that happened while the earl was in the military?"

"It's possible," Simonds muttered. His gaze slid toward the photograph again, his expression apologetic.

"What are you not telling us, Mr. Simonds?" Daniel asked.

Simonds turned back to the two men with an air of resignation. "There was an incident, about a year ago. His lordship went grouse shooting in Scotland. It was one of his favorite pastimes. Well, there was an accident."

"What sort of accident?" Jason asked.

"A young lad was killed. One of the beaters. He was shot in the back."

"By the earl?" Daniel asked.

"It was impossible to know for certain who shot the boy, but the parents blamed the earl. He'd organized the shooting party, so it was his responsibility."

"Did the earl make any reparations to the family?"

"He did, yes. He compensated them handsomely, but the boy's father, Rob McLeod, made verbal threats."

"And how did his lordship react to these threats?" Daniel asked.

"He said the man was grieving for his boy and he wouldn't press any charges."

"So, you think this Rob McLeod followed the earl first to Surrey and then to London to avenge his son's death?"

"It's the only scenario I can countenance," Simonds replied earnestly.

"But how would he know he'd murdered the wrong man?" Jason asked.

"Perhaps he'd been watching the family. I saw someone lurking just outside the gates on Saturday."

"Why didn't you say anything sooner, Mr. Simonds?" Daniel demanded.

"I have only just thought of it now."

"And why would the earl go out to the stables to meet this man if he suspected McLeod meant him harm?" Daniel asked.

"Perhaps he wanted to settle the matter somewhere it wouldn't upset his wife and children."

"Surely if the man had come all this way to avenge his son's death, he would have been better prepared, instead of relying on a conveniently placed pitchfork," Jason mused.

"Perhaps he never meant to kill his lordship, only to demand payment," Simonds suggested.

"And both times, he decided to attack the man with a pitchfork?" Jason asked, his expression one of utter incredulity. "And how would you account for the first victim being in the stables at the time of McLeod's visit?"

"I'm not a policeman, your lordship," Simonds replied, a touch acidly.

"Right. Thank you, Mr. Simonds," Daniel said. "I would like to speak to the footmen now."

"I'll send them in."

The two footmen, when they entered the room, were nearly indistinguishable from each other, having obviously been chosen for their height and good looks. They were both fair-haired, blue-eyed, and slender without appearing scrawny.

"Good morning, gentlemen," Daniel said. "Which one is which?"

"I'm John Mulch," the one on the left said.

"Walter Reedy," said the other.

"Did you accompany the family to Surrey?" Daniel asked.

"Yes," Reedy replied for them both.

"Were you there when the first murder occurred?" Daniel continued.

"We were on the premises, sir," Mulch said.

"How well do you know Thomas Grady?"

"Well enough. He's a good lad," Mulch said defensively.

"Where was he last night?" Daniel demanded.

"In the servants' hall, with us. We had our eye on him the whole evening, sir," Reedy said. "Stills was there too. We all were. Too cold out there to do much else."

"Where is your room?"

"Next to Grady and Stills's, sir," Mulch said.

"Did you hear anyone leave the room after lights-out?" Jason asked.

"No, sir. We all went up at the same time and got up at the same time this morning, when the bell went. Well, except for Stills. He likes to dawdle," Reedy supplied.

"Did you serve at dinner last night?" Daniel asked.

"Of course, sir," Mulch said.

"And how did the earl seem?"

"Aggrieved, sir," Reedy replied. "On account of the murder last week."

"He discussed it openly in front of his children?" Jason asked.

"No, sir, but we've worked for his lordship for years now, and we know all his moods, don't we, John?" Reedy said. "He was understandably upset."

"How did this anxiety manifest itself?" Jason asked.

"The earl drank more than usual and snapped at his son when the boy spoke across his mother."

"Did you notice anything else about his behavior?"

"No, sir. He just seemed tired and irritable," Mulch said.

"Thank you, gentlemen. Dismissed," Daniel said.

He turned to Jason. "Well, that was illuminating," he said, not bothering to hide his sarcasm. "We'll have to find this Rob McLeod and question him."

Daniel didn't relish a trip to Scotland at this coldest, darkest time of the year, all the more so because it would bring back memories of another death, and another case that had ultimately resulted in personal tragedy. Jason seemed to sense his mood.

"Perhaps we can question one of the other guests of the shoot first," he suggested. "Get their version of events before we go flying off to Scotland."

"Yes, that's a good idea," Daniel agreed, relieved at this unexpected reprieve. "And we should speak to Edward Frey's coachman and valet, but first, let's see how the countess fares."

Adams opened the door to the withdrawing room but did not permit them to enter.

“We’d like to speak to the countess, Miss Adams,” Daniel said, irritated with the woman for acting as gatekeeper.

“I’m afraid her ladyship is not—” she began.

“Let them in, Adams,” the countess called weakly from within, so Adams reluctantly stepped aside.

Chapter 25

The countess was reclining on a green velvet chaise and looked even worse than last time, her face waxy and her gaze devoid of emotion as she stared into the flames in the hearth. If not for the rhythmic rising and falling of her chest, she might have been mistaken for someone recently deceased. Without asking for permission, Jason approached the chaise and took hold of the woman's wrist. She didn't protest. In fact, she didn't seem to have any reaction at all.

"What did she take?" Jason asked, turning to the maid.

"A tincture of valerian root, sir. That's what Dr. Platt prescribed when he was summoned this morning."

"Well, I suppose it's better than feeding her laudanum," Jason grumbled. "How much did she ingest? Her pulse is dangerously slow."

"I'm sure I don't know, sir," Adams replied defensively. "Her ladyship did not consult with me."

"Where's this tincture?"

"Just there, sir." Adams pointed to the spindly table situated within arm's reach of the chaise.

Jason reached for the bottle, opened it, sniffed the contents, and made a face. "Take it away." He handed the bottle to Adams. "And bring her ladyship a cup of coffee. That ought to revive her."

"I don't care to be revived," the countess moaned, her gaze still fixed on the flames. "I don't understand," she muttered, almost to herself. "I just don't understand."

Daniel and Jason waited patiently until Adams brought a cup of coffee from the other room and held it to her mistress's pale lips. The countess took a few sips and pushed the maid's hand away, spilling the hot coffee on the woman's wrist and staining the cuff of her sleeve. Adams hissed but didn't utter a word of reproach and set the cup down on a nearby occasional table.

"It's vile," the countess complained, but the caffeine, or maybe the bitterness, had restored her somewhat, and she fixed her gaze on Daniel.

"Ask what you will and leave me in peace," she exclaimed, her voice trembling with emotion. "I can't bear to go through this twice in one week." She began to cry and buried her face in her hands. Her shoulders quaked, and tears dripped onto her black lace fichu.

"We are terribly sorry for what you've been through," Jason said gently, "but we must find out who's responsible for your husband's death."

"Why?" the countess cried, turning her blotchy face toward them. "What's the point? Damian is dead. For real this time. Someone had obviously had it in for him, and when they failed the first time, they came back to finish the job."

"The killer must be brought to justice," Daniel said. The words sounded inadequate in the face of the woman's suffering, but that was the least they could do for her. She would come to appreciate that in time. Knowing that whoever killed her husband had been punished would bring her and the children peace.

"Hanging that monster won't bring my husband back," the countess retorted through sobs.

"No, but it might keep you safe," Jason said quietly.

That got her attention. She looked at him, understanding dawning in her dark eyes. "You think we're in danger? My son…" she croaked.

"Your son is now the Earl of Granville," Daniel said. "If someone has a grudge against his father, they might not be satisfied to leave it there."

"Oh, dear God!" the countess wailed. "What could they possibly hold against a mere child?"

"That's what we need to ascertain, my lady."

Daniel and Jason exchanged eloquent glances. If a grief-stricken father was responsible for the murder of Edward Frey, he might not stop there. He might wish to harm the son as well.

"Ask me anything," the countess wailed. "I have no secrets."

"Why don't you take a moment to compose yourself, Lady Granville," Jason said as he handed her his handkerchief.

The countess nodded her thanks, dabbed at her eyes, then blew her nose before taking a long, shuddering breath. "Go on," she said. "I'm ready."

"Tell us what happened when your husband returned," Daniel invited.

Euphemia Langley closed her eyes momentarily, as if wishing to unsee whatever she was recalling, then began to speak. Her voice was low but firm, her self-pity quickly turning to anger.

"Damian had gone north to Yorkshire. We own textile mills in Shipley. When he returned and learned of the murder, he was livid, and horrified what the children and I had gone through in his absence."

"Did he offer any explanation for why he had lied to you and told you he was on his way to Hastings?" Jason asked softly.

The countess nodded miserably. "Damian said the man who was murdered was his half-brother, a product of a youthful indiscretion that took place when his father visited one of the mills. It seems the man had been threatening Damian, demanding restitution for the way he'd been treated. He'd been raised in an orphanage, you see," the countess said, looking from Jason to Daniel. "His mother died when he was but an infant, and he was placed in the orphanage by the local vicar. He hadn't had an easy life and blamed Damian for his circumstances."

"Why would he blame your husband?" Daniel asked.

"Because he couldn't blame his natural father. My father-in-law died years ago. Anyway, Damian had decided to confront the man once and for all and put the matter to rest."

"I see," Daniel said. "And did his lordship keep any of the letters?"

He didn't believe there were any letters, but if the real Damian Langley had, in fact, written to his brother demanding a meeting, the letters would be irrefutable proof of a connection between the two men. They might also mention something that might help Daniel to decipher a motive for the murders.

"No, he'd burned them, he said. He saw no reason to acknowledge the man's threats," the countess said haughtily.

"So, this man, your husband's half-brother, had tracked you down to your country seat while your husband was searching for him in Yorkshire," Daniel summarized, wondering what load of codswallop the earl had fed his gullible wife to explain away his brother's existence and subsequent death.

The countess looked at Daniel as if he were a simpleton. "Precisely."

"Yet he told you he was going to visit his aunt, who's been dead for several years," Jason pointed out.

"He didn't want me to worry," the countess replied. She shot Jason a baleful look, but he wasn't quite finished.

"Why would you worry that he went to visit a mill in Yorkshire?" Jason pressed.

The countess pursed her lips as spots of color appeared on her previously pale cheeks. She was growing visibly exasperated and glanced toward Adams, who was sitting quietly in the corner, pretending not to listen. If the countess was hoping for some sort of rescue, there wasn't much Adams could do to help.

"So, the earl left you and your children alone in the country, knowing that a man who'd been sending him threatening letters might come to call?" Daniel asked.

The countess looked at him, clearly furious. "How could he have known that ruffian would turn up at Christmas?"

"Why did the earl not inform the police when he began receiving threats?" Jason asked.

"He wished to avoid a scandal," Euphemia replied with an expression that said the answer should be obvious.

"Assuming it happened just as you say, who do you believe killed him?" Daniel asked.

"Grady, obviously," the countess snapped. "He came across the rogue in the stables and used whatever he had to hand to fend off an attack."

"Then who do you think killed your husband?"

Euphemia looked utterly exasperated as she sat up and planted her feet on the floor, which enabled her to face both men at eye level. She dug her hands into the velvet seat, holding on so tightly that her knuckles turned white, and leaned forward, her eyes blazing with anger.

"His accomplice, of course. Must I work it all out for you, you brainless oaf?" she cried, addressing Daniel. "Clearly, he wasn't acting alone. Someone brought him to Surrey, since there was no horse or buggy found anywhere in the vicinity. When his accomplice realized what had happened, he fled, but then returned to finish the job. He must have demanded money, and when Damian refused, he killed him out of sheer spite."

"In exactly the same way?" Daniel growled, just barely managing to control the urge to tell this high-handed creature exactly where matters stood, both with her marriage and with her son's claim to the earldom.

"Poetic justice, if you will," Euphemia pronounced spitefully. "Just as it would be poetic justice if you were dismissed and publicly disgraced for failing to prevent my husband's death. And you," she said, turning to fix her sullen gaze on Jason. "You do not have my permission to perform a postmortem on the earl. I should think the cause of death is obvious. His body will be turned over to Albright and Sons, and they will prepare his remains for the funeral. Is that understood, *my lord*?" she snarled.

"Quite, my lady," Jason replied, his tone maddeningly calm.

Daniel drew in a deep breath to steady himself. He was angrier than he'd been in a long while. He could hardly blame Euphemia Langley for her shrewish outburst. She held him responsible for her husband's death, and maybe he was, to some extent. The investigation seemed to be going in circles, with the only two people who had a tangible motive for murder both dead. He'd seen no evidence of an accomplice, and there was no reason to believe that any link between the brothers had ever existed. In fact, he couldn't think of a single person who stood to benefit from the death of the current earl.

"I think we have all we need," Jason said, giving Daniel a pointed look. "We'll leave you to rest."

The countess lay back on the chaise and nodded to Jason. "I didn't think I'd ever sleep again, but I feel utterly depleted." She turned away, closing her eyes.

Thus dismissed, Daniel followed Jason from the room and into the foyer, where Simonds awaited them.

"We'll interview the coachman and valet now," Daniel informed the butler.

"Very good, sir. I'll send them to the library."

Daniel had no desire to speak to anyone and felt overwhelming melancholy settle over him now that his anger had cooled, but he could hardly leave without questioning the two men who'd been with Edward Frey throughout the past week. He sighed heavily and momentarily averted his gaze to block out the butler's derisive stare. Now that Edward Frey was dead, the palace would demand answers and it would be Daniel who'd be sacrificed on the altar of Ransome's ambition and sense of self-preservation. He would be dismissed from the police service and ridiculed in the papers, painted as the bungling dolt who allowed both sons of the late Earl of Granville to die in unbearable agony while he pursued far-fetched theories and chased up nonexistent connections. He would be disgraced, his days as a policeman over. And how would be live? What else was he qualified to do? His mother-in-law would take him and Charlotte in, but he couldn't bear to live off her charity and face the judgment he'd see in the eyes of the villagers he'd grown up with.

Daniel's wretchedness must have been obvious because Jason placed a hand on his shoulder. "Daniel, why don't I speak to them?" he suggested softly. "You can wait in the carriage. I think you need a moment."

"Would you mind?" Daniel asked with more desperation than he'd intended.

"Not at all. I'll join you shortly."

A maid he hadn't previously met handed Daniel his belongings, and Simonds walked him to the door.

"Keep all doors and windows locked," Daniel said, more in an effort to recapture some measure of authority than because he really believed a home invasion was imminent. "And make sure everyone remains indoors."

"Not to worry, Inspector. We will remain vigilant."

Daniel headed out into the overcast afternoon. Thick flurries danced on the chill breeze and landed softly on the lapels of his coat. Daniel thought they'd have at least a few inches of snow come morning. He found Jason's carriage by the gate and climbed inside after nodding a wordless greeting to Joe, desperately grateful to Jason for this short break and relieved that Ransome's driver had returned to the Yard as soon as he'd delivered Daniel to the crime scene.

Daniel shut his eyes and leaned against the padded seat, allowing his mind to empty itself of everything but the image of Rebecca as she had looked last night in the gentle glow of the flames from the hearth. The memory soothed him, and he found that he was feeling calmer and rather ashamed of himself for allowing his insecurities and wounded pride to get the better of him during an investigation. He was just about to leave the sanctuary of the carriage and return to the house when the door opened and Jason climbed in.

"Lunch, I think. There's a restaurant I quite like not too far from here. My treat," he hastened to add, as he must have realized that Daniel couldn't afford to patronize pricy establishments on a detective's salary.

All Daniel could do was nod.

Chapter 26

Once they were seated at a corner table at Frederick's in Piccadilly, both Daniel and Jason ordered the Scottish salmon with a cream dill sauce, roasted potatoes, and buttered peas. Jason asked for a glass of water, so Daniel followed suit, even though he wouldn't have said no to something stronger. But he was on duty, after all, and it was best to keep a clear head, especially in view of what they had learned—or more accurately, had not learned.

"The coachman and valet have corroborated what we had learned from Dr. Rothman and Mr. Potter at the Red Lion," Jason said once the waiter walked away. "Edward Frey went to Kent, to the Rothman Institute, after receiving an urgent communication from his lawyer. After his meeting with Dr. Rothman, he checked into the inn for the night and would have left the following day had he not received a message informing him of the murder and advising him to delay his return."

"Who sent the message?" Daniel asked.

"Neither man knows."

"Or isn't saying."

"I didn't get the impression they were lying to me. They weren't offered an explanation for the trip to Kent, only warned to keep it quiet if questioned. They would have said they'd been in Hastings, as planned, had they not learned that we've been to Hastings and know all about Lady Seton's death and the earl's mistress."

"Was Yorkshire mentioned at all?" Daniel asked once the waiter served their luncheon and left them to enjoy the meal. What if there was another illegitimate child, a son who craved retribution?

"No. I think that was just something Frey told his wife to keep her in the dark."

"That would have made perfect sense yesterday," Daniel replied, "but given the events of today, I'm having difficulty joining the dots."

Jason's eyebrows knitted as he considered Daniel's dilemma. "Let us backtrack, then," he suggested. "Go all the way to the beginning and consider only what we know for certain."

"That sounds like a good plan," Daniel agreed, and applied himself to his fish, happy to let Jason do the talking. Perhaps hearing the facts spoken out loud and in order would help him to organize his thoughts and form a plausible theory.

Jason set down his fork and began, keeping his voice low and confidential. "Edward Frey received a communication from his lawyer, Mr. Quinlan, informing him that his half-brother, the rightful earl, had escaped from the Rothman Institute and was possibly coming to find him. Terrified the truth would get out, Edward Frey told his wife he was going to Hastings to visit his ailing aunt and hightailed it to Kent in the hope of resolving the situation quickly and quietly." Jason paused before continuing. "We have no way of knowing for certain if Edward Frey knew of the existence of his brother before his conversation with Nanny Briggs, but we do know that his wife was aware of his reasons for going to Hastings. She assumed he had gone to visit his mistress and was none too pleased."

Jason took a sip of water and went on. "Edward Frey visited the institute and was informed by Dr. Rothman that his brother was still at large, at which point he adjourned to the Red Lion and took a room for the night, either to consider his options or because it was too late in the day to travel back. That night, Damian Langley was murdered in Surrey. His body was found early the following morning, and a messenger was dispatched to advise the earl to stay away. Since the message reached the earl before he left Sevenoaks, we have to assume that it was sent by a member of the household at about the same time as a messenger was sent to Scotland Yard."

"Not necessarily," Daniel interjected. "Mr. Quinlan might have been informed of the murder at about the same time as Scotland Yard, which would give him ample time to send a messenger to Sevenoaks to forewarn his client."

"Yes, I suppose that is possible, but let's keep to the facts," Jason replied sternly. "Once Edward Frey felt it safe to return, he arrived at home, heard all about the murder and the investigation to date, probably from Simonds, then went on to spin a tale his wife was sure to believe. He told her a partial truth that explained the man's obvious resemblance to him, his quest for justice, and a possible reason for his murder."

"Which is where it gets tricky," Daniel said. "Edward Frey was now safe, his troublesome brother was dead, and the earldom was secure, for him and his son. The remains had been dealt with, and as far as he knew, the investigation was winding down, since no one much cared about the death of a nameless tramp."

"And then he gets murdered in precisely the same way as Damian Langley," Jason said, shaking his head in disbelief.

"Which turns the case on its head, since we can no longer entertain the possibility that Damian Langley was killed to protect the man who'd unwittingly stepped into his shoes. Or even by a frightened groom who believed he was acting in self-defense."

"The obvious answer is that the first murder was a case of mistaken identity and the killer meant to kill Edward Frey all along."

"But why?" Daniel asked, punctuating the question with his hands. "The only person we know of who might have had a grudge against Edward Frey was Harry Quimby, who was safely in custody at the time of Damian Langley's murder and still is. I had asked Sergeant Oldham of Division E to inform me if Quimby was to be released. The sergeant sent a message to the Yard yesterday to advise me that the man Quimby attacked has died of his injuries and Quimby has been charged with murder."

"There's Rob McLeod, the bereaved father who blamed the earl for his son's death, according to Alfred Simonds," Jason reminded Daniel, but he sounded skeptical. "If McLeod is indeed the killer, why had he waited all this time to avenge his son, and how would he have known that the earl and his family would be at their country house over the holidays?"

"Suppose he did discover that the family would be in Surrey over Christmas and sent a note, asking the earl for a private meeting," Daniel suggested.

"In the stables after dark?"

"It's as good a place as any to meet privately."

Jason shook his head, rejecting Daniel's theory. "It doesn't add up. First, what are the chances that Damian Langley would show up, and how would Rob McLeod know that he'd killed the wrong man if the story never made the papers? Only the family, the staff, and the policemen involved knew of the mix-up."

"Perhaps he had an informant within the household," Daniel suggested.

The men stopped talking when the waiter returned to take their empty plates. "Can I get you anything else, gentlemen?" he asked. "A sweet, perhaps."

"Daniel?" Jason asked.

'Not for me."

"I'll have coffee," Jason said.

"Make that two," Daniel hurried to add.

He didn't really want coffee, but Frederick's was a lovely restaurant and a much better place to discuss the case than either the frigid street or Jason's brougham, where they had to sit side by side instead of face to face.

Jason waited for the waiter to depart and continued undaunted. "And why would a man who'd traveled all the way from Scotland to presumably mete out justice kill the earl with a pitchfork? Surely he would have come armed with either a pistol or a knife, something portable enough to carry beneath his coat. Why resort to a pitchfork both times unless it has some special significance?"

"If the story Simonds told us is true, then the boy was shot rather than killed with a pitchfork. I fail to see the connection."

"As do I," Jason agreed. "Although we must verify the whereabouts of Rob McLeod, I think that the murder was committed by someone close to the family."

Daniel nodded, feeling no more enlightened than he had at the start of the meal.

"I hate to say it, Daniel, but we're missing a large chunk of this puzzle."

"Let's call on Mr. Quinlan once we're finished here," Daniel said. "Now that the earl, or presumed earl, I should say, is dead, his solicitor will have no choice but to cooperate with the police for the sake of the family."

"His allegiance will now lie with the new earl," Jason pointed out. "He will not reveal anything that might damage the family's reputation."

The waiter arrived with their coffee and poured out from a silver pot. Jason added a splash of cream to his cup, but his expression suggested his mind was elsewhere.

"Given that Edward Frey was not the true heir to the title, who is legally next in line?" he asked as soon as the waiter was out of earshot.

Daniel was about to take a sip but set down his cup, the coffee left untasted. That was a good question, one he hadn't stopped to consider. The son of an illegitimate son could not be the rightful heir. Perhaps there was someone out there who had a legal right to the earldom and was about to come forward to claim the title and the estate, which would give them a motive, indeed.

Chapter 27

Horace Quinlan, Esquire, turned out to be a lot younger than Jason had expected. He was a tall, slender man with carefully oiled dark hair, a neatly trimmed moustache, and round gold-rimmed spectacles. He wore a rather beautiful pocket watch attached to his claret and silver waistcoat by a sturdy chain. His clothes were of the finest quality, and his shoes polished to such a shine that Jason was in no doubt he'd be able to see his own reflection if he bent down to examine them more closely.

The office looked as expensively appointed and fastidiously maintained as the man. There wasn't a speck of dust on either the heavy mahogany furniture or the law books arranged on the shelf according to size and color. The brass inkwell gleamed in the weak winter sunshine filtering through pristine net curtains bracketed by red velvet panels tied back with cords of braided gold silk. The studded leather guest chairs were elegant and comfortable, and the whimsical carriage clock on the mantel was Limoges. Jason knew this because Katherine had pointed out a similar clock to him the last time they'd gone shopping in Oxford Street. She had thought it beautiful, and Jason had made a mental note to purchase one just like it for their wedding anniversary in June.

"How may I be of service?" Horace Quinlan asked.

The clerk that had greeted them upon arrival had already informed the solicitor that he would be speaking to a Scotland Yard detective and a member of the nobility, and his solicitous smile was just a little too tight.

"Mr. Quinlan, your client, the Earl of Granville, was found dead this morning at his property in Park Lane. Murdered," Daniel elucidated. "I'm charged with conducting an investigation into his death and need to ask you some questions."

"I'm afraid there is the matter of the legal advice privilege," Quinlan replied, smiling in a manner that meant to show regret at being unable to help.

"And I'm afraid there is the matter of obstructing a police investigation," Daniel countered. "I'm sure your clients would be most distressed to hear that you had been arrested. Might make them question the wisdom of continuing to avail themselves of your services."

"Yes, there is that," the solicitor agreed, his smile fading.

"Two men who both held a claim to the title were brutally murdered within a week, stabbed through the abdomen with a pitchfork," Daniel announced, watching Mr. Quinlan for a reaction.

"Two men?" Quinlan asked, instantly picking out the one kernel of information that pertained to him professionally.

"That's right, but then you know exactly which men I'm referring to. Do you not?" Daniel asked, pinning the solicitor with his dark gaze.

"I would appreciate it if you would stop playing games and just come out with it, Inspector," Quinlan said testily.

"All right," Daniel agreed. "As you know, the legitimate Earl of Granville was confined to an institution in Kent, from which he had managed to escape just over a week ago. He found his way to his ancestral home in Surrey, where he was promptly murdered. Last night, his illegitimate half-brother, the man everyone believed to be the Earl of Granville, was murdered in exactly the same manner. Now that both men are dead, Robert Langley is next in line, unless there's an interested party we're not yet aware of. Unless I figure out who killed Robert's father and uncle, his life might be in danger."

That seemed to get Quinlan's attention. "Robert Langley is now my client," the solicitor said, "and it is my duty to look after his interests."

"It's in his interests to remain alive," Jason said, thoroughly annoyed with the man.

"Indeed," Quinlan said. "So, what can I do to ensure the boy's safety?"

"First and foremost," Daniel said, "we need to know who the legitimate heir to the earldom really is."

"Robert Langley," Horace Quinlan replied straight away.

"Mr. Quinlan," Daniel said, his tone thick with warning.

Quinlan sighed heavily, as if Daniel were trying his patience. "Inspector, the third Earl of Granville, Martin Langley, was an only son. He had a sister who died of consumption when she was seventeen. His first cousin, Ignatius Langley, passed a mere seven months ago. Kidney failure," Quinlan added.

"Did Ignatius Langley have any children?"

"Yes, two daughters, both unmarried the last time I communicated with the family. There are no other living males of that line."

"So, what happens to the title?" Daniel asked.

"If there's no male heir to inherit, then the title becomes extinct. However, as far as the world knows, Robert Langley is the legitimate son of the late earl and the only male descendant of the Langley line, therefore, he is now the fifth Earl of Granville."

"And would a court of law see it that way?"

Horace Quinlan didn't reply, just smiled in a way that was smug enough to suggest he'd make sure they did, which led Jason to believe that any evidence of Damian Langley's tenure at the Rothman Institute had already been destroyed. A court of law would need definitive proof that the man everyone had believed to be the Earl of Granville was, in fact, illegitimate. Since no such proof existed, other than the word of the housekeeper and geriatric nursemaid, neither of whom would wish to see the boy disinherited, chances were that Robert Langley would retain the earldom.

"Tell us about Martin Langley's last will and testament," Jason invited, wondering what the third earl had planned for his sons.

Another exasperated sigh from the lawyer. "The will was drawn up by my father more than thirty years ago."

"When Martin Langley pulled the switch with his sons?" Daniel asked.

"Yes. The earl had created a secret trust to be administered by Quinlan and Sons until the death of his firstborn, Damian Langley. We were to release funds on a quarterly basis to pay for said son's incarceration at the Rothman Institute and check on his welfare, also quarterly. If we felt that he was in any way mistreated or the Rothman Institute ceased to exist, we were to find a fitting alternative and ensure that the patient's identity was protected."

"What were his provisions for his illegitimate son?" Daniel asked.

"Martin Langley left everything to the late earl, except for a dozen bequests for friends and servants."

"Was Edward Frey aware of his brother's existence before last week?" Jason asked.

Horace Quinlan winced at the use of the man's real name but didn't challenge Jason. "His father saw no reason to burden him with the truth, but I can't speak to what he may have heard from the servants."

"So, as far as you know, the first he heard of his older brother was when you contacted him to inform him that he had escaped from the asylum?"

"Yes. After much consideration and a consultation with my father, who's in ill health, and my brother, who's a partner in the firm, we decided that was the most prudent course of action."

"What was Edward Frey's reaction to discovering the extent of this decades-old cover-up?" Jason asked. He couldn't help but feel furious with Martin Langley for discarding his son, and with the Quinlans for legitimizing the request and covering up the truth all this time.

"I really couldn't say since I wasn't there, and the messenger we sent had no knowledge of what was inside the letter. He did say that the earl appeared shocked and upset and asked the messenger to wait while he composed a reply."

"Which was?" Daniel asked.

"He said that he was heading to the asylum and would make an appointment to see me when he was ready to discuss the ramifications of the situation."

"Meaning that he was waiting to see if his brother would be caught and returned to the asylum," Daniel summarized.

"Precisely."

"Did Edward Frey feel threatened by this newfound knowledge that he had an older, legitimately born brother who had a claim to the title and the estate, do you think?" Jason asked.

"I will not speculate on the feelings of my client, but it would be unnatural for him not to feel threatened and unsettled. I presume he had hoped to meet his brother and judge for himself just how much of a threat he presented."

"In your opinion, Mr. Quinlan, was Edward Frey capable of murder?" Daniel asked.

"Everyone is capable of murder, Inspector, as I'm sure you know. And Edward Frey was a soldier in his day."

“Had Edward Frey made any provisions for his butler, Alfred Simonds?” Jason inquired.

“Why do you ask?” Quinlan asked, clearly surprised by the question.

“Simonds had been his batman for several years and then undertook the position of butler in his household. They obviously shared a bond.”

Quinlan nodded. “Yes, they did. It is my understanding that Simonds had saved the earl’s life, a decision that cost Simonds the life of his own brother. The earl owned Simonds a debt of gratitude.”

“And how did he intend to repay it?” Daniel asked.

“I don’t recall. I must consult the will.” Quinlan rose from behind his desk and walked over to a cabinet from which he extracted a thick file.

He sat back down and leafed through the documents until he found what he was looking for, then passed the will to Daniel. “You may as well see for yourself,” he said, no longer concerned with confidentiality.

Daniel scanned the contents of the will, then handed the document back. “So, Edward Frey had bequeathed Simonds an annual pension and a cottage in the village of Ripley. I see there’s also a provision for Mrs. Frey. Did Edward Frey have any inkling that Mrs. Frey was his natural mother?”

“Not at the time we drew up the will,” Quinlan replied. “He simply wished to reward her for years of service.”

“There’s a rather generous bequest to Thomas Grady. What had he done to earn such generosity?”

“I don’t know, to be honest,” Quinlan replied. “The late earl had left several bequests to servants. It’s not unusual to favor certain people, and his lordship was very fond of horses. I suppose

Thomas Grady was the person he trusted most with his equestrian acquisitions."

"Did he spend a lot on horses?" Jason asked.

"He did. In fact, I had just negotiated a contract for an Arabian filly that the earl had purchased for his daughter. That horse cost more than my summer residence," he said with a shake of his head.

"Was that the white horse we saw at the stables?"

"Yes. Viola has a fondness for white horses. She's an accomplished horsewoman."

"The stallion would have fetched a good price if sold?" Daniel asked.

"If someone were to steal it, they would have to ask significantly less than its worth, since he wouldn't have the paperwork to prove its pedigree, but yes, it would fetch a considerable sum."

"Mr. Quinlan, what do you know of the event that resulted in the death of Rob McLeod's young son?"

Quinlan's face tightened. "It was a terrible accident. His lordship was not at fault. The boy was shot by one of his guests, a Lord Melton, who tripped over a protruding root and accidentally discharged his gun as he fell. His lordship felt responsible, since Lord Melton had a history of heavy drinking and was most likely inebriated at the time. A more than generous settlement was arranged for the family on the earl's behalf."

"What of Lord Melton? Did he not feel he should compensate the family in some way?"

"Lord Melton died shortly after when he fell off his horse and hit his head on the cobblestones outside his stables."

"Would there be any reason for the McLeods to hold a grudge against the Earl of Granville?" Daniel asked.

"Not that I can see. It wasn't his fault, and he made restitution, which enabled the family to buy the farmland they had been leasing from a landlord. The death of their son led to the sort of independence they could never have dreamed of, and they have three other boys who stand to inherit once Mr. McLeod is deceased."

"So, you're saying it was a fair trade?" Jason asked, an edge to his voice.

"Nothing can make up for the death of a child, Lord Redmond, but if you are going to suffer such a tragic loss, it helps to know that at least something good has come out of it for those who are still living."

"Mr. Quinlan, did Edward Frey have any enemies that you know of?" Daniel asked.

Horace Quinlan made a show of thinking. "Inspector, no man is liked by everyone, and we all invite the ire of others from time to time. Will those people try to murder us? I suppose that depends entirely on the individual we have slighted. The only person I can think of who'd have happily wrung Damian Langley's neck was Harry Quimby, the father of the earl's mistress, but as far as I'm aware, he never made any attempts on the earl's life in the three years his lordship was keeping his daughter."

"Did Mr. Quimby make any demands?" Jason asked.

"He did, both in person and in writing, but his lordship told him, and I quote, to sod off. The man is a violent drunkard, but he's not stupid enough to threaten an earl's life. He knows only too well how that would end for him."

"According to Mr. Quimby, he has nothing left to lose," Daniel said.

"So, you've met him, then?"

"I have. He was in custody for brawling at the time."

"He still has his life," Horace Quinlan replied. "I wouldn't call that nothing."

"Not for long," Daniel replied. "He's been charged with murder."

"Did Edward Frey make any provisions for his mistress?" Jason asked. "There doesn't appear to be anything in his will."

"He did. His lordship bought Miss Lillie a fine house, furnishings, and works of art, and settled a substantial sum on her, which he then helped her to invest. She might be bereaved, but she's far from bankrupt."

"And do you have documents to substantiate all these settlements that the earl made?" Daniel asked.

"I do." Mr. Quinlan looked through the file and extracted the pertinent contracts, laying them out one by one on the desk. He then made a point of consulting his pocket watch, even though he could clearly see the time on the carriage clock. "Now, if there's nothing else—"

"Thank you, Mr. Quinlan," Daniel said once he had studied each document in turn. "You've been most helpful."

"It's not as if I had much of a choice."

"Yes, that seems to be a shared sentiment when talking about the Langley family," Jason retorted. "Good day, Mr. Quinlan."

"My lord," the solicitor replied. To Jason's amazement, he extracted a card from a silver holder and handed it to Jason. "If you ever require legal counsel."

"Thank you, but I already have a good man on retainer," Jason said.

"Pity."

“How are you for time tomorrow?” Daniel asked once he and Jason were back in the carriage. Jason would drop Daniel off at Scotland Yard, then head for home.

“I have a surgery scheduled for nine in the morning, and I will have to remain on hand to monitor the patient afterward. You?”

Daniel shrugged. “I’m not really sure how to proceed. Given the value of that horse alone, theft doesn’t seem to have been the motive. I also fail to see what Rob McLeod would have to gain by killing the earl. The sum he received will keep that family comfortable for generations. Besides, the restitution was made nearly a year ago, so why seek vengeance now?”

“I agree,” Jason said. “I think we need to look closer to home.”

“We’ve interviewed Euphemia Langley and all the pertinent members of staff,” Daniel pointed out.

“Perhaps we need to speak to the children,” Jason suggested.

“Why? What can they possibly have to contribute?”

“Children are observant. They might have seen or heard something.”

“Their mother will never permit it,” Daniel objected.

“She will if she thinks it might safeguard her son’s life.”

Daniel nodded. “I will go back tomorrow and ask to speak to the children, as well as Mrs. Frey. I don’t see that she would have anything to gain by her son’s death, but maybe she was aware of something that may have constituted a threat. I’m sure she was keenly interested in anything that concerned her boy. And her grandson.”

“Good idea. Do stop by tomorrow evening and apprise me of your progress,” Jason invited.

"I will."

Once they arrived at Scotland Yard, Daniel bid Jason goodnight and disappeared behind the stately door, leaving Jason to ponder the case all the way home.

Chapter 28

Wednesday, December 30

Daniel didn't dare call at Park Lane too early for fear of being turned away, so he spent the morning with Charlotte and Miss Grainger, accompanying them to the park for a brief but invigorating walk. After they returned, Charlotte was given her luncheon and whisked off to the nursery to take a nap, and Daniel reluctantly set off, wishing he could remain at home by the fire with the enchanting Rebecca. Although he occasionally indulged in fantasies of a more intimate nature, what he really longed for was her company, her conversation, and the sound of her wonderful laughter. He didn't want to simply copulate with a woman; he craved a partnership, a deep and satisfying friendship, the sort he'd once had with Sarah, and the kind Jason enjoyed with Katherine.

Daniel missed companionably discussing their days, or lying in bed on a Sunday morning, toying with the idea of missing church and then exploding from beneath the covers just in time to make it to the service and giggling madly at how nauseatingly conventional they were. He missed holding each other close after making love and waking up to the one human being who was the closest to him in the world. Now the bed was empty and cold, and there was no incentive to lie in or to miss church. He had nothing better to do on a Sunday morning. At least he got to accompany Rebecca, which made him feel a little better about sitting through the long sermon.

Upon arrival, Daniel asked to speak with the countess and was instantly admitted. To his mind, she was now plain Mrs. Langley, but to the world, she was still the Countess of Granville, so he had to treat her accordingly.

Euphemia Langley received him with cool civility. She looked better today, the black of her gown almost becoming, and her cheeks flushed from the heat of the fire. She invited him to sit across from her, her gaze never leaving his face as he settled on the Oriental chair he'd found so uncomfortable the last time.

"Still no closer to apprehending my husband's killer, Inspector Haze?" the countess asked caustically.

"It's a complicated case, my lady."

"Yes, it is, but I had thought you would have made some progress by now."

"I would like permission to speak to the children," Daniel said, ignoring the criticism.

"Absolutely not. I forbid it."

"Someone murdered a man who resembled the earl and then killed your husband as soon as he returned home. I fear that until we unravel the motive, your son's life might be in danger."

The countess went white to the roots of her hair. "Do you truly believe Robbie is in danger?" she whimpered.

"I need to speak to him," Daniel said, pressing his point home. "Perhaps he heard something, or maybe someone tried to approach him."

"My son hasn't been out of this house since we returned from Surrey," the countess protested.

Daniel was about to remind her that both murders had been committed on the earl's property but decided to forgo stating the obvious. She knew that, but there was little she could do to keep her son safe other than ensuring he remained at home, under the watchful eyes of the staff.

The countess nodded. "Very well, Inspector, but you may not interview Viola. She's very upset by her father's death and has hardly left her room. I won't have her interrogated by the police."

"I only wanted a friendly chat," Daniel said somewhat petulantly. Was that how she saw him, as an interrogator?

"You may speak to his lordship," the countess said, using her son's new title, "but I will ask Adams to sit in, since Robert's tutor has the morning off. I would do it myself, but I honestly don't think I can bear it. I…" She made a vague gesture with her hands as the tears began to flow, and she whipped a lace-edged handkerchief out of her sleeve. "I don't know how to go on," she muttered as she wiped away the tears. "I wake up in the morning, and for just a moment, I think that everything is all right, and then I recall the nightmare we've been living for the past week, and my heart breaks all over again." She sniffled loudly and fixed her watery gaze on him, silently asking for his understanding, her earlier disdain forgotten.

"I've always secretly chafed at the mourning rituals," Euphemia said softly. "I thought them too cruel to people who've already suffered so much and were then forced to endure a period of isolation that could only exacerbate their melancholy, but now that I have lost my dear Damian, I'm grateful for the excuse to hide away and nurse my wounds in private. I don't want to share my grief with the world or distract myself with forced gaiety. I only want to be left alone so that I can eventually find the strength to face the future, if not for myself, then for my children's sake."

"I completely understand, my lady," Daniel said, her words cutting him to the quick because they so closely mirrored his own feelings in the weeks after Sarah had died.

The countess wearily got to her feet and walked over to the wall, where she yanked on the bellpull. When Adams appeared, Mrs. Langley asked her to fetch the earl and bring him to the drawing room. Daniel vaguely wondered if Euphemia Langley was secretly relieved that her son was too young to take up the reins of the earldom. Robert would most likely welcome her guidance until he came of age, at which point, he just might ask her to move to the Dower House and stay there.

Adams escorted Robert Langley into the drawing room a few minutes later. He was dressed in a black suit and wore a black puff tie, his appearance that of an underage undertaker. It was fitting that he should be dressed for mourning, but Daniel thought black always looked that much more macabre on children. Robert Langley was the spitting image of his father, a fact that made Daniel feel somehow more sympathetic toward him. He was achingly young and seemed frightened as he took the seat his mother had vacated. Adams found a seat in the corner, where she could silently observe.

"I'm sorry for your loss, my lord," Daniel said. It felt absurd to call a child *my lord*, but he had to follow protocol, especially if he hoped to put the boy at ease.

"Thank you," Robert said. His voice was thin and quavery, and Daniel feared he might cry, but he inhaled sharply and fixed Daniel with a bullish stare. "I don't know anything."

"I thought perhaps you might have noticed something. When I was your age, I hated that the adults never told me anything of importance, so I made it my business to know what was going on. By any means necessary," Daniel added with a smile of encouragement.

"Is that why you became a policeman? Because you like to snoop?" Robert asked.

"I simply like to know the truth so that no one can pull the wool over my eyes. Nothing wrong with that."

"No, I suppose not," Robert agreed. "I like to know things too."

"So, what do you know?" Daniel asked.

Robert remained silent, the only sound the ticking of the carriage clock on the mantel. Then Daniel thought he heard rustling behind the closed door of the drawing room. It was probably just the servants going about their daily chores, but he wished they would move on. Robert looked conflicted, so this was a pivotal moment when he might either tell Daniel what he thought he knew or clam up and refuse to share his observations.

"I know that Papa is dead," the boy said at last, "and I am now the Earl of Granville. He always said I would be the earl one day, but I thought it would happen once I was a man and Papa was very old. Mama says I now have to look after her and Viola, which is really strange because I want them to look after me," Robert said miserably.

"I'm sure your mama will guide you and help you for as long as you need," Daniel assured him.

"I suppose so. Or Mr. Quinlan. He was Papa's solicitor. He will see to things until I'm old enough to understand."

It sounded like someone had been coaching Robert and offering reassurance in the process. Probably Nanny Briggs, who'd raised enough children to understand how bewildering this new reality had to be for an eleven-year-old boy.

"Did you see or hear anything the night your papa died?" Daniel asked.

Robert shook his head. "No. He'd only just come back, and he was upset, so I was sent up to my room directly after supper. He needed to talk to Mama. By the next morning, he was gone. Dead," Robert said with unflinching finality.

"What about Lady Viola?"

"She went up to her room too. For real that time."

"What do you mean?" Daniel asked.

Robert looked as if he'd been caught out, but then shrugged to himself, as if he had nothing left to lose. "Viola is mad for horses. Always has been. I like horses, but they scare me. They seem so big when one looks up at them, don't they?"

"Yes, they do. I'm not very fond of horses myself," Daniel confided.

"Viola nearly wet herself when Papa presented her with Snowflake."

Daniel heard a sharp intake of breath from Adams, but she didn't dare to rebuke the young earl for his choice of phrase.

"Snowflake?"

"That's what she named it. The new horse. Because it's white," Robert explained. "She loves that horse. A lot more than she loves her fiancé," Robert added, his lip curling in an impish smile.

"And did she like to visit it?" Daniel prompted.

Robert nodded. "She went to the stables several times a day. Early in the morning, in the afternoon, and then in the evening to say goodnight. But on the day Papa returned, Viola went directly to her room after supper. I saw her. She sat in the window seat, reading."

"Robert, did Viola go to the stables when that other man was killed?" Daniel asked gently.

Robert nodded. "She sneaked out. She was so excited about the new horse, she said she wouldn't be able to sleep unless she kissed it goodnight." He scrunched his nose in disgust.

"And did you see her when she got back?"

Robert nodded. "She went to her room and shut the door."

"Did she mention if she saw anything?" Daniel asked.

"No."

"How was she the next morning?"

"I don't know. When I came down to breakfast, only Mama was in the dining room. Papa had gone away to visit Aunt Hermione, and Viola was still in her room. Then Simonds came in to speak to Mama. I heard him say he'd sent for the police, but I didn't understand why. It was only later..." Robert's face crumpled as though still reeling from the realization that his father really was dead this time.

"Thank you, my lord," Daniel said, instinctively knowing the boy couldn't take any more.

Robert nodded and fled, Adams on his heels.

Chapter 29

Having finished with Robert Langley, Daniel made his way to the servants' hall, where he asked to speak privately with Mrs. Frey. She led him to her private parlor, which was warm and cozy, and shut the door, staring at him blankly as he settled across from her in a green velvet wingchair.

"I'm afraid I can't help you, Inspector. I don't know anything," she rushed to inform him.

Daniel studied her for a moment. She must have been very young when she gave birth to Edward, since she looked to be no older than fifty-five. If he had hoped to see a striking resemblance between mother and son, he was doomed to disappointment. Edward Frey must have taken after his father. He would have to have done to resemble his half-brother so closely. Daniel studied Mrs. Frey's closed expression and decided he had no more time for dissembling.

"Mrs. Frey, I know of your relationship to the late earl, so please, let's just cut to the chase, shall we? Did Edward know you were his mother?" Daniel asked, deliberately using the name she'd given her boy in the hope of startling her into honestly.

"No, he never knew," she said, almost in a whisper.

"Did anyone else?"

"Only Nanny Briggs."

"How is that possible in a house this size?" Daniel asked.

"Martin—I still think of him as Martin, even all these years," she said wistfully. "Well, he was a clever man, and a devious one. He was not the sort of person to do anything by halves. He could have dismissed me when Edward was born, but instead, he sent the child to live with a couple he'd found, who were only too happy to take him in. Martin paid them handsomely to take good care of our boy, and he kept me close. I think he genuinely liked me," she said, smiling for the first time.

"What happened then?"

"Martin spoke to me of his son, Damian. He was worried and angry. He was ashamed of him and felt the countess had let him down by giving birth to such a disappointing child."

"Did you ever see Damian?"

"Very rarely. He was kept in the nursery, with Nanny Briggs. She was the only one who truly cared for him."

"And then Martin Langley decided to switch the children," Daniel said.

Mrs. Frey nodded. "I was horrified at first, but then, of course, I saw the benefit to my son and gave my word that I would keep quiet. How could I not?" she asked, looking at Daniel as if pleading for his understanding. "My boy, who was born out of wedlock, was going to be the Earl of Granville."

"At the expense of his brother," Daniel reminded her.

"Yes, but Damian wasn't mine to worry about. Edward was, and I did what was best for him. Not that I had a choice, really," she said. "Martin would have done what he wanted anyway. He didn't need my permission or my blessing. Edward and I were completely dependent on him."

"And did anyone suspect?"

"No, the exchange was seamless. Only Nanny Briggs knew, and of course, the countess. She died shortly after."

"And the couple who looked after your son?"

Mrs. Frey shook her head. "They were told Edward was going to live with his mother and her new husband. I don't think they ever knew my name."

"And Edward?" Daniel asked. "Did he ever ask any questions?"

"Edward was too young to understand what was happening. He cried for the first few days, as any child would when torn away from the only home he'd ever known, but Nanny Briggs took good care of him, and soon he grew accustomed to his new surroundings."

"Were you permitted to visit him?"

"No, but I did anyway. Nanny Briggs allowed me a few minutes with my son once a week, but once Edward got older, I could no longer explain away my forays into the nursery, so I loved him from afar."

"So, Edward never knew the truth of what had transpired?" Daniel asked. He hoped to catch Mrs. Frey out, but she stuck to her story.

"*Damian* never knew. He ceased being Edward the day he was brought to Langley Hall to take his brother's place."

"And you never once let anything slip once his father passed?" Daniel tried again.

"No, never. I comforted myself with the knowledge that I had given him a priceless gift and he would thank me if he knew."

"I'm sure he would have."

She nodded. "Had Martin not taken him, he would probably be in service, like me."

"And did you and Martin Langley…?" Daniel didn't want to pry, but it was important to find out if there had been other children.

"Martin lost interest in me once I got with child, but at least he didn't have me sacked. He was an honorable man in his own way, believe it or not."

"Yes, so I heard," Daniel replied, unable to hide his sarcasm.

"He did right by our boy, and maybe by his own boy, as well," Mrs. Frey said. "If he was truly mentally deficient, then perhaps an asylum was the best place for him."

"I never met the man," Daniel said, "but from what I heard, he wasn't all that impaired."

Mrs. Frey dismissed that with an indifferent shrug. As she had pointed out, Damian Langley was never hers to worry about.

"Do you know of anyone who might have wished to harm your son…the earl?" Daniel amended.

"I knew little of his life. I rarely saw him, Inspector. I wish I could help you, but I told you the truth. I know nothing."

"Thank you, Mrs. Frey. And I'm sorry for your loss."

She nodded, the closed look returning now that she was ready to rejoin the staff.

A maidservant fetched Daniel's coat and hat, and he left the house by the servants' entrance. He wasn't sure where he was headed, but he needed to walk, even though he'd be chilled to the bone before long. It was hours yet before dusk would settle over the city, but it felt like evening, the sky low and gray, and the windows of the houses Daniel passed glowing with light from the lamps that had to be lit so early in the afternoon.

Huddling deeper into his coat and muffler, Daniel set off at a brisk pace toward Scotland Yard. Ransome would expect an update, even if there wasn't much to tell, and he needed a destination.

Chapter 30

Daniel must have walked along Park Lane for at least ten minutes, his mind shuffling and reshuffling what he knew so far like a deck of cards, when he became aware of being followed. He had no idea if the person behind him was simply walking in the same direction or trailing him on purpose, but there were few people in the street, so it was hard not to notice that someone had been walking behind him for a good while now.

Daniel stopped and knelt to tie his shoe, and the man behind him stopped as well, bending his head to consult a piece of paper in such a way that the upper part of his face was obscured by the brim of his bowler and the lower by a thick green muffler. He was at least twenty feet away, so it was impossible to make out anything that might offer a clue to his identity. His coat and hat were black, and he wore black gloves. He looked like countless other men who weren't distinguished by either their poverty or their wealth.

Feeling none the wiser, Daniel straightened and continued to walk, increasing his pace slightly. The man behind him maintained his distance but began to walk a little faster as well. Why would someone follow him? He hadn't learned anything even remotely helpful, except that Robert had seen his sister sneaking out to visit Snowflake. Viola had returned unharmed and had most likely seen nothing, since she would have told someone at the time, especially if she believed the victim to be her father. She was sixteen, old enough to realize that the information might be valuable.

There was one obvious reason Viola hadn't said anything, which was that she'd seen nothing out of the ordinary, the killer being someone she knew, like Thomas Grady. She'd have no reason to fear the groom, nor would she think anything of him being in the stables in the evening. He could have come up with a perfectly believable reason for returning to the stables either before or after his evening meal. And had he told the others he was going outside to use the privy, no one would question his absence, even if he was gone longer than usual. An upset stomach was all the explanation he'd need to put an end to any speculation.

Daniel sighed and peered into the darkening afternoon, hoping an empty hansom would come along on its way to the cabstand in Piccadilly. He was numb with cold and unnerved by the individual still walking behind him. He was probably being ridiculous. The man was simply heading toward his destination, just like Daniel, but something about the steady presence at his back made Daniel shiver with apprehension.

The street was empty except for the two of them, the handful of pedestrians having either gone inside a building or entered the park. Daniel cursed under his breath and turned back to see if a cab might have appeared at the end of the street. He really was freezing. There was no cab, but the man was still there and looked down the moment Daniel turned around, once again obscuring his visage. Daniel swore under his breath and continued, eager to reach the junction with Piccadilly no more than twenty feet away.

It took him a moment to realize the man behind him was running, and just as Daniel was about to turn around, he felt a burning pain in his lower back. As the man rushed past him, Daniel noticed the gleam of light hair between the bowler hat and the green muffler, and then the man reached the end of the street and turned the corner.

The pain came as a surprise, an intense, pulsating wave of torment that blurred Daniel's vision and drained the strength from his body. He fumbled with the buttons of his coat and managed to open a few and slide his hand inside. When he brought it back out, his fingers were crimson with blood. He felt it trickle down his back and into the waistband of his trousers. Daniel barely noticed when he fell to his knees, or when the pavement had come up to meet his head, the ground rough against his cheek.

Rolling onto his back would probably make the blood flow faster, but he wasn't thinking straight, and the pressure from the freezing pavement against his back relieved the pain somewhat.

Daniel stared into the glowering sky, time of no consequence. Soon, it began to snow, and the flakes settled on his face and clung to his eyelashes.

He no longer felt pain, only an overwhelming desire to close his eyes and sleep. His thoughts were fuzzy, and time seemed to have stopped, but his last coherent thought before the world went dark was of Charlotte. And Rebecca.

Chapter 31

It was dark, and there was a strange smell of carbolic and something foul and metallic that seemed to hover just nearby. Blood and pus. Daniel shifted infinitesimally, and a sharp pain sliced through him, sweeping away the cobwebs in his mind. He drew in a ragged breath, willing himself to remain calm.

He was in an unfamiliar room, lying in a bed and dressed only in his woolen undergarments. The blanket was scratchy and thin beneath his fingers, the sheet starched to the point where an edge could probably do some real damage. Daniel's feet were bare, his heels chafing slightly against the stiff linen.

He gingerly moved his arm beneath the blanket and lifted his hand just enough to touch his middle. Thick bandaging extended from his pelvic bones to his breastbone, and it was the gauze that had to be the source of the evil smell. Daniel shut his eyes and tried to focus. He knew he was in a hospital ward, but he couldn't recall how he'd got there or what had happened. Try as he might, the memory just wouldn't come.

Charlotte. The name seemed to explode inside his brain, lighting the darkest corners of his mind. His breathing became labored, so he willed himself to relax, repeating again and again that Charlotte was safe. She was with Rebecca. They were at home, snug in their beds. Rebecca would be worried about him, he thought anxiously. He had to let her know where he was and that he was alive.

Daniel turned his head just in time to see a middle-aged woman striding toward him. She carried an oil lamp that illuminated her face from beneath and gave her a slightly demonic appearance. The nurse set the lamp on a bedside table and leaned over him.

"Inspector Haze, I'm Nurse Lowe. How do you feel?"

"Where am I, Nurse?" Daniel asked.

"You are at St. George's Hospital."

Daniel nearly cried with relief. Jason's hospital. Jason would know he was here. "What time is it?"

The nurse consulted a small watch pinned to her uniform. "It's twenty past three in the morning."

"Dr. Redmond?" Daniel whimpered, desperate to see Jason.

"I will get him for you. I had convinced him to take a rest. He'd been by your side ever since you were brought in. That would be almost twelve hours ago now."

"Thank you, Nurse Lowe. Please, don't disturb him if he's sleeping."

"I'm not sleeping," Jason informed him softly as he materialized at the foot of the bed. He looked tired and anxious. "Daniel, how do you feel?"

"Like I've been stabbed in the back," Daniel said with a groan.

"Then you feel exactly as you should," Jason replied with a warm smile. "I'll look after him, Nurse," he said to the duty nurse, effectively dismissing her.

"Of course, sir." Nurse Lowe walked away, leaving Daniel and Jason alone with a dozen sleeping men. Daniel had only just realized that the ward was full, every dark hump a sleeping patient.

Jason pulled up a chair and sat down next to the bed. He reached out and took hold of Daniel's wrist, taking his pulse as he studied his face.

"What happened?" Daniel asked.

"You tell me."

"I can't seem to recall. How did I come to be here?"

"A civically minded couple found you and summoned a constable. Had they not come along..." Jason didn't need to finish the sentence. Daniel knew exactly what he was trying to say. "Daniel, I'm terribly sorry, but I wasn't able to save your kidney. But you can live a long and healthy life with just the one."

Daniel filed that bit of news away for the moment. He'd have to think on it later, but right now he had to tell Jason what had happened.

"Jason, I interviewed Robert Langley, then Mrs. Frey. After I left the Langley residence, a man followed me down Park Lane. He stabbed me."

"He clearly knew what he was doing," Jason said with obvious disgust. "John Ransome sent for me right away, then personally interviewed the couple that helped you."

"I don't understand why anyone would wish to—" Daniel couldn't finish the sentence. He wanted to say *hurt*, but the reality was that the man had tried to kill him. Had the kind couple not happened upon him, he would have died there in the street. "Jason, I—"

Jason had finished taking Daniel's pulse some time ago but hadn't removed his hand, and it rested on Daniel's wrist, warm and comforting.

"Daniel, I don't want you to worry about a thing. You must rest and recover."

"Charlotte—"

"Charlotte is safe. John Ransome instructed Miss Grainger not to leave the house with Charlotte for the next few days. Just as a precaution. And not to open the door to any strangers." Jason drew in a deep breath. "Daniel, did Robert Langley say anything that might have precipitated this attack?"

"The only thing he said was that he saw his sister sneaking out to the stables to see her horse on the evening Damian Langley was murdered. She returned unharmed and was still in her room the following morning when the news broke that the man they had believed to be the earl had been found dead in the stables."

"Hmm," Jason said.

"Hmm, what?"

"Nothing. Nothing at all." Jason pulled back his hand and stood. "Get some sleep. Doctor's orders. I will change the dressing in the morning and check on the incision. Are you in pain?"

"Yes," Daniel admitted. His back burned and throbbed, and if he moved even a fraction of an inch, the pain was so sharp, it felt as if someone were sliding a razorblade across his tender skin.

"I will ask Nurse Lowe to administer a dose of morphine to help you rest. Now, I must return home and sleep for a few hours. I have much to do in the morning."

"What do you have to do?" Daniel asked.

"First, I will check on you. And then, I will solve this case."

Chapter 32

Thursday, December 31

By morning, Daniel was burning up. The bandages, when Jason carefully removed them, were saturated with blood and pus, and the skin was hot to the touch. The area around the incision was badly swollen, a deep mottled redness spreading outward like some post-apocalyptic sunrise. Jason had thoroughly cleaned the area before and after the surgical procedure to remove the damaged kidney, but it was very possible that the knife used in the attack had been rusty or covered with a substance that had introduced bacteria into the wound. Some surgeons of Jason's acquaintance believed that the presence of pus meant the wound was healing, but Jason knew better. He'd lost too many men to septicemia after operating on them in field hospitals to know that once an incision had festered there wasn't much a surgeon could do but swab the area, drain the pus, and hope that the patient's organism was strong enough to fight off the infection on its own.

Jason instructed the matron to keep a close watch on Daniel, clean the area with alcohol, and swab it with iodine every hour, no matter how much Daniel protested. If the wound continued to fester, the infection would spread and eventually turn septic. Once that happened, Jason would be helpless to save Daniel's life.

Leaving Daniel's bedside, Jason exited the ward and made his way to the hospital's pharmacy. Mr. Morris, the chemist, sat on a stool behind a table, his shoulders hunched, all his attention fixed on a whitish compound he was grinding in a mortar. A wood-and-brass pill cutter stood within reach for when he was ready to make tablets that would dispense just the right dose of the medication.

Mr. Morris was a thin, elderly man with wispy gray hair and intelligent brown eyes that were unnaturally magnified by the thick lenses of his horn-rimmed specs. His fingers were stained yellow from coming in contact with various compounds, and he always smelled of camphor, valerian, or carbolic, depending on the day.

"Good morning, Dr. Redmond," Mr. Morris said, looking up from his task. "How can I help?"

Mr. Morris wasn't given to small talk, a trait for which Jason was grateful. Jason had no desire to talk about the weather or discuss new advancements in medicine. If he came to the pharmacy, it was because he was concerned about a patient and in need of a remedy.

"Do you happen to have any bromine, Mr. Morris?" Jason asked.

"Bromine, you say?" Mr. Morris's graying eyebrows lifted in surprise. "Can't say that I do. We don't keep it on hand."

Jason sighed in frustration. Bromine wasn't routinely administered at the hospital, being considered too painful and dangerous to the patient, but Jason had been forced to use it during the American Civil War to treat some of the more severe infections, with mixed results. Bromine was known for its bacteria-killing properties but caused agonizing pain at the injection site and often resulted in irreparable tissue damage, but when the alternative was death from sepsis, Jason thought it worth the risk. Swabbing the area with alcohol and applying topical ointments only went so far when dealing with a gangrenous wound.

"Can you obtain some?" Jason asked, watching Mr. Morris intently. If not, he'd have to find it himself.

Mr. Morris tilted his head to the side, his gaze sympathetic. "Is this for Inspector Haze, then?" There were few people at the hospital who didn't know of Jason's involvement with Scotland Yard or his friendship with Daniel.

"It is. The wound's festered, I'm afraid."

"Iodine, applied topically, is a safer alternative," Mr. Morris replied.

"Yes, I'm aware of that, but iodine will not save his life if this infection continues to spread. I will not inject Inspector Haze with the tincture unless he gives me his express permission," Jason added to reassure Mr. Morris. The chemist wouldn't want to be held accountable for a failed experiment.

Mr. Morris nodded. "Very well. I will prepare it for you, Dr. Redmond, but perhaps you should wait a while longer before using it. It does have unpleasant side effects, you know."

"I know, Mr. Morris, and I'm prepared to give it a few hours, but after that, I must act."

"I will have the tincture made up for you by three o'clock, shall we say? Would that suit?"

"I will come back then. And I would appreciate it if you would keep my request confidential."

"I will not lie for you, Dr. Redmond," Mr. Morris said. "If someone asks me, I will tell them who requested it."

"Understood. Thank you, Mr. Morris."

Having left the hospital, Jason went directly to Scotland Yard. Sergeant Meadows nodded when Jason entered and looked like he was about to inquire if he might be of assistance, but Jason walked right past him toward Superintendent Ransome's office. The door was ajar, but Jason knocked on the doorjamb to announce his presence, since Ransome's attention was focused on a document he was perusing.

"Ah, Lord Redmond. Do come in." Ransome gestured toward the guest chair. "How's Haze?" he asked once Jason was seated.

"He's lost a kidney, and the wound has festered."

Ransome paled. "Are you suggesting—?"

"I'm suggesting nothing of the sort. I will do everything in my power to see that Daniel recovers."

"Will he be able to function with only one kidney?"

"He will. But if the other kidney fails…" Jason had no wish to even entertain the possibility.

"Seems his attacker knew what he was about," Ransome remarked.

"He probably thought he had a better chance of piercing the kidney than penetrating the heart," Jason said flatly. An experienced killer would know precisely where to aim to puncture the heart, but it was difficult to make out the ribs when the victim was wearing a thick woolen coat. The knife could strike bone, and since Daniel's attacker had one chance, he had decided on a more accessible target.

"Thank you for the update, your lordship," John Ransome said, obviously thinking that was the only purpose of Jason's visit.

"I would like you to arrest Alfred Simonds and bring him in for questioning."

John Ransome's eyebrows lifted in astonishment. "On what charge?"

"Attempted murder."

"Of?"

"Daniel Haze."

"What makes you think it was Simonds?"

"Once Daniel's condition stabilized after the surgery, I took it upon myself to visit Division T in Kensington. Constable Seth Peters, who's attached to that station, was first on the scene and got Daniel to the hospital on time. I wanted to thank him and also ask him a few questions. He had gone for the day, but I obtained his address and called on him at home."

"And did he tell you something that wasn't in his report?" Ransome asked, clearly intrigued.

"He did. It's a minor detail, but it put me in mind of Alfred Simonds."

"How so?"

"Constable Peters recalls the woman saying she saw an older man with light hair and wearing a green scarf hurrying away as they exited the park. Gray hair can easily be mistaken for light hair when seen from a distance."

"That's it? That's the only reason?" Ransome could barely hide his surprise.

"Given the timing and the description, I believe Simonds followed Daniel."

"All right," John Ransome said. "I have no cause to doubt your reasoning, Lord Redmond. I will send Constables Napier and Collins to pick him up right away, but I would like to be present when you question him."

"You don't believe I have the wherewithal to question the man on my own?" Jason bristled.

"If this man attempted to kill one of my detectives, then it is my duty, as well as my wish, to be there to charge him."

"I see," Jason replied, somewhat mollified.

"Have you breakfasted, my lord?" John Ransome asked, rather unexpectedly.

"No. I was in a hurry to get to the hospital."

"Then what say you we adjourn to the coffeehouse down the street and enjoy a hearty breakfast? We can discuss the particulars of the case while we await Mr. Simonds's arrival."

"Thank you," Jason replied. "It would be my pleasure to join you for breakfast."

By the time they returned, Simonds had been waiting for nearly half an hour, but Jason saw no reason to rush, giving the man time to stew and grow anxious. His anger would work in their favor. It was agreed that Jason would conduct the interview, with John Ransome looking on until his input was required.

Simonds nearly exploded out of his chair when the two men finally entered the room. "Why am I here?" he exclaimed, his attention fixed on the superintendent, who remained impassive.

Jason's gaze slid toward the coatrack in the corner, where Simonds had hung up his coat and hat. A dark green scarf was draped over the coat. "Because you are about to be charged with attempted murder," Jason said calmly once he sat down.

"Attempted murder of whom?" Simonds hissed.

"Of Inspector Haze."

"And why would I wish to try to murder Inspector Haze?"

"Because he got too close, Mr. Simonds," Jason said, watching the man intently. He saw something shift in his gaze and felt emboldened. He was sure he was on the right track. He expected Simonds to deny the charge, but the man remained silent, staring daggers at Jason, whom he realized was the one to watch out for in this interview.

"Lady Viola saw you the night the real Damian Langley was murdered, didn't she?" Jason asked.

"And who is the *real* Damian Langley?" Simonds demanded, mimicking Jason.

"The rightful Earl of Granville, whom you stabbed with a pitchfork to protect your master. Did you then blackmail Edward Frey, whom you knew as Damian Langley, but he refused to pay up?"

"You got it all wrong," Simonds said smugly. "Lady Viola saw nothing because I wasn't there. And no, I didn't blackmail the earl, because I wasn't aware of his true identity until you just revealed it to me. I had assumed the victim was a relation, but I had no idea he was the rightful heir."

"Then why attack Daniel Haze?"

"Who says I did?"

"He recognized you, Mr. Simonds, and named you as his assailant. I'd say that's proof enough." Jason was bluffing, but Simonds paled, another nail in his coffin as far as Jason was concerned. "If Lady Viola cannot implicate you in the murders, then why did you feel threatened by what Inspector Haze had learned when he questioned Robert Langley yesterday?"

Simonds lowered his head, refusing to look at Jason. "No comment," he finally said.

"What did Lady Viola see? Or hear?" Jason amended.

"No comment," Simonds said again.

"Mr. Simonds, you're going to be charged and then you will go to prison. And if Inspector Haze dies of his injuries, you will hang for murder. This is your chance to explain yourself," Superintendent Ransome said.

"Why?" Simonds demanded, his eyes blazing with anger. "Does the reason matter?"

"It might have bearing on your sentence," Ransome replied, using his most reasonable tone.

"Really?" Simonds scoffed. "I'm not a fool, Superintendent. All you have is the word of a dying man, who was delirious with pain when he named me. That's hardly enough evidence to send a man to jail, or to the gallows for that matter. You want me to incriminate myself and make your case for you."

"The case is already made, Mr. Simonds," Ransome replied calmly. "We know you stabbed Inspector Haze with the intention to take his life."

"And now you want me to admit to a double murder so that you can make sure I hang?" Simonds cried. "Well, I didn't do it."

The desperation in his eyes took Jason by surprise. He turned to Ransome. "I'd like to interview Viola Langley," he said, loud enough for Simonds to hear him clearly.

If Ransome was surprised, he hid it well. "Yes, I think that's a good idea. But perhaps we should interview her at her home to avoid any unnecessary unpleasantness."

Simonds looked shocked but didn't say anything.

Ransome stood and squared his shoulders, his gaze fixed on Alfred Simonds. "Please stand."

Simonds rose to his feet, instinctively copying Ransome's stance. The two men looked like they were about to fight a duel of honor.

"Alfred Simonds, you are hereby charged with attempted murder, as contrary to Common Law," Ransome intoned. "You will be transported to Fleet Prison, where you will await trial. Until then, you will be held here, so if you have anything to add, do let the duty sergeant know."

Simonds nodded in understanding and fixed his attention on the small window until Constable Napier came to take him down to the cells.

"Not how you expected it to go, eh?" Ransome said once Simonds was out of earshot.

"I wasn't expecting a full confession, but we now know that Simonds did indeed try to murder Daniel Haze, and that could mean one of two things. He was either protecting himself or someone he loves. Since he refused to answer our questions, it stands to reason that he was protecting someone else."

"I was thinking along the same lines," Ransome said as he pushed to his feet. "Shall we call on Lady Viola?"

"By all means, but I would like to stop at the hospital to check on Daniel first," Jason replied.

"Of course," Ransome said. "We'll take my carriage to speed matters along."

Chapter 33

John Ransome wasn't permitted on the ward, so he opted to take a brief walk while Jason went inside. Daniel was asleep when Jason approached his bed, but even without examining the area, Jason could see that Daniel wasn't faring any better. His face was flushed with fever, and his hand, when Jason touched it, was hot and dry.

"What are your instructions, Doctor?" Nurse Lowe asked.

"Please continue to drain and clean the wound every hour. I hate to disturb him, but we must fight the infection with everything we've got."

"Yes, Dr. Redmond. Shall we dispense another dose of morphine?"

"Yes, if it becomes necessary. I will be back this afternoon."

"Dr. Thorpe is coming on duty in half an hour," Nurse Lowe said.

"Inspector Haze is my patient. I don't want anyone else consulting on his treatment."

"I will advise Matron."

"Thank you."

"Fight the infection, Daniel," Jason said softly once the nurse had left. "Do it for Charlotte. And Rebecca," he added. "They need you, and they're waiting for you."

Daniel didn't stir, so Jason let go of his hand and walked away, going in search of Superintendent Ransome, who came hurrying toward Jason as soon as he saw him emerge from the hospital entrance. Ransome's driver, who'd been walking the horses, brought the carriage around, and the two men climbed in, glad to get out of the cold.

When they arrived at the Langley residence, Walter Reedy answered the door. He looked uncertain, since greeting callers wasn't part of his usual duties, but he was obviously relieved to see that the callers were from the police rather than anyone from the earl's exalted social set.

"We'd like to see your mistress," Ransome said.

"I'm afraid she's not at home to visitors," Reedy replied.

"This is not a social call," Ransome barked. "Get her now. Or don't. We wish to speak to Viola Langley."

"I cannot allow you to see Lady Viola without her ladyship's say-so," Reedy replied.

"Then you'd better get her," Ransome retorted as he strode deeper into the foyer and removed his hat and coat, shoving both into the hands of a passing parlormaid, who waited patiently for Jason to divest himself of his coat and hat as well, given that they were obviously staying. Without being invited to do so, Ransome found the drawing room and strode inside, gesturing for Jason to follow.

Ransome paced the length of the room impatiently, his deferential attitude toward the earl's family gone. It was clear his patience with this case was running thin. Jason had noted Ransome's emotional reaction to the news that Daniel was still in the grip of the infection. Despite his brusque manner, John Ransome cared deeply and was raring to get justice for both Damian Langley and Daniel Haze, should it come to that. Whether the sentiment extended to Edward Frey remained to be seen.

"How dare you barge into my house?" Euphemia Langley screeched as she threw open the door to the drawing room. All lethargy of the previous visit was gone, her movements fluid and efficient, and she faced them, hands on hips.

"We need to speak to Miss Viola," Ransome said calmly.

"That's Lady Viola to you, sir. She's the daughter of an earl."

"She's the daughter of your housekeeper's son," Ransome replied cruelly. "Now, you can ask her to come down and talk to us, or we can take her down to Scotland Yard and interview her there. The choice is yours, madam."

The countess trembled with rage but turned on her heel, nearly colliding with Reedy.

"Ask Adams to fetch Lady Viola," she said, her voice quavering. "These gentlemen would like to speak with her."

"Yes, my lady," Reedy replied, and rushed off.

The countess thrust out her chin defiantly and marched over to the settee across from the one Jason occupied. She sat down, adjusted her skirts, and lifted her head, her gaze fixing on John Ransome. "I don't believe I've had the pleasure," she said coldly.

Ransome bowed from the neck. "Superintendent John Ransome of Scotland Yard."

"Good. Now I will know your name for when I report your barbaric behavior to your superior, Superintendent," the countess replied archly.

"I'm only doing my job," Ransome replied, noticeably leaving out the woman's rank. "I would think you'd have a vested interest in seeing your husband's killer caught."

"Do sit down, Superintendent," Euphemia Langley said, her tone marginally less frosty. "You have my full cooperation. I would offer you refreshment, but that would delay your departure," she added, clearly unable to avoid one final dig at the man who'd humiliated her and brought her to heel.

"We are not in need of any refreshment," Ransome said.

"Where's my butler?" Euphemia demanded.

"Alfred Simonds is currently in the cells at Scotland Yard, awaiting transportation to prison," Ransome replied smoothly. "He's been charged with attempted murder."

The self-righteous expression slid off the countess's face like snow melting from a mountain peak. "Attempted murder?"

"That's correct. He followed Inspector Haze when he left your house yesterday afternoon and stabbed him in the back."

Ransome was barely controlling his anger, and Jason felt gratified to see that he was so upset by an attack on one of his officers. Ransome's burning need to punish the culprit would give Jason carte blanche in bringing this investigation to a satisfying conclusion.

Viola Langley, who finally deigned to show, was a pretty young woman with blonde ringlets and wide blue eyes, her expression so blank, it reminded Jason of the porcelain doll Harriet Elderman had sent as a gift for Lily. The doll's staring eyes had so unnerved Katherine that she'd put it back in its box and shoved it atop a tall wardrobe to be retrieved when Lily was old enough not to be frightened.

Dressed in unrelieved black, Viola was tall and slim, with the lean build of an accomplished horsewoman. Jason suspected her thighs were well toned from hours spent in the saddle. She also had a generous bosom that belied her youth and gave her a womanly appearance. He could see why her parents were eager to see her wed. Even in her bereaved state, there was a sensuality about her that was difficult not to notice.

"What is it you want with me?" Viola demanded in a tone so imperious, it took Jason by surprise. "I have no wish to speak to either of you."

"But speak to us you will, Miss Langley," Ransome replied rather forcefully. She winced at the form of address but said nothing. "Sit down."

Viola sat next to her mother and reached for Euphemia's hand, which was readily given. The two women looked like they were on trial.

John Ransome turned to Jason and nodded, giving him leave to begin the interview.

"What did you see when you sneaked out to the stables the night Damian Langley—that's the name of the first victim," Jason clarified, "—was murdered?"

Viola slid a sidelong look at her mother. She was clearly surprised to learn the man's name and that there was a possible familial connection. Euphemia Langley continued to watch Jason, ignoring her daughter. Viola lifted her chin in imitation of her mother's defiant expression.

"I saw Grady hurrying away from the stables."

"Did he see you?" Jason asked.

"I ducked behind a shed."

"Why?"

"Because I had no wish to be seen."

"Did you go inside the stables?" Jason tried again.

"I returned home and went up to my room."

"Why didn't you tell anyone you'd seen Grady when the man we first believed to be your father was found dead?" Ransome asked.

"Because there's nothing unusual about seeing a groom come out of the stables, is there?" Viola replied sharply. "Besides, he had frightened me."

"How did he frighten you?"

Viola looked uncertain, then took a deep breath and plunged in. "He looked odd. Desperate. And there was something on his hands. I saw him trying to clean them with a bit of straw." She stole a peek at her mother and went on. "Papa forbade me to go to the stables by myself, especially at night, so I didn't want anyone to know I'd sneaked out to visit Snowflake. I only wanted to say goodnight," she added, now sounding like the vulnerable sixteen-year-old she was.

"Was anyone else about?" Ransome asked. His eyes had narrowed as he listened to Viola's account.

"No, but I thought I heard something," Viola confessed.

"What did you hear?" Jason asked.

"It sounded like a moan, coming from within. It wasn't a sound a horse would make. It sounded human."

"What time was this?"

"Around nine."

"So, after the servants had finished their dinner?" Ransome asked.

"Yes, they would have finished by then," Euphemia Langley interjected.

"Did you tell anyone about what you'd seen and heard?" Jason asked.

"I told Simonds. I thought he'd want to know," Viola said with an odd smugness Jason couldn't account for.

"Why did you think he'd want to know?" It would be perfectly reasonable to tell the butler, since he was in charge of the male staff, but the sly smile that hovered around Viola's plump lips told him there was another, more pertinent reason.

"Grady is his son," Viola said, her pleasure at revealing this tidbit obvious.

"Thomas Grady is Simonds's son?" Ransome echoed, turning toward Jason to see if he already knew. Jason shook his head.

"Viola," the countess hissed. "How on earth did you know that?"

Viola gave her mother a triumphant smile. "I know everything that goes on in this house, Mother."

The countess gave her a look that implied they'd discuss this at length later, then turned back to Ransome. "Yes, Thomas Grady is Simonds's natural son."

"Who is his mother?" Jason asked.

Euphemia sighed. "The housekeeper. Mrs. Frey."

Jason felt his mouth drop open and quickly closed it. "Why is he called Grady?"

"Because we wanted to avoid awkward questions, obviously. My husband held Simonds in high regard and promised him he'd find a position for his boy. After Thomas was born, he was sent to live with a family on the estate. The Gradys cared for him until he was ten. He then returned and was put to work as a hall boy. He had a fondness for horses, so my husband allowed him to work in the stables."

"Does Grady know who his parents are?" Jason asked as he tried to rearrange the facts in his mind to form a coherent pattern.

"He does," Euphemia replied, ignoring her daughter's snide smile.

Ransome nodded and got to his feet. He walked toward the doors, threw them open, and called for Reedy, who was hovering nearby. "Bring Thomas Grady here straight away."

"Yes, sir." The footman hurried toward the green baize door, presumably to exit the house through the servants' entrance, which would bring him closer to the mews.

"If we're finished here," Euphemia Langley said haughtily as she rose to her feet. Viola sprang to her feet as well, eager to leave.

"Yes, you may go," Ransome replied.

Euphemia Langley looked positively livid to be thus dismissed from her own drawing room but didn't deign to reply. She took Viola by the arm, and they fled, making for the grand staircase in the foyer. Jason and John Ransome followed them out and positioned themselves in the foyer.

Thomas Grady looked bewildered when he came, glancing down at the muck on his boots with obvious horror.

"Thomas Grady, I'm arresting you on suspicion of murder of Damian Langley and the man you knew as the Earl of Granville," John Ransome intoned.

Grady's mouth fell open, his confusion and disbelief obvious. "I didn't kill them, your lordships. I swear," he cried.

Ransome produced a pair of iron handcuffs and secured them on the young man's wrists before leading him out the door and toward his waiting carriage. "Get in," he barked, then followed the groom inside.

There was no room inside for a third man, so Jason sat next to the driver on the bench and braced himself for a frigid ride back to Scotland Yard.

Chapter 34

"I didn't kill anyone," Grady reiterated once he was seated in an interview room, his cuffed hands before him on the wooden table. "Why would I?"

"Mr. Grady," Ransome began, "you discovered both victims. The murders happened in a place where you spend most of your time. And Viola Langley saw you running away from the scene of the crime after the first murder."

"That don't mean I did it!" Grady cried desperately.

"What transpired between you and Edward Frey?" Ransome was clearly losing his patience, but Thomas Grady looked utterly bewildered.

"Who's Edward Frey?"

"The man you knew as the Earl of Granville," Jason supplied.

Grady looked nonplussed. "Nothing. I hardly ever saw him. And why are you calling him by that name?"

"Did you know he was your half-brother?" Ransome asked. "Perhaps you felt you were owed something."

Grady's face said it all. "My what?"

"Edward Frey was born to Martin Langley and your mother, Lucille Frey."

Thomas Grady shook his head. "You're having me on."

"Surely your mother told you her little secret. Possibly even spurred you on, encouraging you to ask the earl for a leg up in the world," Ransome taunted the young man.

"My mother said no such thing, and I don't know what you're talking about."

Ransome sighed. "Mr. Grady, we have enough evidence to charge you."

"But I'm innocent," Grady wailed. "I had nothing to do with the killings."

Ransome was just about to say something when Sergeant Meadows knocked on the door. "What is it, Sergeant? We're in the middle of an interview."

"Mr. Simonds is asking for you. Says it's urgent."

"Tell him to wait," Ransome replied, turning back to Grady.

"The wagon from Fleet Prison is here, ready to take him. He says he must speak to you before he goes."

"All right," Ransome replied, clearly exasperated. "Take Mr. Grady down to the cells and bring Simonds in."

"Yes, sir. Let's go," Sergeant Meadows told Grady, who shuffled away like a man twice his age.

"It's case closed, as far as I'm concerned," Ransome said once the door closed behind Sergeant Meadows. "Thomas Grady killed both men, the first one by mistake, and the second intentionally, probably because his brother refused to give in to his demands. And then his father attacked Haze to keep him from getting any closer to the truth. It's like you said, your lordship; Simonds was protecting someone he loves."

Jason shook his head. "Simonds tried to kill Daniel, no question about that, but I don't believe Thomas Grady killed either Damian Langley or Edward Frey. He had no motive. It's obvious he had no idea of the relationship between them."

"But what if he did?" Ransome retorted. "Edward Frey was the master, for God's sake, and Grady was working in the stables, shoveling horseshit. He wanted something better for himself, and who better to provide that than his half-brother, the fraudulent earl?"

"Still, I don't think he murdered either man," Jason replied stubbornly. "Killing the earl would not get him any closer to attainting his goals."

"No, but perhaps an argument broke out, Frey told him where to shove his demands, and Grady killed him in a moment of blinding anger."

"I don't think that's what happened."

"My lord, I appreciate your help. We would never have made an arrest without your insight, but the case is closed. Whatever Simonds has to say will have little bearing on the eventual outcome."

"Let's just hear him out before we make that determination," Jason suggested.

Ransome's version of events certainly made sense, but Jason had learned to heed his gut instinct when it came to dealing with people, and although he could easily believe that Simonds had stabbed Daniel, the rest didn't sit well with him.

Alfred Simonds looked like a broken man when Sergeant Meadows admitted him to the interview room. His shoulders were stooped, and his gaze was that of a man who'd been robbed of everything that was worth fighting for.

"You wished to speak to us, Mr. Simonds?" Ransome asked once Simonds was seated.

"I did it. I killed the earl," Simonds said without preamble.

"Why?" Jason asked.

"Because he was going to pin the murder of Damian Langley on my son."

"Are you so sure your son didn't do it?"

"Thomas is not capable of murder, and he had no reason to kill either man."

"If he knew the truth of their relationship, he had reason aplenty," Ransome argued.

"Thomas never knew. In fact, I never knew either. Lucille never told me. Like everyone else, I believed the earl to be the legitimate son of Martin Langley and Lady Cecily."

"Why did you and Lucille Frey never marry?" Jason asked, wondering why the relationship as well as their son had to be kept secret.

"Lucille was afraid she'd lose her position as housekeeper if she were a married woman. I told her that wouldn't happen, but she was adamant. She wanted to remain in the earl's employ. Now I understand why."

"And she didn't think that giving birth to your bastard would jeopardize her future?" Ransome demanded.

"That couldn't be helped, but his lordship looked after Thomas, as a favor to me. He owed me. He placed the boy with a family that live on the estate. Thomas was given their surname, but he learned we were his parents when he turned sixteen. We thought he was old enough to understand."

"And did he?" Jason asked.

"He was understandably angry at first, but he came round to the idea of having two sets of parents who love him."

"That's rather a convoluted family tree," Ransome remarked.

"More than I ever realized," Simonds admitted.

"So, if your son didn't murder Damian Langley, who did?"

"I don't know," Simonds replied, but there was something evasive in his gaze that aroused Jason's curiosity.

"It would be understandable if Thomas was spooked by the presence of a stranger and felt the need to defend himself," Jason said. "I bet as soon as Damian Langley began to speak, he realized he wasn't dealing with the earl."

"That sounds feasible, but that's not what happened," Simonds insisted.

"So, what did?" Jason asked.

"I honestly don't know, and neither does Tom. He left the stables, as he said, and went up to the house for supper. He remained in the servants' hall all evening, as numerous people have confirmed."

"Viola Langley says she saw Thomas leave the stables around nine. No one would have questioned a trip to the necessary, giving him enough time to go to the stables," Ransome replied.

"No, they wouldn't, but why would Tom go back, and how was he to know that someone would be there at precisely the time he'd chosen to return?" Simonds demanded.

"Perhaps they had a prearranged meeting."

Simonds scoffed. "With all due respect, Superintendent, you're trying to shove a square peg into a round hole, and I think you know that."

Ransome's mouth twitched with amusement at the butler's turn of phrase, but he quickly got hold of himself. "Right. You have confessed to the murder of Edward Frey, and that's good enough for me. Let's say it's a round peg in a round hole," he said nastily. "Until we figure out who murdered Damian Langley, your son will remain in custody."

"You can't hold him without evidence," Simonds protested.

"I can," Ransome replied. "There's enough evidence to consider him a suspect, and until I'm certain he's innocent, he stays in the cells."

"Please, be good to him. He's just a boy."

"He will be treated with kindness," Ransome promised. "Now, I believe you have a ride to catch."

"And I have a patient to see," Jason said, rising to his feet. He was eager to return to Daniel and prayed there'd been an improvement.

Chapter 35

Jason found Daniel awake, still flushed with fever, his gaze glazed with pain. Nurse Lowe had helped him to turn onto his side to take the weight off the infected area. Daniel stared at Jason as he approached the bed and pulled up a chair.

"Did you get Simonds?" Daniel asked, the raspiness in his voice at odds with his normally soft-spoken tone.

"We did."

"Why did he attack me?"

"Because you got too close."

Daniel's confusion was obvious, his brow furrowed. "But what did he hope to accomplish by killing me? Even if he had succeeded, someone else would be assigned to the case."

"Perhaps he did it on the slim chance that another detective wouldn't get as far as you did," Jason said. "Or maybe he hoped to buy some time."

"Time to do what?"

"To get his son to safety."

"His son?" Daniel echoed, now even more bewildered.

"Forget about the case for now," Jason replied. "We need to talk about you."

"What about me?"

"The infection is spreading, Daniel."

Daniel nodded miserably. "Jason, please, promise me you'll look after Charlotte should the worst happen. I know Harriet will raise her, but she's getting on in years, and Charlotte will need someone she can rely on and look up to."

"You have my word that I will look after Charlotte, but I'm not ready to give up on you just yet."

"What do you propose?" Daniel rasped.

"A dose of bromine. Possibly more than one. I won't lie to you. The injection is painful. I've never experienced it myself, but I was told by numerous men that it felt like liquid fire was consuming their flesh, and the sensation lasted for quite a long time. Some also reported a loss of feeling in the area once the infection had been contained, but, on the upside, they lived to tell me about it. I will not administer the bromine without your consent."

Daniel looked exhausted, his breaths coming in short gasps. "Do what you must, and do it soon. I can feel this poison spreading through my body, and I feel like I'm burning already, so it can't get much worse."

"It can, actually, but I would advise you to take the chance. The alternative is—" Jason couldn't bring himself to speak the words.

"You needn't mince words with me, Jason. Please, do it."

"I will be back shortly," Jason promised, and took himself off to the pharmacy.

Mr. Morris was there, still seated at the table, a mug of milky tea and a ham sandwich before him. He hastily rewrapped the sandwich in brown paper and pushed it aside.

"I had no time to eat this afternoon," he explained once he'd swallowed.

"I didn't mean to interrupt your lunch," Jason apologized. "I know I'm early, but the situation is dire."

Mr. Morris nodded and slid off his stool. He reached for a brown bottle on the highest shelf of the cabinet behind him. The liquid within looked murky and dark, much like iodine, which was in the same chemical family.

"This should be enough for four doses," Mr. Morris said. "I sincerely hope you will not require more."

"So do I, Mr. Morris. And thank you."

Jason returned to Daniel, whose eyes were closed now, but his fingers were wrapped around the iron bedstead to keep himself from rolling onto his back, which would be agonizing.

"Daniel," Jason said softly. Daniel opened his eyes.

"Are you ready?"

Daniel nodded.

Jason filled the syringe he'd brought along with ten milligrams of bromine and came behind Daniel. He carefully pulled down the bandages to expose the red, pus-spewing volcano that was Daniel's lower back, and pushed the needle into his tender skin. Daniel inhaled sharply but made no other sound. Not wishing to prolong the torture, Jason depressed the plunger and injected the area with the solution.

Daniel gasped, his hands trembling as the drug set about its work. His face took on a grayish tinge beneath the flush of fever, and he whimpered miserably and buried his face in the pillow to stifle his groans of pain.

"I'm sorry," Jason said. It was woefully inadequate, but that was really all he could offer. He swabbed the site of injection with alcohol before adjusting the bandage, then placed the used syringe on a metal tray by Daniel's bed that held alcohol, iodine, and clean bandages.

"How soon will we know?" Daniel forced out between his pale lips.

"We should begin to see an improvement within the next twenty-four hours."

Daniel nodded. “What if it doesn’t work?”

“We do it again.”

“Oh, Jesus!” Daniel exclaimed. It was clear he was in extreme pain but tried not to show it as he hid his clenched fists beneath the covers. His forehead broke out in a sheen of sweat, and his eyes filled with tears.

Jason stopped the bottle of bromine and slid it into his breast pocket, then sat down next to Daniel, determined to remain by his side until he felt stronger.

“Jason, tell me about the case,” Daniel said weakly.

Normally, Jason would advise the patient to rest, but focusing on something other than the pain would help Daniel to cope.

“Tell me,” Daniel said again.

“Viola Langley claims to have seen Thomas Grady leaving the stables on the night of Damian Langley’s murder. She said he looked anxious and that there was blood on his hands.”

“Was Grady arrested?” Daniel asked eagerly.

“He was, as was Simonds, who was charged with attempted murder.”

“I still don’t see why Simonds would want to kill me.”

“It seems that Thomas Grady is Simonds’s natural son. And would you care to guess who his mother is?” Jason asked, grinning despite the dire situation.

“No!” Daniel cried, and was rewarded with a stern look from a passing nurse, who put her finger to her lips to urge him to keep his voice down.

“Oh, yes. The very fertile Lucille Frey. So, Thomas Grady and Edward Frey are half-brothers.”

"Good Lord!" Daniel sputtered.

"Simonds confessed to killing Edward Frey," Jason continued.

"But why would he kill him?" Daniel asked as he gingerly pushed himself up on the pillows, the pain momentarily forgotten.

"Edward Frey had intended to pin the murder of Damian Langley on Thomas Grady in order to derail the investigation. Simonds couldn't allow his son to be sacrificed to protect Frey's secret."

Daniel nodded. "I doubt Grady would get the death penalty if he pleaded self-defense, but jail time for certain."

"Possibly decades," Jason mused.

"Depends on who the judge happened to be. To some, murder is murder, regardless of the reason. If Grady had the misfortune to come before a 'hanging judge,' he may have got the noose or been transported to Australia."

"I hear they're abandoning that particular punishment," Jason said. "It was in the papers."

"A convict ship, *Hougoumont* it's called, went out just a few weeks ago," Daniel replied. "It should be docking in Botany Bay soon, assuming it made the crossing without incident. Let's hope it was the last one of its kind." He leaned deeper into the pillows, clearly tired, so Jason made to get up, but Daniel raised his head, his expression pleading. "Please, don't go. Not yet."

"I'll stay until you fall asleep," Jason promised, and shifted his weight in the uncomfortable chair.

"Do you think Grady committed the first murder?" Daniel asked.

"I think Grady is a convenient scapegoat."

"But if Thomas Grady didn't kill Damian Langley, who did? It couldn't have been Edward Frey. He had a solid alibi for the night of the murder and was the only person to have a clear motive. Thomas Grady had no reason to kill the man, and neither did anyone else if they had no inkling of who he really was."

"My thoughts precisely," Jason said. "I can just about believe that Simonds killed Edward Frey to protect his son, although I have my doubts, but I see no obvious connection between Damian Langley and Thomas Grady."

"Why do you have doubts that Simonds killed Edward Frey?"

Jason considered the question. Why did he have doubts? Was it not utterly plausible that a father would kill to protect his son? Deep down, he knew he'd kill to protect Lily, but the explanation just didn't sit well with him.

"Alfred Simonds and Edward Frey's relationship went back years," Jason said, eager to share his reservations with Daniel." They had been in the army together and had forged a strong enough bond for Frey to offer Simonds employment on discharge and leave him a generous bequest in his will. Why would he sacrifice his friend's son in order to sabotage the investigation? Surely he could have framed the other groom, Stills, or just let the murder go unsolved. Whoever killed Damian Langley had rid Edward Frey of a problem he didn't know he had."

"That's very true, but once Edward Frey learned from either Dr. Rothman or Mr. Quinlan that we were aware the true heir to the title and estate had been another man all along, he'd never feel safe, so he wanted the investigation closed before the story made the papers," Daniel argued.

"Yes, I suppose that makes sense," Jason agreed. He was about to add that the real killer was still at large, but Daniel's eyelids began to flutter, and his hand relaxed on the blanket, the fingers uncurling.

Jason waited until he was sure Daniel was asleep, then stood and quietly walked away, intercepting Nurse Lowe on her way to change Daniel's bandages.

"Let Inspector Haze sleep until he wakes up," Jason said. "He needs his rest."

"Yes, sir."

"And please send for me at home if there's any change for the worse."

"Yes, sir," Nurse Lowe replied.

Jason left the ward, collected his hat and coat from the doctors' lounge, and descended the wide staircase that led to the vestibule. He stepped out into the purple glory of a December twilight and took a deep gulp of fresh air, needing to clear his lungs after the overwhelming stench of putrefaction that had pervaded the area around Daniel's bed. Jason wasn't a very religious man, but as he briskly walked toward a cabstand, he prayed that the pain he'd inflicted on Daniel wasn't in vain.

Chapter 36

When Jason returned home, he found a pleasant domestic scene. Micah was reading by the drawing room fire, while Katherine sat perched on the settee, a tea tray on the low table before her. Judging by the empty cups and plates, Jason had arrived too late to enjoy a slice of Mrs. Dodson's freshly baked cake. He settled in a wingchair across from Katherine, who reached for the teapot, but Jason shook his head. He didn't want tea. He needed something stronger.

As if reading his thoughts, Micah set aside his book, got to his feet, and walked over to the sideboard, where he poured Jason a generous brandy. He handed it to him wordlessly. Jason lifted his glass in a silent salute and tossed back the drink before holding the glass out for a refill. Micah obliged, then resumed his seat. Katherine gave them both a mildly disapproving look.

"How's Daniel?" she asked, her gaze anxious.

Micah was watching Jason with a similarly worried expression.

"It's too soon to tell, but I'm hopeful."

"Oh, Jason," Katherine said with feeling. "I can't stop thinking about him. And poor Charlotte. She so recently lost her mother."

"Daniel is not lost to us yet," Jason replied, secretly wishing he could have a third drink but knowing he really shouldn't, in case he was summoned to the hospital.

"Miss Grainger came by earlier," Katherine said. "She's frantic. I think..." Katherine's gaze slid toward Micah, and she let the sentence trail off.

"You don't have to mince words on my account," Micah said petulantly. "I'm not a child."

"No, you're not, and you're right, Katie," Jason said. "I think Miss Grainger and Daniel have feelings for each other."

Katherine smiled sadly. "She loves him, Jason. It's plain to see. I hope…"

"One day at a time, Katie," Jason said, not ready to engage in a conversation about Daniel's love life. Just then, he was more interested in Daniel's life.

"Have you caught the killer?" Micah asked, clearly bored with talk of relationships.

Jason was just about to reply when Fanny walked in. "Lily is awake," she said, a smile spreading across her face.

Both Jason and Katherine sprang to their feet, eager to see the baby.

As soon as Jason lifted Lily out of her cot, she angled her body downward, her gaze on her wooden blocks. Jason set her on the floor and sat next to her, ready to help her build a tower, but Lily snatched the block he'd picked up from his hand and glared at him from beneath the lacy trim of her bonnet, eager to build a tower herself. She stacked the blocks, then knocked them over with a glee Jason found endearing.

"Do you think our daughter has destructive tendencies?" Katherine asked as she watched Lily demolish her second creation.

"I think it means she has a sense of fun."

"And she's territorial," Katherine said, clearly still bothered by Lily's refusal to share her toys.

"She's a nine-month-old baby." Jason picked up two blocks and began to juggle while Lily gaped at him in speechless wonder.

"You know, no matter what Lily does, I'll still love her unconditionally, and that astounds me," Katherine said philosophically.

"Why?" Jason asked, putting the blocks down.

"Because I've never known that kind of love, not even for my mother or sister. My mother was a kind, generous woman, but she wouldn't tolerate disobedience or any complaints about Father. As far as she was concerned, her husband was never to be questioned, only obeyed and respected. And Anne, well, she could be petty and unreasonable sometimes, which is normal in adolescent girls, I suppose."

"Katie, everyone has faults, but that doesn't mean they're not worthy of love. And when it comes to children, some parents tend to be blind, either because they don't care to correct them or due to an inability to see their flaws clearly. When I look at Lily, all I see is perfection." Jason smiled broadly at Lily, who was banging two blocks together.

"Are you saying you would never correct her?" Katherine asked, scrutinizing Jason over the top of her spectacles in a way that made him want to kiss her senseless.

"I'll leave the discipline to you," he teased.

"And what if she did something truly unforgivable?" Katherine pressed.

"Why would our child do something unforgivable? And why are you thinking these awful thoughts?"

"I've had a letter from one of Father's parishioners, asking me for advice."

"What about?" Jason asked.

"She asked me to keep her confidence, but suffice it to say, her daughter has irrevocably broken her heart. There's no coming back from what she's done."

"Lily will never break our hearts, because no matter what she does, we will love and support her." Jason stood and lifted Lily off the floor, tossing her up in the air and making her giggle madly. "Right, Lily? You will remain perfect."

"Dada," Lily cried joyfully, and for the very first time.

"I always knew she loves you more," Katherine said with an indulgent smile.

"What's not to love?"

Katherine leaned against Jason and smiled winsomely at Lily. "Say Mama."

"Ma," Lily cried triumphantly.

Katherine reached out and caressed the child's silky cheek. "I will love you always," she whispered. "And I will do anything to protect you, no matter what mischief you get up to."

Wiping the tears from her eyes, Katherine returned to her no-nonsense persona. "Now, it's time for Lily's supper, and I think Micah is feeling a bit listless these past few days, especially in view of our cancelled New Year's Eve plans."

Katherine had invited the Powells as well as Daniel to join them for a New Year's Eve supper and champagne toast at midnight. She had asked Adelaide to bring along her widowed younger sister and twelve-year-old niece to make up the numbers but had written to her friend to cancel as soon as she heard about the attack on Daniel. No one was in the mood to celebrate, least of all Jason. They would be on their own tonight, while the servants had their own celebration in the servants' hall downstairs.

Jason smiled and handed Lily over. "I'll ask if he'd like to join me in a game of chess before dinner."

"What a very good idea. I'll see you later," Katherine said, and swept from the nursery.

Jason returned downstairs and gave Micah three games, all of which he lost because his mind was on Daniel, and the case.

Chapter 37

Friday, January 1, 1869

Jason rose early, breakfasted alone, and headed straight to the hospital to check on Daniel. The sun had not yet risen, but Jason thought it would be a fine day, clear and bright. And very cold. He felt hopeful since there had been no word from the hospital, but he still felt a pang of trepidation as he entered the hospital vestibule and jogged up the stairs in his eagerness to get to Daniel. Jason divested himself of his coat and hat in the doctor's lounge, then hurried to the men's ward. The ward was busy, the nurses removing nightsoil, serving breakfast, and doling out morning doses of medication.

Daniel greeted him with a wan smile and a reassurance that the pain had diminished somewhat, but Jason wasn't taking his word for it. He removed the bandages, closely examined the incision, and was exceedingly pleased to see that although the area was still red and puffy, the infection was no longer spreading, and the skin wasn't as hot to the touch. The circumference of the swelling had shrunk, and the incision wasn't as angry or putrid as it had been yesterday afternoon.

Daniel waited patiently for Jason to swab the wound and apply a clean bandage before asking, "May I have some breakfast?"

"Of course. Hunger is always a positive sign." Jason hedged a little, hating to broach the subject. "Daniel, I think it would be prudent to administer one more dose. Just to be sure the infection is contained. I will inject a lower dose, but I'm afraid the body's reaction to it will not be very different. In fact, it might be more painful the second time."

"Do what you must. You have my complete confidence."

"Nurse, I require a clean syringe," Jason said softly to Nurse Pritchard, who had appeared at his side.

"Yes, Doctor."

Once Nurse Pritchard returned, Jason administered a second dose of the tincture and instructed the nurse to bring Daniel breakfast.

"I will be back in a few hours. Try to rest," he told Daniel.

"Where are you going?" Daniel asked.

"I have an errand to run," Jason replied noncommittally. He didn't want Daniel to worry, only to get better.

It was the height of social impropriety to call on someone before noon, but Jason presented himself at the Langley residence in Park Lane at just after eleven. Reedy once again opened the door, looking not only exasperated but fearful. Perhaps it was the arrests of two members of staff, or possibly the gossip that ran rampant in any household, even in that of an earl—or unlawful earl, as the staff were bound to have discovered by now. Secrets didn't last long in such a closely contained environment. They were like a chemical experiment, ready to boil over once heat was applied.

The house was unnaturally quiet, the mirrors and paintings draped in black crape and the curtains only partially open, the rooms gloomy. The servants passed by on silent feet, their eyes downcast. It was the start of the new year, but this household would be frozen in time for a long while, mourning the death of its patriarch.

Euphemia Langley looked angry when she entered the drawing room, the black of her taffeta gown and lace cap making her look spectral in the dim light of the unlit room. She sat down, and Jason followed suit, settling across from her so he could clearly see her face.

“I didn’t expect to see you again so soon, or so early, my lord,” Euphemia said pointedly.

“And I didn’t expect to return, but there are things we need to discuss,” Jason said.

“Oh?” Euphemia’s hands were clasped in her lap, and her face resembled a death mask, still and expressionless.

“Why did you do it?” Jason asked, watching her intently.

“Do what, exactly?”

“Murder your husband.”

Euphemia Langley’s face went even paler, her eyes betraying the truth of Jason’s accusation. “How did you know it was me?” she whispered, not bothering to deny it.

“I didn’t. You just told me.”

Jason thought she might slap him, but given her current status, he was now above her on the social register and had connections to Scotland Yard. Adding assault to the list of charges wouldn’t do her any favors.

“Was it because you were trying to protect Viola or because you had reasons of your own for wanting him dead?”

“Protect Viola?” Euphemia echoed.

“It was Viola who killed Damian Langley. She went to the stables that night to visit her beloved horse and came face to face with a man who resembled her father but clearly wasn’t. Damian must have approached her and possibly tried to explain, but he was cognitively and socially impaired, and his explanation would have made little sense to her. Perhaps he came too close to Viola or tried to prevent her from leaving, or perhaps he did nothing other than stand there, as shocked by the unexpected encounter as she was, which would leave her no less terrified. She was alone with a stranger in a dark stable, and she understood only too well what that could mean.”

Euphemia Langley hadn't moved, but everything about her had changed. She seemed to have aged before Jason's eyes, going from an attractive woman in her prime to a shrunken crone. Sympathy for her tugged at his heart, but he had no choice but to continue.

"Desperate to escape, Viola grabbed a pitchfork and lunged. She is tall for a woman and fit. It wouldn't have taken much to overpower Damian Langley, who was malnourished and weak. She then returned to the house and pretended that nothing had happened, going up to her room to prevent anyone from asking any uncomfortable questions. She's young, but as the daughter of an earl, she understands the value of an unsullied reputation, especially when she's about to be married."

Euphemia's hand flew to her mouth at that. There would be no wedding now, no glittering future for her daughter.

"After the police had finally gone, leaving you in shock at having been suddenly widowed, Viola told you the truth and assured you that the man she had killed wasn't her father, but you had already dispatched a message to Mr. Quinlan, knowing you would require legal counsel regarding the earl's estate. Mr. Quinlan, who knew the truth of the matter, sent a messenger to Sevenoaks, charging the man with visiting every public house until he located the earl."

Euphemia Langley's demeanor reminded Jason of the soldiers who'd survived canon fire. They were often physically unharmed but stunned and unable to focus, lying in a fetal position on the ground or stumbling away on legs that barely held their weight, the ringing in their ears preventing them from responding to offers of help. She stared at Jason, watching his mouth as if she couldn't quite understand what he was saying.

"H-h-how?" she stammered at last. "How did you know?"

"It was something my wife said yesterday about our own daughter. It made me realize that the one person who had the strongest motive was you. Your husband had been unfaithful to you for years with a woman nearly half your age. He had lied to you, had come to your bed only in the hope that you would conceive another son, and had wounded your pride. But you were willing to put up with it all for the sake of your social position and your children's prospects. Your daughter was contracted to marry a wealthy and influential man, and your son would be the next Earl of Granville.

"And then, suddenly, you discovered that everything you believed was a lie. Your husband confessed that he was not the rightful Earl of Granville. He was plain old Mr. Langley, or more accurately, the illegitimately born Mr. Frey, and if this information got out, your daughter's engagement would be broken and your son's future uncertain. And that was when you snapped. So you asked him to meet you in the stables and killed him. I expect your husband was so inebriated, he didn't put up much of a struggle. Or perhaps you had slipped some of your valerian or laudanum into his drink to make certain he didn't fight back. You forbade a postmortem just to make sure I didn't find any traces of either drug, or perhaps because you knew I'd discover that Edward Frey wasn't really circumcised and that whole revelation was nothing more than a ruse to cover your initial mistake and get rid of the body quietly and without too much fuss since you already knew your husband was still alive."

Jason inhaled sharply and continued. "Now that a second man had died in exactly the same way, it would be obvious that the first murder had been a case of mistaken identity and someone had been after the earl from the start, removing all suspicion from Viola. But once you had calmed down, you realized that killing your husband might have been a mistake, because now the police would redouble their efforts. You had no way of knowing just how much Inspector Haze had uncovered, or if a legitimate heir would come forward to claim everything you had taken for granted all these years. You had to act.

"First, you tried to use Thomas Grady as a scapegoat because it was convenient, but then you realized that there was a better way. By allowing Viola to slip into the conversation that

Grady was Mr. Simonds and Mrs. Frey's son, you very effectively drew Inspector Haze's attention to the fact that the men were brothers, making Grady a suspect for both murders. But you didn't count on Simonds going after Inspector Haze, did you?"

Euphemia Langley shook her head. "No." Her eyes blazed with hatred. "I detest Simonds, just as I hate Mrs. Frey and Nanny Briggs. My husband forced these people on me in my own household because he felt a loyalty to them. Well, I had hoped I might get rid of all of them once and for all now that *his lordship* was gone." She spat out her husband's title as if it were poison.

"And what would you have done had a legitimate heir to the title presented himself? Would you kill him as well?"

"I wouldn't have to. He would have to prove his case in a court of law, and Mr. Quinlan would make certain his claim would be dismissed."

"It wouldn't be, though, would it?" Jason replied. "There is now sufficient proof that the first victim was the rightful earl, and your husband had no claim to either the title or the estate."

"My husband was his father's chosen heir," Euphemia replied. "He had acknowledged him both in life and in death. His last will is testament to that. My son is now the Earl of Granville, and will continue to be. And there are no other claimants, according to Mr. Quinlan."

Jason sighed. He wasn't there to debate succession. He was there to make an arrest. "Mrs. Langley, I'm afraid I must place you and your daughter under arrest and deliver you to Scotland Yard, where you will be charged."

Euphemia's eyes filled with tears, her entire body leaning toward Jason. "Please, Lord Redmond," she pleaded. "You don't understand. That man frightened Viola out of her wits. She thought he was going to ravish her. He kept talking about getting to know her, to love her. He kept trying to touch her. She was terrified. Surely no one can blame her for protecting her virtue, and possibly her very life."

"No, but they can blame you for trying to cover it up and then murdering your cheating husband to keep your secrets."

"Can they?" Euphemia Langley exclaimed. "Can they really? You don't know what I've had to put up with these past few years. The deceit I've had to turn a blind eye to in order to prevent anyone from guessing the extent of my husband's betrayal. Damian never loved me, but he was civil and considerate, and we had managed to build an affectionate and respectful relationship. But since he met that whore, Rosamunde Lillie, he'd given up all pretense of being a husband to me. Oh, yes, he came to my bed, but he taunted me with being too old to give him another child and even said that if I no longer stood in his way, he'd marry his mistress. She was young and beautiful and knew how to please a man in all the way that mattered. He even went so far as to mutilate his manhood. Oh, yes," she cried. "He really was circumcised. He thought it would enhance his sexual pleasure and increase his prowess in bed. Have you ever heard of such poppycock?"

She was crying openly now, her nose red and running. Euphemia Langley whipped a handkerchief out of her sleeve and dabbed at her eyes viciously, making them look red and swollen.

"What will happen to us?" she asked.

Jason sighed. He condemned her actions, but he could understand how the pain of betrayal and a need to protect her daughter had led her down such a dark path.

"Perhaps Viola will be spared a prison sentence, but I'm not a lawyer, and I don't know what constitutes self-defense in a court of law," Jason said.

He had read something about the concept of reasonable force, which he thought to mean that a person had the right to use what they believed to be reasonable force if under attack, but Damian Langley had never actually assaulted Viola. He had certainly frightened her, which Mr. Quinlan or another defense lawyer could argue was justification enough, but Jason couldn't promise her mother that Viola would not receive a custodial sentence.

As far as Euphemia herself, Jason had no doubt that she'd get the death penalty, given the brutality of the murder, the lies, and the attempt to pin the crime on an innocent young man. There was only so much even the best lawyer could do.

As if reading his thoughts, Euphemia Langley leaned forward and grabbed Jason's wrist, her wild gaze fixed on his face. "Please, I implore you, don't tell them."

"I beg your pardon?"

"Don't tell them about Viola. I will claim responsibility for both murders. Please," she wailed. "I must protect my daughter. None of this is her fault. She's a victim of circumstance, and she will be ruined by prison. Her life will not be worth living by the time she's free."

Jason considered her request. As a father, he could sympathize, and although Viola had resorted to unspeakable brutality, he could understand only too well how threatened she must have felt when cornered by a man with Damian Langley's disabilities, who had likely never meant her any harm but came off as a madman in his attempt to explain why he was trespassing on the earl's property. And since she didn't know the man was really her uncle, she would, of course, have feared for her virtue. And who was to say that she was wrong? Jason had no idea what Damian understood of sexual relationships or why he'd attempted to touch his niece. Perhaps he'd only wished to give her a hug, or perhaps his intentions had been more sinister, and Viola had realized that.

"Please, your lordship. I beg you," Euphemia wailed. "Spare my girl. Her fiancé will most likely end the engagement, but at least she will still have a chance. Her brother and Mr. Quinlan will look after her, and eventually the scandal will blow over. She's still so very young."

"Mrs. Langley," Jason began, but Euphemia interrupted him.

"I will stand up in court and say I committed both murders. The judge will have no reason to doubt my word. I will do whatever it takes to protect my daughter. Please, spare her the ordeal she will have to face if charged with murder. Surely, as a father, you can understand how I feel. Would you not do everything in your power to protect your child?"

Jason turned away from the weeping woman and stared out the window. A weak sun had emerged, the light desperately trying to penetrate the gloom of the drawing room. Jason sighed heavily. He was terribly conflicted, but he could understand only too well what Euphemia Langley was going through. Viola had acted in self-defense; that was clear. Was it an act of justice to destroy her life?

"All right," Jason said at last. "As long as you claim responsibility for both murders, I will not say a word about Viola. But you must come with me now. Willingly."

Euphemia Langley nodded. "You have my word. May I say goodbye to my children? In private?"

"You may say goodbye, but I'm not leaving you alone."

"I understand. And thank you, Lord Redmond. You're a kind man."

Jason nodded for lack of anything to say.

A short while later, he escorted Euphemia Langley out the door and into her carriage, which had been brought around to the front. Having spoken to her children, one at a time, she seemed calmer, accepting of her fate.

Jason caught a glimpse of two pale ovals in the drawing room window and felt a pang of pity for the Langley children. Their lives would never be the same, having lost both parents in the space of a week and about to be stripped of the cocoon of security they'd grown up in. He hoped Mr. Quinlan would guide them into adulthood and help them to cope with the scandal that was about to break.

Epilogue

February 1869

The day was unusually mild for February, a hint of spring in the air. Jason knocked on the door and was instantly admitted by Grace, who smiled warmly at him.

Daniel was in the parlor, occupying his favorite chair by the hearth. Miss Grainger sat way too close to him, given the number of vacant seats in the room, and blushed prettily when Jason was announced. She instantly sprang to her feet, excusing herself to go check on Charlotte, who was napping upstairs, leaving Daniel and Jason to speak privately.

"How are you feeling?" Jason asked as he settled himself in the other chair.

"I am absolutely fine, as I try to convince you weekly," Daniel replied, his mouth twitching with good humor.

"How is the incision?" Jason asked, ignoring Daniel's response.

"There's some numbness and scarring around the area, but otherwise, it's healed cleanly."

"The numbness and scarring were exacerbated by the bromine," Jason grumbled.

"Jason, you saved my life. A bit of scarring is a small price to pay. I don't blame you. Honestly," Daniel promised.

Jason saw the newspaper folded on a side table and knew it was safe to broach the subject, since Daniel had obviously already read the article. Following his gaze, Daniel quickly surmised what was on his mind.

"She's better off," Daniel said. "The poor chap who smuggled in the razor will pay dearly for violating the rules, but if Euphemia Langley offered him enough of a bribe, he'll probably still think it was worthwhile."

"Yes, I suppose you're right. It was either dying on her own terms or facing the gallows. I would do the same in her place."

"Any word on the children?" Daniel asked.

"I spoke to Mr. Quinlan after Euphemia Langley's arrest. He's still their family solicitor, but I think he'll be happy to discharge that responsibility, given everything that has transpired."

"Has he refused to represent their interests?"

"No, but he's made arrangements for them to go to Philadelphia. Euphemia has a cousin there. He's offered to take them in. I think they'll be better off, given the amount of publicity the case has received and their uncertain future. Legally, Robert is still the Earl of Granville, since he's Martin Langley's grandson and his grandfather had recognized his father as his heir despite his illegitimate status, but in the court of public opinion, Robert has been stripped of his legacy. And Viola's fiancé called off the engagement as soon as the story appeared in the papers. Sometimes anonymity can be a blessing, especially for a child."

"Anonymity and a healthy bank balance," Daniel said. "Viola and Robert will be all right in time. They're still better off than some."

"I'm not sure I agree, given what they've had to endure these past weeks, but there's nothing more anyone can do for them," Jason replied. "So, I hear you're going back to work."

"I am," Daniel replied happily. "Monday."

"Excellent. I'm glad to hear that you're fully recovered and enjoying the ministrations of your women," Jason said with a smile.

Grace and Rebecca had been fussing over Daniel since the day Jason had brought him home from the hospital, tending to his every need, both physical and emotional. Even Charlotte had been behaving like an angel, sitting by Daniel quietly as he read her stories and then laying her little dark head on his shoulder and napping by his side.

Jason strongly suspected that Charlotte wasn't the only one laying her head on Daniel's shoulder, but he dared not ask. It wasn't his place, and Daniel would tell him if there was anything going on between him and the lovely Rebecca if and when he was ready.

Daniel began to say something when there was a loud knock at the door, followed by Grace's hurried footsteps. Jason heard a gruff voice out in the corridor, and then Sergeant Meadows entered the parlor, his expression apologetic.

"I'm terribly sorry to disturb you, Inspector. I know you're still on sick leave, but I'm afraid there's been a suspicious death, and we're rather short-handed at the moment. Since you're coming back to work the day after tomorrow…"

Daniel sprang to his feet, his face aglow with purpose. "What happened, Sergeant?"

"A woman was pulled from the river, sir."

"So how do you know she was murdered?" Jason asked.

"Because someone whacked her on the back of the head and laid her out in a boat. Doubt she did that herself." Sergeant Meadows looked sheepish. "She looked like a mermaid, sir."

"How do you mean, Sergeant?" Daniel asked as he accepted his coat and hat from Grace, who had deduced which way the wind was blowing and hurried to send her employer off.

Sergeant Meadows blushed at the memory of the woman. "She was naked, sir, with her hair flowing loose and fresh flowers in her hair. And her legs were wrapped in a blue shawl, so at first glance, it looked like a fishtail."

"Who found her?"

"A ferryman spotted her drifting past and towed the boat to shore. I left Constable Napier to watch over her."

"Jason, are you coming?" Daniel asked, unnecessarily, since Jason had already put on his coat and was about to jam his shiny new topper onto his head.

He was dreadfully sorry a woman was dead, but the sight of Daniel, fully recovered and eager to get back to the business of policing, warmed his heart. Jason followed Daniel out the door and climbed into the hansom Sergeant Meadows had left waiting at the curb. A new case was about to begin, and he felt the familiar tingle of anticipation. He couldn't wait to get started, and by the looks of him, neither could Daniel.

The End

Please turn the page for an excerpt from Murder of a Mermaid

A Redmond and Haze Mystery Book 11

Notes

I hope you've enjoyed this installment of the Redmond and Haze mysteries and will check out future books. Reviews on Amazon and Goodreads are much appreciated.

I'd love to hear your thoughts and suggestions. I can be found at

irina.shapiro@yahoo.com, www.irinashapiroauthor.com,

or https://www.facebook.com/IrinaShapiro2/.

An Excerpt from Murder of a Mermaid

A Redmond and Haze Mystery Book 11

Prologue

The morning was cold but clear, the rising sun setting the deep gray waters of the Thames aflame and wrapping the still-dark buildings in a mantle of crimson light. It was a sight that took one's breath away, and Dick Hawley got to enjoy it nearly every day.

He sucked the last few drops of gin from his dented tin flask and pulled his knitted cap lower, but it would take a lot more than that to warm him up. He was near frozen, and his joints ached mercilessly, reminding him of his advancing years. But he wasn't ready to quit yet. What would he do with his time if he did, and who'd look after him once he got too old to work the oars?

There were few boats on the river, but Dick liked having the river to himself, if only for a short time. When asked, he said he was a ferryman, and he was, for a few daylight hours, but it was his nighttime activities that kept him fed and watered. He went out nearly every night, making sure to pass close to the bridges and listening intently for the telltale splash that often preceded a fortuitous find. What was it with people throwing themselves off bridges? he wondered as he rowed along hour after hour, hoping to spot a floater. Surely there were easier ways to die if one had a mind to end it all. But if they'd chosen to drown their sorrows permanently, or if someone had given them a helping hand, there was always something to find on a fresh corpse.

At best, the poor sod still had his purse and valuables on him. At worst, the coat and shoes could be sold to a rag and bone shop once they dried. Sometimes there was even a fancy waistcoat or a snuffbox still full of tobacco. Even now, Dick's pockets held a pretty timepiece and the purse he'd lifted off some posh cove he'd spotted not two hours ago. The silly bugger was hardly more than a boy, and there were sure to be parents and possibly some young woman who was about to learn she was now a widow. Shame that, but it would have been a waste had the valuables been lost to the murky waters of the river, or worse yet, picked by another boatman.

Dick peered into the shimmering sunrise, surprised to see another boat. He hadn't noticed it before, but it must have been there for some time. It was drifting slowly, leisurely, the prow nosing its way toward him. Dick shielded his eyes with a hand clad in a worn fingerless glove and fixed his gaze on the dinghy. At first, he took it to be empty. It might have come untied and drifted away from its hapless owner. But then he spotted a mass of copper curls, the tresses glinting like a freshly minted coin in the rays of the rising sun. Gripping his oars tighter, Dick rowed toward the tiny craft, his mouth opening in shock once he could see inside.

A woman lay in the bottom of the boat, her face serene, her eyes closed, her breasts bare beneath the thick tendrils of glorious hair that had been adorned with flowers. Dick leaned forward, craning his neck to get a better look at the rest of her. Her bottom half was wrapped in silky blue fabric, making her legs look like the tail of a mermaid. The woman was breathtaking, but her beauty was nothing more than a momentary illusion, for death was already her master, and it had started about its ugly work.

Despite the cold, Dick pulled off his hat and held it to his chest in a moment of silent acknowledgement of the person she had been only a few hours before. Then, he reached for the hook he used to harpoon the floaters and pulled the boat closer, tying it to his own so he could tow it to shore. He'd summon a constable once he tied up. He owed her that much, he decided, for she was his very own mermaid.

It was only when he'd pulled the dingy onto the thick mud of the bank that he noticed the gold band on her finger. It glinted in the sun, taunting him with its promise. Well, he'd be hurting no one if he took a little souvenir, Dick reasoned. This lovely no longer had any use for it, did she? Dick slid the ring off the woman’s finger, then yelled, “Oi!” when he noticed a ragamuffin child hovering in the shadow of the bridge.

“Come ’ere, boy. I’s got a job for ye,” Dick cried, and held up a sixpence.

Chapter 1

Thursday, February 11, 1869

The morning was pleasant, the sun that shone benignly from a pale blue sky having burned off the soupy fog of the night before. The river wound into the distance, a shimmering ribbon speckled with vessels of various shapes and sizes. Boatmen called out greetings to each other as they rowed past, and there was the usual cacophony of noise from traffic along the embankment: carriages, dray wagons, carts, and hansoms all vying for space on the too-narrow road, and street vendors calling out to passersby as they tried to hawk everything from fresh buns to morning papers.

Jason Redmond and Daniel Haze alighted from a cab near the New London Bridge and made their way down the stone steps that led to the riverbank. Sergeant Meadows, who'd come to summon them not half an hour ago and had been forced to sit squeezed between the two men, led the way. Despite the time of year, the air was heavy with the reek of wet mud, rotting fish, and various other organic matter that Jason chose not to dwell on as his feet sank into the slippery muck. The Thames looked picturesque from a safe distance, but up close, the turbid water and awful smell were testament to centuries of abuse. The river swelled with sewage and corpses—human and otherwise—and everything from broken furniture to capsized boats littered the riverbed. Occasionally the river gave up its revolting contents after a particularly bad storm that left the banks strewn with debris.

Sergeant Meadows, who was tall and lean, jumped from one bit of flotsam to another like a mountain goat, managing to keep his feet dry and his helmet from sliding into his eyes, while Daniel moved gingerly, having only just recovered from major surgery. This was to be his first case since the stabbing that had robbed him of a kidney last December, and although eager to get back to work, he was understandably nervous.

Constable Napier, who was stocky, fair-haired, and at the moment pink-cheeked from the cold, stood on a chunk of board. The hems of his trousers were muddy and wet, and he looked miserable, but the young man straightened his shoulders as soon as he spotted the approaching group and smiled, obviously relieved that his watch was nearly over.

"There she is," Sergeant Meadows said unnecessarily, pointing to the weathered dingy that had been pulled up onto the bank.

"Where's the boatman who found her?" Daniel asked, since there were no other people in the immediate vicinity, although a small crowd had gathered along the embankment, the onlookers gawking at the odd scene on the riverbank.

"He went off," Constable Napier complained as he made an expansive gesture toward the opposite bank. "Said he was too tired to hang about and that he had nothing more to add."

"What did he say, exactly?" Jason asked.

"Why, nothing much, sir," Constable Napier replied. "Just that he saw a dinghy drifting toward him and rowed over to investigate. Once he realized the woman was dead, he towed her to shore and found a street urchin to go fetch a constable."

"That's very civic-minded of him," Daniel said sarcastically. "Had he taken anything off her?"

"The old geezer swore he never touched her," Constable Napier replied. "If he had, he would have taken the shawl. Pure silk and sure to fetch a few bob."

"Did you take his name and address?" Daniel pressed the constable.

"He wouldn't give it, sir."

"I wager his pockets were filled with ill-gotten gains," Daniel muttered, his lip curling with disgust. "Robbing the dead is a lucrative occupation."

"Keeps him in gin," Constable Napier agreed. "The old boy reeked of spirits."

Daniel sighed in obvious frustration. "Has Mr. Gillespie been summoned?" he asked, turning to Sergeant Meadows. It wouldn't do to move the body before the police photographer took photos.

As if on cue, a man Jason had never met hurried toward them, the tripod in his hand and the bulky boxed camera slung from his shoulder identifying him as a photographer. He wore a felt-top hat, a navy wool pea coat, and dickersons to keep his feet dry. Jason thought he might be from a newspaper that had got whiff of the story, but Sergeant Meadows raised a hand in greeting and addressed him by name.

"Good afternoon, Mr. Braithwaite. She's over here," he said again, as if the man could possibly miss the body. "Mr. Gillespie was unavailable," Sergeant Meadows explained to Daniel and Jason, and performed the introductions.

Jason ignored Mr. Braithwaite's obvious surprise when the two men were introduced. People were frequently confused by his noble rank, American accent, and inexplicable willingness to perform pro bono work for the police, but Jason felt no need to explain himself. He had grown accustomed to his newfound station, relished his work at the hospital, and was happy to offer his services to Scotland Yard, particularly on cases that were assigned to Daniel Haze. In return, Daniel encouraged Jason to participate in the investigations and treated him as a partner rather than the bored aristocrat his peers regularly assumed he was. It was a happy outcome for all concerned.

Once the social niceties were out of the way, everyone got to work, each member of the group intent on his own grim task. Jason sat back on his haunches and studied the woman before him.

She was laid out in the dingy, her head resting against the prow. Dark red hair was spread about her shoulders, the curls shimmering in the sunlight. She was one of the most beautiful women Jason had ever seen, her skin like porcelain, her features perfectly drawn. Her eyes were closed, the lashes as thick and red as fox fur.

The woman's torso was bare, her breasts full and tipped with rosy nipples. A silky peacock-blue shawl was wrapped around her lower body, hiding her pelvis and legs, and giving her legs the appearance of a fishtail. No wonder the old boatman who found her had thought she resembled a mermaid. Several colorful blooms were tucked into her hair, and a few more were scattered across her chest and stomach. There were no marks on the alabaster skin or any obvious signs of violence, but there was no doubt in Jason's mind that this woman had not died a natural death.

"She's beautiful," Constable Napier whispered on a sad sigh. "What a waste of a young life."

"She is that," Sergeant Meadows agreed as Mr. Braithwaite set up his tripod and mounted the camera.

Jason stepped aside, then carefully turned the woman over once Mr. Braithwaite had taken the initial photos. The hair on the back of the woman's head was matted, the strands glued to the skull with dried blood. Mr. Braithwaite took two more photographs before closing the camera and packing it away in its case. No one spoke.

At last, Daniel asked, "What do you think, Jason?"

"I think someone has a good imagination," Jason replied.

"Is that what killed her?" Daniel inquired, his gaze on the bloodied contusion on the back of the woman's head.

"I won't know for certain until I open her up and determine the cause of death. Let's get her to the mortuary."

Daniel turned to Sergeant Meadows. "Have you sent for the police wagon?"

"Should be here any minute, guv," Sergeant Meadows replied. "We'll get her there safe and sound. Don't you worry."

Jason sighed. This young woman would never be safe and sound again. He turned away and retraced his steps, wishing only to get away from the sight of that haunting face.

Chapter 2

Once at Scotland Yard, Jason and Daniel parted ways. Daniel didn't have the stomach to observe a postmortem, so he took himself off to catch up with the colleagues he hadn't seen since December and find a cup of tea. Jason made his way to the basement mortuary, where The Mermaid, as she was already being referred to by the men, was laid out on the slab, her tresses sliding off the table in corkscrew curls. Jason hung up his coat and hat, set his Gladstone bag on a nearby chair, put on the leather apron he wore to protect his clothes, and tucked his hair into a linen cap to keep it from falling into his eyes.

He began by unwrapping the shawl from around the woman's legs and turned it over in his hands, looking for any identifying marks. There was nothing, but Constable Napier had been correct in his assessment. The silk was fine, the shawl fairly new, the fringe not yet frayed. Jason folded the garment and set it aside, ready to turn his attention to the body.

Lying there, the woman looked perfect. Her skin was supple and smooth, her hair lustrous, and her nails clean and unbroken. This was a woman from a well-to-do family, someone who had not only enjoyed a plentiful and varied diet but had been waited on hand and foot. These were not the hands of a servant or a sempstress. They were the hands of a genteel woman, a wife, Jason thought when he noticed the slight indentation on the fourth finger of her left hand. Her ring had either been stolen at the time of death, or afterward by the boatman who'd brought her ashore. And it had probably been pure gold.

Jason lifted each hand in turn and examined every finger closely before leaning over until he was almost nose to nose with the deceased. He sniffed experimentally, then pushed his fingers into the mouth and probed before removing his hand. The teeth were intact, and there was nothing lodged inside the mouth. Jason smelled his fingers to be certain the woman had not vomited before death. She hadn't.

After wiping his hand on a linen towel, Jason lifted the eyelids to examine the woman's eyes, which were a vivid blue, the irises almost an exact match to the color of the shawl. Nodding to himself, he turned her over. Her back and thighs were unblemished except for an indentation where the bare back had pressed against the rowing bench, and the skin just over the left temple where the head had rested against the prow. The feet were soft and clean, the nails carefully buffed.

Jason parted the hair at the back of the head and examined the wound closely, noting its shape, size, and severity. He then turned the body back over and pushed apart the milky white thighs. It would be negligent not to check for sexual assault. Satisfied with his initial findings, Jason reached for a scalpel. He was ready to begin but couldn't seem to bring himself to make the first cut. He didn't normally get emotional about the cadavers he worked on, but something about this woman made him question the ethics of taking her apart and destroying something that until mere hours ago had been nearly perfect. Annoyed with himself for giving in to this uncharacteristic sentimentality, Jason pressed the scalpel into the cool flesh and sliced, making the Y incision that would open her chest and allow him a glimpse into the inner workings of her body.

Three hours later, Jason emerged from the mortuary. He found Daniel, and together they made their way to Superintendent Ransome's office. Jason hadn't seen Ransome since they'd made the arrests in the case that had nearly claimed Daniel's life, and found that he was actually glad to see the man. John Ransome had his flaws—he was arrogant and unapologetically ambitious, eager for the power that climbing the chain of command would bring—but he cared deeply about his men and about justice and was a good man to have in your corner in times of trouble. It wasn't widely known, but Superintendent Ransome had insisted that Daniel be paid a full wage during his convalescence as he had been hurt in the line of duty.

John Ransome pushed to his feet and reached across the desk to shake Jason's hand. "Pleased to see you again, Lord

Redmond. I've already had the pleasure of welcoming Inspector Haze back to the fold," he said, settling back in his chair. "Gentlemen." He indicated the guest chairs.

Jason hung up his coat and hat on the rack in the corner, set down his bag, and settled in the proffered chair.

"So, what have we got?" Ransome asked, directing his question to Jason.

"The victim is a woman in her early to mid-twenties. Rigor is well established, so she's been dead for more than twelve hours. Of course, given that the body was left out in the open, it's difficult to say for certain. I think it's safe to say that she died sometime last night. She came from a well-to-do household, and I believe she was married. A ring was taken off her hand either by her attacker or by the boatman who found her this morning. She was in fairly good health but suffered from endometriosis."

"Which is?" Ransome interrupted.

"It's a condition in which extraneous tissue begins to grow on the outside of the womb. This can lead to infertility or complications if the woman does become pregnant."

"Is this condition relevant to her death?" Daniel asked.

"No."

"So, what killed her?" Ransome demanded.

"There's a fracture on the back of her head that corresponds to the subgaleal hemorrhage over the left parietal bone. The contusion is about six centimeters in diameter and is circular. The victim was struck on the back of the head with a blunt object. It could have been a cudgel or possibly a round stone. The impact would have almost certainly stunned her and possibly rendered her unconscious."

"Is that the official cause of death?" Ransome asked.

“I think it’s safe to say that the victim died of a subdural hemorrhage caused by the blow to the head, but it’s possible that she was still alive when she went in the boat. There was a thick fog last night, and it was cold and damp, more so on the river. Had she still been alive, the hypothermia would have almost certainly killed her, since no one would have noticed her until the fog lifted this morning.”

“Could she have been saved?” Daniel asked, clearly thinking back to his own recent brush with death.

Jason considered the question. “Perhaps, if she was brought to a hospital immediately and the attending physician was able to alleviate the pressure on the brain caused by the hemorrhage, which wasn’t as severe as one would expect given the size of the contusion.”

“Meaning?” Ransome asked.

“I don’t believe she was hit with great force,” Jason speculated.

“What does that tell us about her killer?”

“Perhaps the person couldn’t achieve a favorable angle, or the weapon was too heavy, or they didn’t mean to kill, only to incapacitate.”

“Well that last theory doesn’t stand up, does it?” Ransome scoffed. “If they didn't mean to kill, then why take off her clothes and leave her floating on the river?”

“Perhaps they thought they had killed her and needed to dispose of the body. How the victim was displayed says a lot more about the killer than the method of the murder. I would hazard to guess that the victim either knew her attacker or was taken by surprise.”

“What makes you say that?” Daniel asked, giving Jason a sidelong glance.

"I found no evidence of a struggle. There are no defensive wounds, no bruising on the wrists, and no particles of skin beneath the fingernails. She never saw it coming."

"The poor woman," Ransome said with a heartfelt sigh. "I hear she was quite beautiful."

"She was," Jason said. "A woman like that will always attract unwelcome attention."

"Is that it, then?" Daniel asked, clearly disappointed. "That's not much to go on."

"No," Jason agreed. "But I did find something else that might be of interest."

"Tell us, man," Ransome invited, leaning forward in his eagerness.

"There is bruising and tearing to the vagina and evidence of recent sexual intercourse. I also found twin bruises on her hip bones that would correspond to thumbs. It would appear that someone had gripped her hips with considerable force."

"So, she was raped," Daniel concluded. "Perhaps after she was knocked unconscious, which would explain the lack of defensive wounds."

"The amount of semen present would indicate that she either had sexual relations with one man several times within a short period or she was used by several men, either before or after the head trauma was inflicted."

"Perhaps she was a streetwalker who had taken several clients within a short time," Ransome speculated.

"If she was a prostitute, she was very new to the profession," Jason replied. "There are no visible signs of the abuse such a lifestyle takes on the body. Her skin is supple, her hair lustrous, her teeth in excellent condition, and there's not a mark on her, except for the contusion on her head. Prostitutes rarely have such well-tended and unblemished bodies."

"But there is the tearing to the quim," Ransome pointed out.

"Which might have been the result of ardent sexual intercourse, possibly with her husband."

Ransome nodded and averted his eyes, his lean cheeks turning the telltale pink of someone who was embarrassed. Perhaps he was recalling an ardent experience of his own. Jason had never met Mrs. Ransome but had heard she was a force to be reckoned with, much like her husband. Two such strong personalities often led to strong feeling, and passionate lovemaking.

Unlike Ransome, who seemed a bit hot under the collar, Daniel's expression was pained.

John Ransome cleared his throat. "And the presentation of the body?" he asked, moving from the physical to the abstract. "I do declare, the killers in this city are becoming more creative by the day."

"The only thing I can state with any certainty is that the shawl was relatively new and of good quality. The flowers were still fresh, so probably purchased shortly before the murder."

"So, what sort of individual are we looking for?"

"I really couldn't say," Jason replied. "But the victim was laid out with obvious care. Perhaps it was someone who'd admired her in life."

"Was there anything on the shawl to give us an inkling of who she was?" Daniel asked.

"No."

Ransome nodded. "Right. I will send runners to the other divisions to check if anyone fitting the woman's description has been reported missing. If she died last night, then surely by now someone will have realized that she's not come back. With any luck, we'll have a name for her before long. In the meantime, I will wish you gentlemen a good day. I have a meeting with the commissioner, and I will be late if I don't leave now." He grinned, the smile lighting his dark eyes. "Good to have you back, Haze. Try to keep from getting stabbed this time, eh?"

Daniel gave the man a tight smile. "I will do my best, sir."

Jason and Daniel retrieved their things and left, heading directly out into the street.

"That's all we can reasonably do for today," Daniel said. He looked tired and pale after spending the last six weeks mostly indoors.

"Get some rest, Daniel. Perhaps we'll have more information tomorrow."

"Perhaps," Daniel agreed. He pulled on his gloves, tipped his bowler, and melted into the gathering dusk of the winter afternoon.

Chapter 3

When Jason arrived at his home, Katherine was in the drawing room, mending the family's linen. She might be a noblewoman by marriage, but she was still a vicar's daughter at heart and felt she shouldn't be idle if there was work to be done. Katherine put aside one of Lily's baby gowns and rose to her feet, coming to meet Jason.

"I was beginning to worry," she said, looking at Jason anxiously. "You've been gone for hours. Is Daniel all right?"

"Daniel is absolutely fine," Jason replied as he kissed her tenderly. He then led her over to the settee she'd just vacated and settled in next to her. "We were called out on a case."

"But Daniel wasn't due back at work until next week," Katherine protested.

"It seems there was no one else available, and this case promises to be a corker."

"Tell me," Katherine urged.

She liked hearing about the cases Jason worked on and often held forth, not only on the victim but on the investigation. Normally, Jason was more than happy to listen. His wife was one of the most astute, practical women he'd ever met, and her insights often led to unexpected breakthroughs, but he hated sharing the more gruesome details with her, especially when the victim was either a woman or a child. But if he tried to spare her any unpleasantness, she'd accuse him of treating her like a feeble-minded woman who'd get the vapors at the mere mention of violence. He sighed in resignation and plunged in.

"A young woman was found on the river, her body arranged in a dinghy. She was nude, except for a silk shawl wrapped around her hips and legs. There were flowers in her hair, which is a glorious red, and petals were scattered across her stomach."

"Was she murdered?" Katherine asked, clearly shocked by Jason's description.

"I'm afraid so."

"How did she die?"

"She was struck on the back of the head. If she didn't die of the head injury, she would most certainly have died of exposure to the elements," Jason replied.

"And you say she was drifting along, adorned with flowers?" Katherine asked.

"Yes. Why?"

"It makes me think of Ophelia."

"From *Hamlet*?"

"Yes, but I'm referring to the painting by John Millais. Did you ever see it?"

"Can't say I've had the pleasure. Did you?"

Katherine shook her head. "I was only six when the painting was exhibited at the Royal Academy, but my mother had seen it and told us all about it. She said it was beautiful, but very sad and dark."

"Tell me about it," Jason invited.

"Well, you know Ophelia drowns in the play," Katherine reminded him. "One is never really sure if her death is intentional or accidental. In the painting, Ophelia is depicted lying half submerged in the water, her face serene, her body adorned with flowers. And her hair is red," Katherine added. "But she's fully clothed."

"And you think there's a connection?"

"Not an obvious one, but a young, redheaded woman floating along and decorated with flowers is not so very different, is it?"

Jason considered this for a moment. Katherine was right. There was something serene and beautiful in the way the woman had been displayed, as if whoever had laid her in that boat had tried to create a work of art out of death.

"Why do you think someone would want to put her on display like that?" Jason asked, hoping for more insights.

"I think it was a tribute. They wanted to show the world how beautiful she was, and possibly make her immortal."

"How so?"

"Did the police photographer not take photographs?"

"He did."

"Well, there you have it. Tomorrow these photographs will be in the papers, and everyone will see this *artwork*. Perhaps it will even be archived, so future generations might refer to the case."

Jason looked away for a moment. "Her legs were bound with the shawl," he said quietly. "So it's not all beauty and serenity."

"Perhaps the bondage is a symbolism of sorts," Katherine said.

"Symbolism for what?" Jason asked, wondering if Katherine was reading too much into an act of barbarism.

"The role of women in society," Katherine said without missing a beat. "Women are bound from the moment of birth, by their fathers, their husbands, the limitations society sets on them, the lack of rights over their life, property, and even the physical body and offspring. Should I go on?" she demanded hotly.

"Do you feel bound by me?" Jason asked. He felt irrationally wounded by his wife's anger, even though he didn't think it was directed at him.

"No, but I am bound *to* you. By choice," she added, smiling sweetly at him. "But not all women marry the man of their dreams, or if they do, he often turns out to be not quite what they expected and asserts his rights as soon as he has control over their finances and person."

Jason nodded. Katherine was right, of course, in everything she'd just said. "That's an intriguing theory, Katie. I hadn't considered it."

"Will you explore it?" Katherine asked, giving him the gimlet eye.

"I will share it with Daniel and see what he thinks. But we must follow the evidence, first and foremost."

"Do you have any evidence?"

"Not a shred," Jason confessed.

"I will be more than happy to consult on this case," Katherine offered playfully. "I might even charge you a fee."

"Oh, really? What's your price, Lady Redmond?"

Katherine leaned forward and kissed him. "Your complete surrender, Yank."

"Ooh, I like this game," Jason purred, and was about to show Katherine just how much when Fanny appeared at the door with a tea tray, putting an end to their negotiations.